ELSEWHERE

SARAH TIERNEY

BLOODHOUND
— BOOKS —

www.bloodhoundbooks.com

Print ISBN: 978-1-917214-01-8

BEFORE

CATHERINE

The trip to Scotland with my sister was my husband's idea, though I haven't told her that. A week in his parents' holiday cottage in the Highlands, just me and Anna. He said it would be a good way for us to 'reconnect' and get to know each other again. He didn't like it that I saw so little of my family. He thought it was a shame we'd drifted apart.

'It isn't drifting,' I'd said. 'It's a deliberate departure.' But once Anna had moved back to the UK, he kept mentioning the cottage and the idea of us going there. He'd been with his brother last summer and thought we would benefit from the same 'quality time' together. What he didn't understand was that I'd had all the quality time I needed with Anna when I was a child. We'd shared the same bedroom until I was fifteen. We didn't need to share an equally cramped living space as adults.

I emailed her, certain she would feel the same way. I expected her to send a tactful reply but she called me. We never called each other. Did I have to answer? What was wrong with a text? 'Hi, Anna.'

'Catherine! I just got your message.' Her voice was different. We hadn't spoken in three years. 'I love it! I'm so up for it. I've

1

always wanted to stay in a little cottage in the wilds of Scotland. Whereabouts is it, exactly?'

I didn't know where it was. I hadn't expected her to say yes. 'Somewhere on the west coast. I'm not entirely sure.'

'Where's it near?'

'It's not near anywhere. It's very remote. And basic. No electricity. No phone or internet.'

'Oh my God, it'll be such a relief to be offline. And it's free, yeah?'

'Well, apart from the flights.'

'Let's do it! When can we go?'

I needed a way out of this. I considered how to word it – that the email was just a suggestion for something we could perhaps do at some point in the future, and I didn't have space in my schedule at the moment.

She said, 'What about next week? Can you get time off work?'

'Next week...'

'Yeah. I mean, I love Mum and Dad to bits but I need to get away.'

'You've only just got back.'

'I know. And they're already driving me crazy. Imagine trying to start a new life with Mum giving a running commentary on everything you do. What about the week after then?'

I tried to put her off for a while at least, saying I would find some time later in the year when my workload wasn't so intense. But when I put the phone down, I thought, oh, why not just go? Just go and get it over with and then Joe couldn't complain that I never listened to any of his ideas. I already knew the cottage was empty right now – he'd said nobody was staying there until September. I found flights to Inverness and emailed Anna with the times and the place name she'd wanted. She replied a minute later. *BOOK IT!*

I emailed her back with the flight confirmation.

Another immediate response. *So excited! Can't wait for this. XXX.*

I told Joe that evening when he got home from work. He was looking at his phone, his coat still on. His head darted up when I said I'd booked the flights to Scotland.

'What flights?'

'For me and Anna. So we can go to the cottage. Like you said.'

His mouth was slightly open, like he was struggling to understand. 'When?'

'A week on Saturday.'

He turned his back and put down his phone. I couldn't see his face to work out if he was annoyed or not. When he turned back his expression was neutral. 'How long will you be gone for?'

'A few weeks.'

He paused, thinking something he wasn't going to say. 'Right.'

'It was your idea.'

'I didn't think you'd organise it without telling me.'

He didn't think I'd organise it at all. And now I was going away without him, he wasn't so sure.

He went upstairs to change out of his work clothes. When he came back down, I said, 'I could try and cancel them.'

'No, don't cancel them. It's fine.' He smiled. 'I'll call my mum and ask her to post the keys.'

3

1

CATHERINE

Saturday. Sunrise 04.40. Sunset 22.18

The keys were in my hand luggage now along with our plane tickets and a sketched map from Joe that was reminiscent of a child's drawing. A cluster of triangle-topped squares was a village. The sea was marked by a series of wavy lines. The cottage was an X surrounded by Christmas trees. I compared it to the map I'd printed from Google but there was no correlation between the two. I'd asked Joe to keep his phone on tonight in case we couldn't find it. He'd said I wouldn't have a signal. I knew that. It had just slipped my mind for a moment in the rush as we hugged goodbye.

I checked our departure time on the board and scanned the incoming crowds for my sister. According to her last text message, Anna was 'on her way' but from where, she didn't disclose. We'd agreed to meet at check-in at 3.45pm. It was 4pm and she still wasn't here. She'd phoned this morning, her voice lively but rough, like someone who hadn't transitioned from drunk to hungover. She said she'd been out last night. There was a string of garbled sentences about an ex and missing the last train and sleeping on his couch. She was heading back to Mum and Dad's to pack and wanted to know if she needed her passport because she wasn't totally sure where it was.

We were going to Scotland. We didn't need passports. I said, 'Just bring your driving licence for ID.'

'Right, yeah, I've got that here, I think. Okay. Holiday time! See you in a bit!'

I kept my eyes on the double doors leading from the taxi drop-off. There was no sign of her amongst the streams of families following overloaded luggage trolleys, the hen parties with walk-on bags and co-ordinated T-shirts. They looked drunk and anxious. The nicknames printed across their backs were sexual and crude. I didn't have a hen party, primarily because of T-shirts like those. Joe tried to talk me into it, naming a few of the girls at work (colleagues not friends), a housemate from Cambridge (we'd not spoken in over a year), my sister.

I said absolutely not. She's a liability. I'd spend the entire time looking after her. He didn't argue because he knew I was right, but seven years later, he'd finally succeeded in getting us to spend some time together. If she didn't miss the plane. Ten past. Typical Anna.

I called her but there was no answer. Two more minutes and I would check in without her. I started to imagine the holiday with only me on it. Ten full days of solitude. It would suit me fine. Then I felt a tap on my shoulder and I turned and made myself smile.

'Made it.' She was out of breath. Sweat dampened the edges of her face. She still wore the remains of last night's eyeliner.

'It's quarter past. I said quarter to.'

'Sorry, sorry. Wow, I can't believe it's been three years.' She hugged me, taking me by surprise, and I had to let go of my suitcase to steady myself. She said, 'You've not changed a bit.'

I didn't contradict her. 'Your accent is different.'

'It can't be. I've totally been milking the English thing in Canada. I found myself talking like Gran at one point, calling people duckie and pet. They love all that shit over there.'

And you look older. And you don't know it yet. I checked the time on my phone. 'We need to check in.'

The queue had cleared so we went straight to the desk. Anna took her passport from the back pocket of her jeans.

'You found it, then.'

'It was still in my rucksack. Mum went tearing through my stuff looking for it. I told her you don't need a passport to fly to Scotland but she was fretting that someone had stolen it and were already setting up credit cards in my name.'

'It happens.'

'Not with my credit rating.'

The check-in lady stuck labels on our bags and returned our passports. We joined the queue for security. Anna was peering at me as if she was still adjusting to seeing me again after so long. I asked her what she'd been doing in Banff before she left.

She wrinkled up her nose. 'Not much. Working in a bar. Living in a van. Dating a mountain biker. More than dating, I guess. But we broke up.' She sighed and looked away. 'Anyway.'

It was impossible to know whether to offer sympathy or not. I said, 'Well, you're back now.'

'Yep. Back in England.'

'You had to come back some time.'

'I could've applied for residency.'

'Why didn't you?'

'I was homesick.'

'Homesick?'

'Yes.'

For what? Our parents? The depressing northern town we grew up in? She set the alarm off going through security. House keys in her pocket. Then she needed the toilet and they were already calling our flight to the departure gate. It was not the most relaxing start to a holiday but I refrained from saying anything. On the plane she accepted the window seat, then put an eye mask on and fell asleep before we left the ground. She had slotted her passport and phone into the seat pocket, along with a spiral-bound sketchbook. I eased it out to have a look.

Line drawings of my mother watching TV. My father eating toast at the kitchen table. On one page a list that read: *Find somewhere to live. Get a job. Make some friends. Buy sunglasses.* As though an entire adult life is something you can pick up at the supermarket. As though dating is a relationship and mountain biking a job.

She shifted in her seat. I waited until she had settled again and carefully put the book back. I took out my journal and filled a few pages before zipping it away in my bag. Then, with my phone on flight mode, I had nothing to do but think. I don't sleep during the day.

Strong, bright sunshine. Puddles shrinking on the tarmac as we walked from the plane to Arrivals. I was uncomfortably hot beneath my coat and jumper. Then the sun was hidden behind a cloud and it was June in Scotland again. Breezy with rain in the air. At the luggage carousel I turned on my phone and waited for the ping of updates. Anna looked over at my screen.

I said, 'I'll meet you outside if you want to smoke.' She had already collected her rucksack. Her hand kept going to the cigarettes in her pocket.

'Yep. Cool. I'll be just outside the doors.'

At the car hire office, we chose the cheapest option then had a discussion about who would drive. I said I would, because I wasn't tired. By which I meant, I wasn't hungover like her. Anna said she didn't mind paying extra to put us both on the insurance, but when the man told us how much it would cost, she changed her mind. I could see that she didn't want to rely on me for transport but she didn't have the money to change it, so that was how it would have to be.

We drove out of Inverness and onto the road that followed the shore of Loch Ness. Scenes familiar from a hundred shortbread tins and jigsaw boxes. I felt like I'd been here before even though I hadn't. Anna talked about life at our parents' house. Mum fussing over what time she ate breakfast, what she ate for breakfast, after she'd had breakfast, what she was planning to do with her day. She said Dad had narrowed his already telescopic mind. 'He voted Leave. It's like he actually believes what he reads on Facebook.' She sighed. 'Listening to him going on makes me want to move back to Canada. I don't feel at home at home anymore.'

I said, 'So why did you come back?' I wanted to know if she'd give the same answer as last time.

'I guess things weren't really moving forward for me there. I needed a change.'

'Another one?'

'Yeah, another one.'

She'd moved to Canada to escape her life in England. Now she'd moved back to England to escape her life over there. And this holiday in Scotland was a way to escape what she'd moved back to. My sister runs away from running away. I was glad I had control of the car.

The nearest big supermarket to the cottage was in Fort William, though 'near' was hardly accurate. It would be another hour's drive from there, at least. I had a list I'd written a few days earlier, knowing I'd be too tired to think clearly about what we needed now. I'd calculated it would be about £70 each, but I hadn't accounted for Anna adding items to the trolley as we sped round the aisles. Junk food: crisps, chocolate, cakes. Two bottles of red wine, two bottles of white. She asked how far it was to the nearest shop then added four more.

Siege mentality. Functioning alcoholic. On the way out, she bought two packets of tobacco, a box of filters, two envelopes of Rizla. She picked up a second-hand Harry Potter and dropped a pound in the charity box. I ran back for ice to pack around the fresh food. Over the Tannoy, a recorded message told shoppers to go directly to the check-out, they were about to close.

We drove towards the coast on a fast, wide road that weaved between mountains and lochs. It was past ten o'clock and the sky glowed orange and red as the sun slowly set.

'It's beautiful.' Anna gazed out of the window. She was finally running out of conversation after two hours of near constant chatter.

I could only look away from the road for snatched moments, and I found myself feeling disorientated when I did. This region seemed more water than land and I couldn't tell what was loch and what was sea. Kelp crept up a shoreline to our left, but we were enclosed by mountains on all sides. As we turned off the highway onto a narrower road, I glimpsed a faraway skyline rising out of misty blue. Island or mainland, hills or cloud, I couldn't tell.

We had crossed from one side of the country to the other and now we were heading south, following the jagged line of the west coast. Anna's excitement about the view increased with every mile. 'Oh my God, that sunset is amazing,' she said for about the third time. 'Can you pull over? I want to get a picture.'

I stopped at the next lay-by and she got out with her phone. The sun gleamed between low clouds. I could see it was beautiful but I felt very tired and I just wanted the drive to be over.

I looked at my phone but there was no signal and I didn't know how long it had been gone. Joe was vague about how far I'd have to drive from the cottage to get reception. He'd suggested I have a 'digital detox' while I was away, and although the idea appealed to me in theory, I would need to check my emails daily. Also my social profiles. There would surely be wi-fi in the village.

We set off again. The other traffic had all but disappeared and the radio played only static. We passed road signs warning of ice and deer. A car drove up fast behind us and overtook, disappearing around a bend as suddenly as it had appeared.

Eventually we came to the village; it was little more than a pub, a shop and a few houses. A few miles later, we turned off onto a road that was single-lane and potholed and shaded by oak trees. I saw a fishing boat in a field, lichen hanging from silver birch, purple rhododendrons in flower. The road descended and rose and twisted back on itself. The satnav said we'd arrived but there were no houses in sight. The trees became thicker and I lost my sense of direction again. Were we heading inland or closer to the sea?

We bumped over the cattle grid marked on Joe's map. A lopsided gate came into view. I stopped the car and Anna got out to open it, swatting at midges as I drove through.

She jumped back in. 'Jesus Christ, they were eating me alive. It's like they were waiting for us.'

Finally, a clearing with a low, white-painted building which seemed to glow in the dusk. It had a rusted iron roof and a blackened chimney. At the front, a picnic table sunk into the grass at a slant. We parked up beside a pile of logs covered in a tarpaulin.

'It's remote,' Anna said.

'I did warn you.'

'I know, I'm not complaining. Our little hideaway. Come on, let's get in.'

Midges prickled my face as soon as I stepped outside. I hurried to push the key into the padlock on the front door. It wouldn't turn.

I tried again. It didn't give. It was rusted shut.

'What's up?' Anna was waiting behind me.

'It's stuck.'

'How are we going to get in?'

I said nothing. The midges clouded the air around us.

'I need my hoodie.' She ran to get it out of the car and covered her head, then tucked her jeans into her socks. 'Let me have a go.'

I handed her the key, wondering why she thought she'd be able to open it when I couldn't. I watched her trying and failing. She lit a cigarette and waved it around, trying to disperse the midges. 'Are there any other doors?'

I walked around the cottage's perimeter. It was backed with reeds and long grass and odds and ends of building materials. At the front, Anna looked hopefully at me. I shook my head.

'We need something to bash the lock with. Stupid fucking thing.' She found a stone and banged it repeatedly against the key, holding her cigarette in her mouth.

She looked deranged and desperate and I saw very clearly what a mistake I'd made by organising this trip. I'd agreed to one of Joe's ideas and this was what it had led to. We had a running joke about how, when it came down to it, I was pretty much always right, and it was as true now as ever.

'Thank the Lord.' Anna held the open lock in her hands. 'I really didn't fancy sleeping in the car.' She pushed the door and I followed her inside, closing it behind me fast to stop the midges getting in.

There wasn't much light but I could make out plastic patio

chairs stacked double in the middle of the room. A fireplace filled by a solid iron stove. One corner was a kitchen. There was a table in another covered in a jumble of objects. Mugs, plates, pens, an OS map and a pad of paper. A couple of candles and a box of matches. I lit one and saw the table was covered with little black dots. Tiny dead flies. Thousands of them.

Anna lit another candle. The carpet of flies extended across the stone floor. The room must have been swarming.

'Fly-mageddon,' she said. 'Fuck it, we can sweep them up in the morning. Let's get our stuff in and have a drink. Please tell me there's a corkscrew. If not, I know a way.'

I lit candles that were already dotted about the two rooms, on windowsills, sideboards, fastened with wax to the iron frame of a bunk bed. The cottage grew then shrank around them as we saw how small it was. From the kitchen, a badly-fitted door led on to a bath and toilet. The only bedroom doubled up as storage space. I saw a barbecue, a mop, an axe. The mattresses on the bunk bed were thin and damp. The pillows too.

Joe would be lying diagonally across our bed like he did when I got up before him in the mornings. I wanted to call him to say night-night. No signal. He'd be asleep anyway.

I asked Anna which bunk she wanted, already knowing the answer.

'Top. Like when we were kids.'

And when we were teenagers. We brought in our bags. I put my journal under my pillow and my pyjamas on top. The rest could wait until tomorrow.

In the living room, Anna was looking out of the window into the clearing in front of the cottage, a mug of wine in her hand.

'I think I saw a deer,' she said. 'I saw its eyes glowing in the woods over there. In Banff, they'd walk down the main street in the middle of the day. It was a totally normal occurrence.' She filled another mug with wine and handed it to me. 'Happy holidays.'

'Happy holidays.' We were here, at least.

'This was such a good idea, Catherine,' she said. 'We never see each other anymore.'

'You moving to Canada didn't exactly help that.'

'But I'm back now. And you're living up north again. We can meet up. Hang out.'

Last night, my suitcase packed, reading in bed, I'd asked Joe if he thought I should tell her.

He was still for a moment. 'Tell her what?'

'You know what.' I picked up my book, thinking I'd been stupid to ask.

Then he said, 'Maybe you should.'

But how do you start a story like that?

Anna refilled her mug. I rehearsed a line in my head: *You know what happened, when I was fifteen.* I didn't say it though because another line followed. It said: *Once you tell her, you can't untell her.*

I joined her at the window. I could see the crooked table and the trees that circled the clearing. Down here at ground level it was night but when I looked into the sky, a persistent grey light lingered. Anything could happen out here in the woods. I didn't know how long I'd be able to keep her in the dark.

2

___

ANNA

Sunday. Sunrise 04.28. Sunset 22.18

I love it when you arrive somewhere new late at night and you don't know what you'll find when you wake up in the morning. Yesterday we'd driven through dusk made darker by the woods and found our way around the cottage by candlelight. I saw dead flies and the deer's glowing eyes and Catherine's still face when the padlock wouldn't open.

I leaned over the bunk rail to see if she was awake but her bed was empty and I felt a little bit cheated because I like to be first up, even if it's only because I've not been to bed. I'd choose a sunrise over a sunset any day. Last night though. Driving down the coast road, that path of gold reflected on the sea. My eyes twitched with tiredness but I couldn't look away.

Catherine wasn't in the other room either so I opened the door and saw what was blurred by twilight yesterday. The cottage was enclosed on three sides by woodland so green and thriving the trees looked like they'd just burst into life that morning. Beyond the clearing at the front, rough fields gave way to a distant sea, wind-whipped and glinting in the sun. It was faraway enough to look like a painting, but close enough to make me want to run down there as soon as I'd found my shoes. I could make out a fishing boat surrounded by gulls. Hazy blue mountains floating on the horizon and they were so out of reach and mysterious, I could barely believe they were real. It was the kind of view you'd look forward to for weeks, and photograph endlessly when you were there, and dream of when you'd gone.

There was no sign of Catherine. I didn't know where she'd gone but I really hoped it was to do with getting the stove going, because the two things I wanted most in the world right now were a bath and coffee. I found my flip-flops and went to track her down, looking round the back of the cottage where there was a tumbled stack of firewood and a whole load of junk. Plastic pipes, empty buckets, a bag of sand. And Catherine, holding a battered-looking ring binder, looking up at the roof.

'What's happening?'

She sighed. 'It says we need to uncover the chimney before we light the stove. Otherwise the cottage will fill up with smoke.'

'We don't want that, do we?'

'No, we don't. There's a ladder under the bed. I didn't want to wake you up to get it.'

'I'll go and see.'

It still felt weird, talking to her, spending time with her. I awkwardly carried the ladder out of the bedroom and back to her, leaning it against the wall. 'I'll go up,' I said. 'You hold it steady.'

The view from the roof was even better. Behind me rose hills and crags. Ahead of me, the sea. I reached over to the block of wood positioned across the chimney and weighed down with rocks, then shouted to Catherine to shift out of the way so I could chuck them into the grass.

Back inside, she struck a match and tossed it into the furnace in the stove. Firelighters sprang into flame, then the kindling around it.

I said, 'I'm glad you know what you're doing. I'd be useless at this on my own.'

'I thought you were used to this kind of thing, living in a van.'

'There was electricity at the camp-ground. We had a TV. Wi-fi. A fridge.'

'We've got a fridge.'

Catherine had got it working last night. It ran off a gas canister and was only big enough to chill one bottle of wine. We also had a gas lamp that hissed when it was lit and filled the space around it with a warm, vanilla glow. And a stove which did everything else: heating, cooking, hot water.

'So who gets first bath?' I asked.

'You do, if you want. But the water won't be warm yet.'

I wasn't too fussy about that. I didn't like to tell her I hadn't washed since Friday. I'd been tempted into town by an invite on Facebook. Got drunk on rum cocktails. Woke up late at a one-time boyfriend's flat. (Nothing happened, thank the Lord.) Then I had to run around in a crazy panic trying to get home, get packed, get to the airport in time.

Catherine would have been all packed a couple of days before. Joe would have dropped her off at the airport at the suggested two hours before take-off. Probably half an hour earlier, just in case.

She is organised and reliable. I am disorganised and likely to let you down. She's sensible and practical and gets things done. I bumble along. She'd be a good person to know in an apocalypse. I'm a good person to know, well, the rest of the time.

That's the official Bradley family version anyway. The girls according to Mum and Dad. It's pretty accurate, I suppose. I'd like to get her drunk to see what she's like when she loses control. Either that or mellowed out on some gently mind-altering drugs. Nothing too extreme. Just something that would make her let go and relax fully for a moment.

I had a lukewarm bath while Catherine made breakfast, and stepping out of the dark cottage, with clean, wet hair into the morning sunshine, to see a mug of coffee and a bacon buttie waiting for me, was a good feeling. Catherine had her legs stretched out across two plastic chairs, sunglasses on.

I carried out a chair and placed it next to hers. We watched as two chunky lambs ran towards their mother in the field below. She'd been calling to them and now there was sudden quiet as they mobbed her for milk. It made me think of the time I fed a lamb at a petting farm when I was little. I was shocked at its power; it was way stronger than me, its legs all muscle, its head pushing against my knees. It got the teat in its mouth, yanked the bottle out of my hand, and ran off with it, while I was stood there wondering what to do.

I turned to Catherine. 'Do you remember that time we went to that farm place in Scarborough and fed the lambs?'

'Vaguely.'

'The lamb nicked my bottle of milk and drank the whole lot in a corner without me. I feel like it scarred me for life.'

She looked at her book. 'I don't remember that part.'

I said, 'So how come you've never been here with Joe? Didn't you say his parents have had this place ages?'

'We just never have the time. We've got a list of countries we want to visit before we start a family.'

'A pre-baby bucket list?' Before you die, before you have a child. 'Are you...' I couldn't think of the word and she wasn't helping me out. 'Trying?'

She nodded quickly, avoiding my eyes. 'We thought we'd

come here afterwards, for family holidays. There's a sandy beach near the village. Joe said it's just right for little kids.'

I was thinking of those countries gradually being ticked off the list as the years went by. Did they add a new one after each holiday in case it got too short? They'd been together seven years. Catherine was four years older than me. Thirty-eight.

I tried to think of another subject of conversation. I couldn't handle worrying about my sister's fertility as well as my own. 'Maybe we can go there today? Have a day at the beach?'

'I'm not intending to move from this spot. I want a day of doing nothing.'

'A full day?' I'm not good at doing nothing. And I like to explore when I'm in a new place. 'Maybe we can have a walk to the village this afternoon?'

'It'd be a long walk.'

'We could take a picnic. Or drive.'

'Let's go tomorrow. I need to relax.'

'You could relax at the village?' I was imagining ice creams, homemade cakes, a pint in that pub we'd passed.

'I need some alone time. I want to decompress after the journey.'

Alone time? Did that mean without me? I had a flashback to being eight years old and failing to persuade her to play Connect Four.

She picked up her book. Flicked through it to find her place. 'Why don't you do some drawing?'

'What of?' I was practically sulking.

'The view?'

'I draw people.'

'Well, don't draw me. I don't like being watched.' She put her sunglasses on and stared down at the page.

Catherine has always been quiet but I think she's got quieter. Last night, working my way through the wine and too many cigarettes, I'd felt like I was talking to myself half the time. Or maybe she was listening and taking it all in. I don't know. I've no idea, really, what goes on in her head.

And the thing is, I need people to chat to, on a fairly regular basis. Unlike my sister, I'm naturally sociable. Ade used to wonder at my ability to strike up friendships with neighbours and bartenders and people on trains. How do you get to the point where they know your name? he'd asked, and I had no idea. It just happened. He said when he tried small talk in the local shops, it would end in awkwardness and covert 'save me' looks at co-workers. With me it progressed on to shared interests, invites to coffee, or in the case of Ade, who I'd met while waiting for a ferry, a two-year relationship. But that was the exception. Usually it's just a little lift to your day, and someone to say hi to the next time you're passing.

But still, I didn't have the stamina for a five-mile hike to the village and back today. I'd explore around here instead. I packed some water and my sketchbook and set off down the track, then took a path that led through a marsh in the direction of the sea. I brushed through ferns uncurling at waist height, followed a peaty black stream. Occasionally I caught a glimpse of the bay and the sudden blueness of it reminded me of walks I'd done with Ade through the forests on Vancouver Island.

To pass the time, I started imagining I was talking to him and it was nice for a while, until the imaginary chat turned into an imaginary argument, and I had to imaginary break up with him again, as if doing it in real life wasn't bad enough. I remembered his short, sharp laugh when I tried to explain why I was going back to the UK.

'I feel like I've outgrown it here,' I'd said.

'You've outgrown Canada? Next you'll tell me you're moving back to your tiny little island because you need more space.'

I meant the lifestyle not the landscape. The floaty sensation you got from living in a place where you had no family, or shared history, or friends who knew you when you were a kid. Perhaps if he'd been offering something to keep me there, something to tie me down, I wouldn't have felt like I was drifting. But he wasn't. He cried when I packed up my stuff, but he didn't do anything to try and make me stay.

Fuck it, I was away from all that now, and this was just a morning stroll to the sea. I didn't have to spend it reliving our break-up. I tuned into the sound of birdsong and humming insects. Water trickling unseen in the reeds. I looked up and, as if it was a reward for breaking my introspection, I saw a massive bird of prey rising in slow circles over the heather.

The path weaved between crags dotted with cotton-grass then it began to climb. I reached the brow of a hill and the view opened up before me. One hundred and eighty degrees of blue. The sea, the sky, just a few wispy white clouds. And that rugged skyline anchoring your eyes on it. From here you could see it was two islands, one in front of the other. The first was a straight-edged slab, sloping up to a sudden drop into the sea. The mountains of the further away island zigzagged above it.

The path dropped steeply through a wood of sycamore and oak, moss and ferns and clovers, and everything was so alive and verdant, you could almost see it racing upwards towards the sun. I weaved between tree roots and rocks until I saw a stile, and behind it, a small, low building with a chimney. I was approaching someone's house, and I wasn't sure whether I was about to walk into their back garden. Though surely nobody could live out here? There was no road. I climbed over. The windows were boarded up and grass grew high against the walls. I waded through to the front. There were more.

I looked down on a marshy pasture between the hills, sloping towards the sea. Dotted around the edges were six or seven small, squat buildings of grey stone like the one I stood beside. A village. But without any people. Just some sheep who had stopped grazing to stare at me.

I passed another house; this one in a state of disrepair. Roof tiles lay in the grass. The door was gone entirely and there was sheep wool caught on the frame. The path became a rotting wooden walkway across the marsh. I was still trying to get to the sea. Surely there was a way down from this place. Whoever had lived here and left must have fished or travelled by boat. Was it one of the villages emptied by force in the clearances? Were there families in America and Canada who kept an album of photographs of these falling-down houses where their ancestors had lived?

The walkway divided into two. One path led up to a white-painted house with what looked like a whalebone fixed to the wall. I was singing to myself, the Beatles song 'Honey Pie'. It had been in my head since I woke up and I felt like if I stopped I might hear something underneath the buzz of flies. The creak of a door or the tread of footsteps. I walked a little faster, until the houses were behind me. I could hear the sea now; low and soft and constant, and temptingly close. I just wanted to dip my toes in the water, maybe go up to my ankles, walk on sand. But the path came to an abrupt stop above a cliff face. Far below waves lapped against black rocks dotted with gulls. There was no way down, and it was like being thirsty or hungry or craving a cigarette, which thinking about it, would be nice, but I'd left them at the cottage.

I let my eyes rest on the blue for a while before I walked back up to that first empty building on the edge of the woods. I stopped there and drank some water. It was a picture-perfect scene, really. Maybe landscapes were the way forward, for this holiday at least. I took out my pad and pencils and spent some time trying to capture the shades of the buildings and the stretch of water-logged ground between them. I sketched the walkway, the point where it led off to the whalebone house, then paused, pencil mid-air, when something made me stare at a window by the door.

A hand pushed it open, retreated again.

Oh. So I wasn't alone, after all. It broke the stillness, added a sense of normality to the forlorn village. I sat there for another hour or so, drawing, sipping water, half watching the house, but nobody appeared. I left feeling a little disappointed. Lonely, I guess. And then I got back to the cottage and Catherine and the car were gone.

My sister is not the type to go off unexpectedly without leaving a note. Which made me think that she wasn't planning to be gone for long. I had no idea where she'd gone or why, especially after all that talk of clearing her head and enjoying the solitude, but I was sure there'd be a logical reason for it. Like we'd ran out of gas or firelighters or candles (though when I checked, we had all three). Or she'd remembered something she needed to tell her office to deal with while she was away.

I made a sandwich then dragged the mattresses outside to let them air in the breeze. The mustiness of the mildew mingled with the sweet smell of ferns. I lay down, half listening for the sound of a car and the thrum of the cattle grid, and woke an hour later. Still no sign of Catherine.

I bet she had the kind of job where the place started to crumble if she wasn't around. She was a specialist in something to do with disadvantaged children. She'd described it vaguely when I asked, but didn't elaborate much. She probably thought I wouldn't understand what she was talking about, which was probably true, but I still wanted to know.

As a child I'd faded into the background academically, compared to Catherine. She was good at everything: English, Maths, Science, French and it was disconcerting when I started secondary school and all the teachers expected me to be equally smart. At first, anyway. I could see them lowering their expectations as the year went on. At the start of term, they'd call on me in class to answer questions, as if I was going to be the leading light of our tutor group. They expected me to know things they hadn't even taught us yet, as if they thought our family spent the evenings discussing poetry and pollution and the fall of the Berlin Wall. It was depressing, never knowing the answers when they singled me out. Eventually I stopped even trying to get them right, and they stopped asking, and I was allowed to settle to my natural level: average. I got Cs mainly. Enough to get through. One A for Art, which didn't mean much to Mum and Dad. I remembered Dad telling me art wasn't a career, and I'd thought, but it's the only thing I'm good at. It was upsetting. Especially as he turned out to be right.

I'm not blaming him. I mean, what kind of artist lets a bit of resistance from their parents stop them from following their path? A not very committed one. I wasn't exactly burning with the urge to create; I didn't even finish my art degree. I don't know what happened there. I was on course for a 2.1 from the Glasgow School of Art but I messed it up by getting too into this boy, and too into the weed he used to bring round every night. It was fucking ridiculous. Total self-sabotage. I meant to resit the final year, but then I ended up working in this bar on Ibiza and I was doing enough painting to feel like perhaps I didn't really need a degree. But then work and socialising took over and I spent less and less time on my art. Months would pass between picking up my brushes. And that's kind of where I'm at now. I've started drawing again recently because it's easy to carry a sketchbook around, and having it in my bag makes me feel more like me. I see it and feel more substantial, somehow. Like I've carved out a slightly bigger space in the world, just by having some blank paper and a pencil with me. I know that makes no sense.

But what I think is, if I'm still drawing, and I still feel like an artist, after all these years then that says something in itself. I've got longevity. It's not a phase; it's what I do. It's just that sometimes I go for months without actually doing it.

Where the hell was Catherine? I made coffee, smoked a cigarette and decided to do something to make our holiday home a little homelier.

The place had an unloved quality to it, like it was purely functional, nothing more than a roof over your head. There were no pictures or ornaments or rugs or cushions. No attempts at comfort at all. It was very male, which made sense, as it belonged to Joe's very male family. He had four brothers, which made me think his mum must have been desperate for a girl, to keep trying like that. We'd been on the same table at Joe and Catherine's wedding, and she'd fussed over Catherine like she was her actual daughter. She had probably been hoping for a granddaughter to dress in pretty outfits. I wondered whether she still was.

The ring binder Catherine had this morning was on the sofa. Inside was a diagram of the Rayburn stove, maps showing walks from the village, leaflets for castles and monuments. And halfway through, some pages titled *Fàilte* that had been done on a typewriter.

Firstly, well done for finding us. Especially if you arrived in the dark. And if it was dark, then it must be winter, and you must be cold, so we'll start with the stove. The last inhabitants ought to have made up the fire for you, but if they didn't (Charlie!) they should have at least made sure there's wood in the wood pile. And if they haven't even done that, there's an axe in the bedroom, though my advice is to warm yourself with a dram of whisky and go to bed until it's daylight.

I guessed it was written by Joe's father. It went on for five or six pages, veering between practical instructions for the cottage, and local history, and wildlife sightings, and suggestions for days out. I slipped it under the sofa, out of sight. I was going to make this place mine. Ours. For this week at least. There was still a scattering of dead flies in the corners and on the windowsills, so I swept them away first. I mopped the floor and cleaned the plastic chairs while I waited for it to dry. Then I went round the two rooms gathering up everything we didn't need. Broken pens. Screwdrivers. Scraps of paper containing shopping lists and ferry times. I put them in a bag, along with an out-of-date calendar, a tube of superglue, numerous corks and lighters and bottle tops, and a whole load of other crap that just didn't need to be hanging around. I would scatter it all about again before we left. I shoved the axe under the bunk bed, put the gardening equipment out the back and wiped away a winter's worth of dirt from all the empty surfaces.

With all the junk gone, the cottage's plus-points started to show. The window at the back by the kitchen sink was made of little squares of coloured glass. The stones around the fireplace glittered with minerals. I found a jug and filled it with the tall yellow flowers that grew by the track, then did the same with last night's wine bottles. There was a plastic tablecloth in the kitchen cupboard. I put it over the picnic table and clipped it in place. What else? A fruit bowl? Cushions fashioned from the spare pillows?

I was loving all this. Playing house. Making it look nice. You have to remember I'd been living in a van for over a year; a small, awkward space made even smaller by Ade's snowboarding gear. I'd spent the last two weeks in Catherine's old room at Mum and Dad's, which was now a guest room, with lamps that matched the curtains, and curtains that matched the bedding. I felt like I was disrupting the colour scheme every time I walked in. I would have preferred my old room, which still had the bunk beds and my scratch 'n' sniff stickers on the wardrobe door, but they didn't seem to want me sleeping in there. I felt like a guest, which was about right really. Dad hadn't asked how long I was planning on staying, but it was there behind the questions about job applications and flat hunting.

One of my reasons for coming back was I'd wanted to feel like part of a family, rather than a lone ranger, thousands of miles from where I belonged. But moving back into the family home wasn't how I'd imagined. I'd thought Mum and Dad might like having me there, for a while at least. I was thinking a few months. They were thinking a few days.

So rearranging the furniture in this remote little cottage was very satisfying to me. I knew it wasn't mine, and I knew we were only there a week or so, but it was the most space I'd had to myself in years. Even if I was still sharing a bedroom with my sister.

Those years when Catherine was a fully-fledged teenager and I was still playing with Lego. At the time, I'd only thought of how annoying it was for me to have to share a room; to get shouted at if a stray felt tip went on 'her side', to have a CD player I couldn't use because she was always revising.

She was possessive about her things and would somehow know if I'd touched anything of hers. She had a collection of snow globes and I swear she knew if I'd shook them when she was out, as if she'd memorised how the flakes had fallen inside. There were about ten of them lined up on her desk and the windowsill beside it. She bought one every time we went somewhere touristy and her friends bought them for her too, so she had snow globes from all over the world; Pisa (from a friend), Paris (from a school trip), Llandudno (from us). One from the Caribbean that her friend Rachel bought her. It had palm trees and a sunset and a boat on the water. I remember saying that it probably never snowed in the Caribbean and she started talking about the hole in the ozone layer. It was the mid-nineties and she was already woke.

My favourite game as a child was to make it snow all over the world, all at the same time. I'd wait for her to go out, then, moving really fast, shake and set down each snow globe so that snow was falling in every scene. It was almost but not quite impossible to get it snowing in the last one before the first one stopped. Then there was a moment or two when the snowstorm enveloped them all, pole to pole, the next ice age, happening right there in mine and Catherine's bedroom.

She had certain favourites: the Eiffel Tower that lit up when you flicked a switch on the base, an Alpine scene of a Heidi-style cabin with pine trees and a log pile in front. It was the only one where snow suited the setting. And she was so precious about them, as if they were going to run out of weather if I shook them too often. I guess we both wanted more privacy than we had. Four years is a big difference at that age. We didn't have whispered conversations at night once she'd started secondary school. We didn't even say good morning. She made a big deal out of buying a diary with a lock and key, and scribbling away in it every evening.

I remember wondering what she wrote about. I was genuinely curious, because as far as I could see, her life was just school, homework, and the occasional outing to the cinema with her two friends, Emma and Rachel.

'Are you writing about me?' I asked once.

'None of your beeswax.'

I'd suspected she was a geek for some time, and when I started secondary school, my suspicions were confirmed.

Catherine was part of a small group of girls whose hang-out spot was the chicken coop. I don't know why our school had a chicken coop built into its grim 1960s architecture but it did. A muddy rectangle of ground between the maths block and the sports hall, with a shed, a few bramble bushes and puddles that joined together when it rained. Catherine and her friends had taken on the job of looking after the chickens for Mr Shaw, the biology teacher. Feeding them, collecting the eggs, cleaning out. It was how they spent their dinner hours.

'Are you writing about the chickens?' I'd asked her once I had this new insight into her life.

'Shut up, Anna.'

'Can you bring some eggs home?'

'You hate eggs.'

'I like them in pancakes.'

She started writing again but slower, as if her full concentration wasn't really on it. Then, a few days later, she did bring some eggs home. Or tried to. One of the lads in her year, a fat bully in a shell suit called Simon Smith, started chucking them across the top deck of the bus once they were out of sight of school. All the girls were screaming. All the boys were laughing. Catherine didn't get hit, being too close to Simon to be in the line of fire, but I could tell she was struggling not to cry as he took egg after egg out of her box and pelted them against the windows and seats.

That night she didn't write anything in her diary. Then in one of those blatant miscarriages of justice that seemed to happen a lot at our school, Catherine and her friends were banned from the chicken coop for a week. They hung out in the library instead and Mr Shaw had to collect the eggs himself.

I wondered if she would laugh if I reminded her about this now. Probably not. And, anyway, *where was she?* I put on another jumper, opened a bottle of wine, sparked up a cigarette.

28

It felt lonely in the cottage. I dabbed insect repellent on my face and sat outside. The breeze had picked up, which at least meant there weren't too many midges around.

I'd left Catherine at about ten o'clock this morning. Now it was coming up to six. It occurred to me that this was the longest time I'd gone without seeing another person in years. Apart from that hand in the window, and I wasn't counting that because I hadn't seen a face. Had the owner of the hand seen me wandering through the abandoned village, peering at those empty houses, nearly walking off a cliff? Or had I slipped by unnoticed? Except I'd been singing. Had the hand been listening?

I finished my drink. Brought the bottle out rather than taking the glass in. I was feeling mildly worried. I had no phone signal and no car. And it would be at least a two-hour walk to the pub. I would just sit here and wait. Catherine would be back soon. I had wine and I had cigarettes. In my personal hierarchy of needs, they were the foundations of the pyramid.

At half eight, I thought I heard a car on the track below and I swore with relief. Finally. But then it didn't appear through the trees, and the tyre sound was gone. Whoever was out there, it wasn't Catherine.

I started to think about that hand again. How desperate would I have to be to walk down there and knock on the door? My instincts were telling me to wait indoors but the night seemed darker from inside so I got my sleeping bag and wrapped it around me at the picnic table, letting my eyes adjust with the fading light.

It wasn't that I don't like the great outdoors. I just prefer to be on the edge of it, with lots of people around me, not alone and surrounded by it on all sides. Deserts, mountain ranges, pathless forests, without company they all unnerved me on some deep, primal level. It wasn't wild animals or wandering psychopaths or fear of getting lost. It was the quiet. People say you can't hear yourself think in the city but in the countryside, you can hear yourself too well. It's like therapy without the reassurance of knowing there's someone else in the room.

It was twelve hours since I'd seen Catherine. Something must have happened. There was no way she would leave me here not knowing where she'd gone. No way.

Except she had. And underneath the worry about where she was and what I was going to do, I was angry. And also, somehow, unsurprised.

At just past eleven I heard a car. A few minutes later, I saw the glow of headlights through the trees.

I'd imagined greeting her with an icy calm, a few barbed comments, and an announcement that I would be leaving in the morning. But I didn't have that level of self-control. She looked surprised to see me sitting outside in a sleeping bag in the near dark, and shivered in the night air.

'What are you doing?'

'Oh my God, Catherine, where have you been? I've been terrified, out here on my own. Where *were* you?'

Her voice was quiet compared to mine. 'I went to the village to call Joe and check my emails.'

'Check your emails? How many did you have? Jesus Christ. I thought you were dead.'

'Why would I be dead?'

Her logical response infuriated me. 'You just disappeared. What was I supposed to think?'

'It was still light. I didn't realise how late it was.'

'I was really worried.'

She looked at me like she didn't know what to do. 'Well, sorry.'

'And *you* said you didn't want to *go* anywhere today. I would have come with you if you'd waited.'

'I only decided after you'd left.'

I shook my head and turned away. In the cottage, the candles had burnt down to stumps. She followed me in.

'I've been to the shop. I bought more wine and crisps.'

I ignored her and went and sat on the top bunk. I could hear the crinkle of plastic bags as she unpacked the shopping, the thud of a bottle being placed on the table, crisps being crunched.

She stood in the doorway. 'Do you want a drink?'

Of course I wanted a fucking drink. I took it from her outstretched hand then sat outside with a cigarette. I watched her through the window, putting food in the fridge, lighting the gas lamp. She looked tired and distracted. I could just about imagine how she had suddenly decided she needed to call Joe, and thinking she'd be back before me, set off without leaving a note. I don't know why it took her twelve hours though.

She joined me outside. I asked if Joe was okay.

'I didn't actually speak to him.'

'Oh.' I tried again. 'Any interesting emails?'

'Not really. Why?'

'Just thought you might have had work stuff to deal with and that's why it took so long.'

'I had a few things to sort out.'

I waited but she didn't say what those things were. I wondered whether she would ask about my day. Two cigarettes later, the question still hadn't come. I told her anyway.

'I found an abandoned village. Except it's not abandoned. I saw a hand, opening a window. I'd thought the whole place was empty. It was weird.' She wasn't listening. 'So anyway, then I came back here and tidied up.'

She didn't answer for a while. Then she said, 'These flowers are nice.'

'Thanks. I thought they'd cheer the place up a bit.'

She nodded. 'They do.'

'Shall I make us some food?'

'I'm really tired, I think I'll just go to bed.'

Maybe it had been a mistake to live abroad for so long. I'd thought I'd just slip back into things when I got home but even talking to my closest family was hard. Though, in reality, it had been hard with Catherine for years. Despite what she'd said, she'd moved away first, long before I did. She went to university in Cambridge, then straight down to London after graduating. She looked down on our town and the people who lived there. She thought it was backwards and inbred. She'd come home at Christmas but she never stayed overnight.

It had gone quiet in the bedroom. Was she asleep already? I was considering trying to find her diary and sneak a look, like I was ten years old again. I looked around the living room but it wasn't there. She probably had it with her. She was probably writing it right now. She was still so secretive. I wanted to know where she'd really been all day, and why she wouldn't tell me.

3

CATHERINE

Monday. Sunrise 04.28. Sunset 22.19

I had been looking forward to the absolute darkness you only find this far from civilisation but even in the middle of the night, milky twilight seeped through the curtains. At 2am I could make out the detail of the clothes Anna had discarded before clumsily climbing up to her bunk. At 3am, I had light enough to write my journal. Soon after, birdsong started from all directions. Eventually I gave up and got dressed in the living room. I opened the curtains. It was 4am but out there it was day.

I turned on my phone even though I knew there was no signal. Habit. Everyone did it. I would go for a walk and see if I could pick one up on higher ground or closer to the coast. It was a forty-minute drive to the village and back. Not something you'd want to do more than once a day. I had not fully considered this before I'd booked the flights.

Joe was always nagging me to curtail my screen time. He didn't like me taking my phone to bed in the evenings. He didn't like me carrying it around in my pocket all day. I had thought this trip was his way of getting me to spend more time with Anna, but perhaps the aim was to reduce the time I spent online. If that was the case, it would make sense that if there was some stray wi-fi signal out here on the peninsula, he wouldn't have told me about it.

I closed the door behind me quietly so as not to wake Anna and started down the steps. Then I stopped and it took me a moment to process what I was looking at. It was our table outside our cottage, but someone else had been here and swept everything on it onto the ground.

The plastic cover was dragged back over itself. Anna's flowers and ashtray were in the grass, several feet away. The stems were broken, and bruised petals and cigarette stubs were stamped into the earth. I looked quickly around me, into the woods, at the track, towards the sea. Was someone watching me react? Could they see that I was afraid?

Anna stumbled onto the steps behind me, still in the long black T-shirt she slept in. Her eyes were scrunched against the early morning light. She'd gone to bed late last night, walking into the bunk bed at one point and banging her head. It was possible this was her work.

I said, 'Did you do this?'

'Do what?'

I gestured towards the dragged tablecloth, the mess on the ground. She peered at it for a moment, not fully awake. 'What happened there?'

'I don't know.'

'I didn't do it.'

'You were quite drunk last night.'

'I didn't drink that much.'

I said nothing.

She said, 'I did not do this. I'd know. I'd remember.' She

frowned at the broken stems on the ground. 'Why would I destroy my own flower arrangements?'

'Well, somebody did.' I took a few deep, calming breaths to try and slow my heart down. 'Did you hear anything last night?'

'No. Did you?'

'No.'

'It could have been an animal? Looking for food? Like a squirrel, or a deer?'

I didn't want to alarm her but at the same time, I didn't want to lie. 'It's too deliberate.' Some of the flowers had been snapped. The ashtray looked like it had been picked up and thrown. And the clips that held the tablecloth in place were on the ground near the car. I said, 'Somebody must know we're here.'

'It's not a secret.' She squinted at me. 'Is it?'

I shrugged. It wasn't a secret, no. But somebody wasn't happy about it.

Anna went to pull the cloth back over the table.

'Wait. Don't touch it.' I took out my phone and filmed the scene; the sabotaged table, the flowers and ashtray on the ground, the stillness of the surrounding trees. Anna stood back until I'd finished then straightened the tablecloth, picked up the fasteners and clipped them back into place.

I said, 'A squirrel couldn't pull those off.'

She gathered up the flowers that weren't broken, and the bottle, and started putting them back in. One of the stems was crooked but she propped it up amongst the others so you couldn't tell. Then she put the bottle back where it had been, in the middle of the table. I watched her gather up the cigarette stubs and rub the ash into the ground with bare feet. She was making it look like nothing had happened. Our parents had taught her well.

'It's too early for this,' she said, kneading her forehead with her fingers. 'What time is it anyway?'

'Four o'clock.'

'Anywhere else, this would be the middle of the night. Why are you even awake?'

'I'm going for a walk to see if I can get a wi-fi signal.'

'Why?'

'There's some work stuff I didn't finish yesterday.'

'Your job must be really full-on.'

I said, 'I'll lock the door behind me.'

'Can't you go later?'

'I'm awake now. I won't get back to sleep.'

'Well, don't be gone for long. Like, not for twelve hours.'

'I'll be back by seven.'

'Seven in the morning or seven in the evening?'

I looked at her. 'The morning. You go back to sleep.'

I set off down the track that led to the narrow road along the peninsula. I found myself looking into the woods as I walked, checking over my shoulder, half expecting to see someone walking behind me. I wasn't afraid, as such, more... alert. Because who did that to our table and why? It was the tone of it that shocked me. I could only describe it as blatant.

I wondered if anything like this had happened before at the cottage. I would ask Joe, though it occurred to me that he may not be honest with his answer. He wouldn't want to worry me. If I told him about the vandalised table, he'd brush over it, say it was probably a squirrel, like Anna did.

I opened the gate and crossed the cattle grid. Whoever it was must have come on foot. The metal bars rumbled beneath car tyres and the gate dragged on the track when you pushed it open. But on foot, you could pass this way in silence. You could approach through the trees, sneak up behind the cottage, stay hidden until you were certain nobody was awake.

It made me even keener to find a phone signal out here. I took a muddy track that led towards the coast, thinking it would bring me closer to the village as the crow flies. It turned a corner and opened out into a clearing on the cliff top. And even this early, somebody was here before me. There was a black saloon car parked facing the sea. I took a closer look; mud splattered up the sides and a stack of dance music CDs on the passenger seat. Was it stolen? Why would it be all the way out here, at this time of day, with no houses around?

I took a picture of the number plate and one of the sea. At the cliff edge I looked down onto a steep, zigzagging path that led through gorse bushes and bracken to a rocky cove swamped in seaweed.

A signal bar came and went on my phone as I started down the path. My instincts had been right. I estimated the village was less than a mile across the bay from here. I could see the boats in the harbour and the houses behind. I heard a dog barking in someone's garden.

I reached the thick tideline of kelp and began picking my way through it towards the sea. It was woven with ends of rope, milk cartons, the sole of a shoe. I stopped and looked around me. So much debris. A length of plastic pipe turned up like a smile. A twisted metal bar that looked like it was straining to escape from the seaweed. A computer monitor, its screen face-down. I kicked it over. It was white, small, intact. It made no sense for it to be here, like that car up there, and that ashtray thrown on the ground.

The sun shone between clouds. On the cliff top, the car

windshield glinted. The movement was unnerving, making it look like someone was in the driver's seat.

I picked up a stick bleached white by the sun and sea and used it to poke through the rubbish strewn amongst the rocks. I flipped over a plastic bottle. Its label was in Mandarin or Cantonese. There was a skull and crossbones boxed off in red.

I took pictures of the beach, the car, the view across the bay. The signal that had appeared briefly had gone. I would drive to the village later, after breakfast.

Anna looked relieved when I got back, as if she wasn't sure who was about to step inside. Had I really left her for twelve hours yesterday? It seemed unlikely. I hadn't told her I'd driven to Fort William. She wouldn't be impressed that I'd been somewhere without her. In truth, I hadn't planned it; I'd only intended to go as far as the village.

I'd parked in front of the pub, overlooking the playground. There was a wi-fi signal but it was weak and the few seconds of delay as each page loaded made me anxious. In the playground two small children flew back and forth on the swings. I could only see their backs, just coats and boots, interspersed with there-and-gone glimpses of their mothers. They pushed from the front, face to face with the children, smiling and laughing like they were the ones weightless and flying.

One of the children started trying to climb out of its seat. The mother steadied the swing to a stop and lifted it out. Then both women looked over at me. They were about my age, perhaps a little younger. I looked back at my phone. One bar. Searching. No signal. That was when I decided to drive further up the coast. The roads loaded seamlessly ahead of me like I was in a video game. Smooth, continuous highway with long sweeping curves. It made me want to keep driving and I only stopped when I reached Fort William.

I bought us a few supplies in the supermarket. Detoured into a shop that specialised in Harry Potter souvenirs. Anna would have loved it. I couldn't tell her, she'd be furious. Later I settled in a hotel bar with good wi-fi and that was where the hours went. I got engrossed, slipped down a wormhole, and the extended daylight didn't help. I only realised how late it was on the drive back when I turned onto the road through the woods. Everything was shadows and darkness and Anna was sitting outside the cottage in a sleeping bag with an empty bottle of wine. She looked homeless and drunk. She was angry at me for leaving her for so long.

She seemed to have got over it now, at least. She was singing to herself by the stove, frying a breakfast of eggs and tomatoes. I took mine outside and sat at the table, which showed no sign of the state it had been in this morning. I was glad I'd filmed it before Anna tidied everything up. I was scrolling through my photos when a movement in the woods made me look up. There was a girl on the other side of the cattle grid, in the shadow of the oak trees, trying to stay out of sight. I stood instinctively and she turned and walked away, back towards the road. Blonde hair. Jeans. A purple cloth criss-crossed around her waist and shoulders. A sling?

Anna came outside just after she'd disappeared from view. 'What are we going to do about these midges?' She had her hoody zipped to the top. Her jeans stuffed into her socks.

'I just saw somebody.'

'Where?'

'She's gone now. She was standing by the gate.'

'Maybe she lives near here?' Anna's voice was hopeful. Was she that desperate for company?

I said, 'She walked off when she saw I'd seen her.'

'Shall I go after her?'

'And do what?'

'Say hello?'

'She was carrying a baby.'

'Then I'll easily catch her up.'

'No. We don't know who she is.'

'That's kind of the point.' Anna looked for a moment like she might head off in search of her, then decided not to bother. 'Do you want anything from inside before I lock up?'

We were going to the beach. 'I'm ready. Let's go.'

We passed the girl further along the track. She was leaning into the back seat of a car parked on the verge, just her legs and back visible. We turned a corner and she was gone.

I said, 'I need to check my emails. Do you mind if we stop at the village on the way?'

'What's the point of paying to go on holiday if you're going to spend it working?'

Anna has never had a job with any real responsibility. Dog walker, sand sculptor, lifeguard. I'm just waiting for the day she joins the circus. She was like those writers who list all their quirky, directionless occupations on the inside cover, except she hadn't written a book.

She said, 'I suppose it's different when your job actually means something to you. I kind of wish I'd got into the charity sector. It was all that volunteering you had to do first that put me off. You used to spend every Saturday working on the recycling round. Then you had that job in Oxfam. Then you went on that hut-building thing in Borneo. I've never done anything like that. I'm just not sure who'd want me as a volunteer. I can't really do anything.'

'You can talk.'

She gave me a look.

I said, 'You could work on the phones for the Samaritans.'

'Isn't that more listening than talking?'

'Or visit lonely old people.'

'Do you think they'd want to talk to me?'

'Depends how lonely they are.'

The radio surprised us with a sudden blast of pop music. It had been on all this time, playing static so quiet we hadn't noticed it was there. The road was busier now. We passed a post van. A campervan. A garage tow truck. I pulled into the car park which looked over the playground. The same two women as yesterday watched from a bench while the children gathered woodchips into piles between their feet.

I opened up my emails on my phone.

Anna said, 'Shall we get a coffee in the pub?'

'There's a signal here.' She was looking at my screen. 'But we can go in if you want.'

I was surprised the pub was open at this time. We were the only ones in there, apart from the barman and an old man sipping a cup of tea. I could tell from the way Anna was looking at him that she was going to start drawing the poor chap. It was almost as awkward as her drawing me. She got her sketchbook out. I keyed in the wi-fi code. I had a new follower on Instagram. A man in a baseball cap with a husky dog. PatrickCruz210. American. Late teens or early twenties. His profile was set to private which always made me suspicious. It was bait. Drawing you in to see what was behind the curtain. I sighed and clicked follow back.

On Facebook, I had a friend request from somebody called Rosy Francis Elliot. I'd already left it twenty-four hours. I clicked Accept. Her request could have been a mistake. It happened, I'd done it myself once. She'd left her personal information blank. Her home page was just cat memes. The blandest of the bland. Everyone liked cats. All ages, all over the world. It said nothing. Her friend list was private.

I clicked back to Instagram. A post from PatrickCruz210 showing a dog asleep on an armchair. I scrolled through his followers. Mainly young women. I clicked one at random. Blonde hair. Pretty. She was on a boardwalk. She was on a balcony. She was sitting on the edge of a bed.

Anna looked over. 'Why is everyone pretending they're in a magazine nowadays? Fair enough do it in private, but for everyone to see?'

'It's a basic human need.'

'Taking selfies?'

'Being seen.'

'Everyone's too busy looking at their phone to notice anyone else. I was on there for a while, Instagram. I started boring myself after about a week, so God knows how my friends felt. Here I am! Here I am again! Wearing the same head as I was yesterday.' She picked out a pencil from her tin. 'And everyone works so hard to look good, even though there's like, millions of beautiful people on there. Why bother, if everyone's beautiful? We might as well all be ugly. It'd be the same thing but less effort for everyone involved.'

'It's how your generation are. It's not okay to just be "okay" anymore.'

'I'm fine with being okay.' Said with the confidence of someone who knew they were better than okay. Anna has been called pretty since she was three years old. In her teenage years, it progressed to 'fit' which in today's vernacular would be 'hot'. Even hungover with greasy hair and an oversized T-shirt that proclaimed *I think I lost it* across the back, she was being watched by the pony-tailed guy behind the bar. You've no chance, I thought. She's only interested in the old man with his weak tea. He's got liver spots on his hands and rolls of fat on his neck. Character.

It took her just a few minutes to get his likeness.

'You could teach life drawing.' She had talent, I had to admit.

'I used to model for a life-drawing class.'

I had no response to that.

'It's good money for sitting there doing nothing.'

'Sitting there naked, doing nothing.'

'Yeah, it was a bit weird. I didn't do it for long.' She took a sip of her coffee. 'It was hard staying still. And the pictures they did. They were just a bit crap. I think that's why I quit. I was offended by how bad the drawings were.'

I clicked on another of PatrickCruz210's followers. A girl of about twenty-two or twenty-three. Tattoos. Brown eyes. Tongue hanging out like a dog.

'It was starting to make me paranoid about my appearance. All these men drawing my tits and thighs all wrong. It wasn't good for my self-esteem. Maybe that's why I started dating Robert, you know, the photographer I told you about. I've got some of his pictures on my phone somewhere if you want to see them.'

I looked up. 'Sorry. See what?'

'Are you even listening? The photographs Robert took of me.'

'Naked photographs?'

'No, not naked. Well, not all.'

'You're insane letting someone take photographs of you naked. Haven't you heard of revenge porn? Or cloud-hacking?'

'Nobody other than me has got a copy.'

'That's what he told you.'

'He wasn't a revenge porn kind of guy.'

'You could still get your phone hacked.'

She looked out of the window. 'It's not very likely though, is it?'

It wasn't likely, no, but it happened.

She said, 'What did you mean, "*your* generation"?'

'Millennial.'

'It's your generation too.'

'It's not.'

'What are you then? A baby boomer? You're only four years older than me.'

I sighed. She paused. 'Can we go to the beach now?'

I called Joe as we walked to the car but it went straight to answer.

At the edge of the village, a sign pointed to Whispering Beach. A bumpy track led along a riverbank until it ended in a car park, empty apart from an open-back truck. We got out into the prickle of midges. Anna ran down a path between tall green reeds, trying to escape them, or was she just eager to get to the sea?

The 'whispering' was the wind through the reeds. Behind them was a beach of white sand streaked with tidelines of black seaweed, and this time there was no rubbish caught amongst it, just shells and feathers and driftwood. A café overlooked the beach, its big windows reflected the water and sky. White plastic tables and chairs filled a veranda in front.

Anna dropped her bag on the sand and started pulling off her shoes and socks. 'I can't believe how lucky we are.' She rolled up her jeans and went down to the water, calling back, 'It's not too bad. It's actually all right.'

The sea was flat and glassy like a mirror. The beach was empty apart from us. She took off her T-shirt and jeans. She was wearing an orange swimming costume underneath. 'Okay. I'm going in before I lose my nerve.'

Further along the beach, there were canoes tied up against a jetty. Across the bay you could see the woods and hills of our peninsula and I thought I could pick out the cove I'd found this morning. I chose a stretch of sand without any seaweed and sat down.

This beach reminded me of my first weekend away with Joe. We'd driven up to Scotland from London, arriving late on a Friday night when the sea was just an absence of light on the other side of the road. We were staying in a holiday flat above a shop on the seafront and you could hear a low rushing sound that could have been waves breaking or could have been the wind. The bed was three deep in blankets and when we turned off the lights at night you couldn't see the walls. The darkness smothered us, like the heavy wool covers, and we were still at the stage in our relationship where we slept holding each other. Joe would sleepily follow me around the bed each night, bringing me back in when we got separated. He was always warm and close and there, and I had adjusted to his presence completely.

That first morning he went down to the shop to buy bread and milk while I stayed in bed. I heard his footsteps descending the stairs. The ring of the bell as he pushed open the shop door. A muffled conversation through the floorboards. I felt a peace and contentedness that still echoes back to me when I walk into a shop with a bell on the door. A sense of safety, of being in the right place, with the right person.

I hadn't had any long relationships before Joe. I hadn't been on holiday with a man before. I'd always gone alone and I'd had to make everything happen myself: plans, conversations, breakfast. I'd had no sense of how it could be any different.

He came back and cooked eggs and by then the sun was shining on the beach across the road. But we went back to bed. Following each other's bodies beneath the blankets, awake this time and meeting each other's eyes.

Later we walked across the bay towards a tidal island in the mouth of an estuary. The sun reflected off the wet sand and water swallowed our footprints moments after they were made. When I turned around, I expected to see them leading back to the shore, but it was like we'd never been there, we were only here.

There were no people living on this island, just birds and a causeway that came and went with the changing tides; it was a raised bed of broken shells that crunched beneath our boots as we followed it onto the surer ground of the island, where families picnicked on the grass and children ran in and out of tunnels in the bracken. We sat at a distance from them, watching the seabirds diving and the children hiding.

Joe took my hand. 'Do you think you'll have kids?'

I wasn't sure what to say. I was a little bit stunned by the question. He was talking about the future but was he talking about our future? I said, 'I'm not sure. Will you?'

'I'd like to, yes. Not now, but you know, some time.'

'You want a family?'

'Yes.'

I said, 'I do too.'

It felt true to say I wanted a family. More so than to say I wanted a baby.

Joe said, 'You'd make a good mother.'

'Why do you say that?'

'Because you're a good person.'

I'd never thought otherwise. But the two things didn't necessarily go together, did they?

Anna shouted something to me. I think it was, 'This is awesome.' She swam parallel to the shore, then flipped over onto her back and lay there lolling in the cold sea like it was a hot bubble bath.

She would like it if I had a cup of coffee waiting for her

when she came out. I got up and wandered over to the café. Inside there was the smell of bleach and coffee. Light flooded through the big windows and bounced off the white walls and tables. Batik cloth with inky blue swirls hung in billows from the ceiling and driftwood was placed artfully in enclosures in the thick walls. There was nobody behind the counter. Then music started. Something electronic and dreamy without words. A door opened and the girl who came out was the girl I'd seen this morning.

Her face showed a split second of surprise, smoothed over so fast I would have missed it if I hadn't been looking when she came through. Her eyes moved from me on to the windows and empty beach, then back to me and away again, as if I was something hard to look at, like the sun or someone you secretly loved. She recognised me. That much was clear.

'What can I get you?'

English not Scottish. Early twenties. Blue eyes.

'Two lattes, please, to take away.'

She spooned coffee into the filter, twisted it into place. The machine churned. There was silence while the liquid trickled out.

I said, 'I saw you this morning.'

Her eyes didn't move from the cup as it filled. She said, 'Are you staying in that place across the bay?'

'Yes.'

'Oh.' She paused. 'What was it you ordered, again?'

'Two lattes.'

'Sorry, I'm still half asleep.' She started the process again. Refilling the filter. Jamming it into place.

I said, 'You were up early.'

'My baby wouldn't sleep. It's better to get out of the house sometimes.'

The bundle in the sling. Where was it now?

She poured milk from a jug, put lids on the coffees. 'Sugar?'

'No thanks. I mean, yes, one, for my sister.'

Her eyes darted out towards the beach again.

I said, 'She's gone for a swim.'

'Brave.' She put a bag of sugar and a stirrer on top of one of the cups. 'Five pounds twenty, please.'

I handed her the money.

'Enjoy the beach,' she said.

'That was amazing.' Anna had seaweed between her toes and wet sand on her calves. 'Why don't you go in?'

I handed her a towel to stop her dripping cold seawater onto me. 'No thanks. I got you a coffee.'

'Thanks. You know, I never knew Scotland was as beautiful as this.' She looked out at the bay, smiling and shivering at the same time. 'I mean, look at the colour of that water. It doesn't even look real.'

I waited for her to dry off and sit down before I told her. 'The girl I saw at our cottage is working in the café.'

'Small world.'

'She said she was taking her baby out because she couldn't get it to sleep.'

'Oh right.' She took a sip of her drink. 'Are you hungry? We could get a second breakfast.'

'Okay.'

Anna dressed, not quite under the cover of a towel. 'Shall we leave our stuff here?'

I picked up my bag. 'I'm not.'

I let her lead the way into the café. It was still empty apart from the girl who was laying out cakes in a glass cabinet across the front of the counter. She flicked her eyes over us and continued with her task. 'I'll just be a moment.'

'No hurry,' Anna said brightly. 'Good coffee by the way.'

'Thank you.'

Anna picked up a menu. 'Are you serving food?'

'I am.' The girl put the last cake out. 'What would you like?'

'Can I have a bagel? Oh my God, a bagel with Marmite. Have you got Marmite?' Anna smiled warmly. She was making friends.

'We have. With butter?'

'Yes please. There's not even a toaster in our cottage. Can you believe that?'

I said, 'You need electricity for a toaster.'

Anna said, 'It's like living in the jungle.'

I said, 'It's not at all like living in the jungle.'

The girl said, 'So, is it just the two of you there?'

Anna answered before I could think of a response. 'Yeah, it's tiny. You couldn't fit any more.'

She nodded. 'Is that everything?' She was looking at me.

'A cup of tea, please.'

She told us to take a seat. Anna chose a table by the window. The girl went through the door behind the counter. I glimpsed the shining metal surfaces of a kitchen as it swung shut. I said, 'Why did you tell her we're staying out there on our own?'

Anna shrugged. 'Why wouldn't I?'

'She could have been something to do with last night.'

'You think *she's* the midnight rambler?' Anna looked unconvinced by the idea. 'Because you saw her this morning?'

'Yes. And the way she was acting. Trying to stay hidden, then walking off when she saw me.'

The girl came back in the room and I stopped talking. When she'd gone again, I said, 'I'm just saying, we don't know who it was so we ought to be a bit careful. That's all.'

'Okay. But–' She sighed. 'Anyway.'

When the girl brought our order over, Anna started chatting to her again. She wanted to know about the canoes at the jetty; were they for hire, who should she speak to? I wondered whether she was deliberately being friendly to annoy me. Then an older lady came in with a baby crying in a carrycot, saying, 'Here's Mummy. Here she is.'

The girl paused, mid-sentence, unsure who to respond to first; Anna's question about canoe hire or the baby, which was crying so loud it drowned out the music. She hurried over to it, unfastened the straps, and lifted it out. She held it under its arms and jiggled it up and down, saying 'Shush now. What's all this about?'

The older lady was saying the baby had drunk two ounces, had slept for over an hour, had just been changed. It peered at us over her shoulder. It wasn't crying anymore and its face became still as it looked at me.

I felt this wave of heat travel up my back and neck and into my face. I thought I was about to be sick. I tried to smile but I couldn't.

The girl glanced at us then turned away just as fast. She lay the baby back in the carrycot and put it on a booth seat near the counter, sheltered from view. My nausea passed. My chest felt cold where my T-shirt was damp with sweat.

'Are you okay?' Anna asked.

'Yeah, I just feel a bit funny.'

'Do you want some bagel?'

'No thanks.'

On the beach, a group of school kids were spreading out in twos and threes. They wandered along the shore with collection jars and fishing nets, wellington boots over leggings and tracksuits.

Anna finished eating and asked if I wanted anything else.

She was getting another coffee. I watched her chatting to the older lady while the girl dried teacups and stacked them on the counter. The lady turned and asked her a question and the girl said something in response. I couldn't hear what it was.

Anna came back and dug in her rucksack for her sketchbook. She took a seat where she could see into the carrycot. She was going to draw the baby.

I tried to read but I couldn't concentrate. I was trying to hear what the three of them were talking about. I could pick up the tone but not the words and it reminded me of when I was a teenager and I'd listen from upstairs when Anna brought all her friends round. Not one or two, but five or six, filling the kitchen. I could smell the sickly chocolate cookies they were baking, and hear snippets of their conversations. Asking if they could go in Anna's room and Anna saying no, because I was home.

'She's always home. Doesn't she ever go out?'

'She went out last Friday, for your information. To the cinema.' Anna's tone was somewhere between mocking me and defending me, like she wasn't sure which way to go.

'Fun times. Who with?'

'Emma and Rachel.' As though even my friends' names were a joke.

'The Chicken Crew. Did Mr Shaw go too? Did they take the chickens?'

'All the chickens following them into the Odeon, pecking at the popcorn on the floor.'

High-pitched laughter. Exaggerated and all exactly the same, like everything they did.

Another asked, 'Has she got a boyfriend?'

'She's never even got off with anyone.'

'She's fifteen!'

Then when they'd gone and Anna had got the house

looking normal again, she didn't even refer to it, as if they'd never been there, laughing about me in the kitchen.

I remembered this, listening to my sister gabbing away as she sketched. I had no reason to think she was talking about me. The baby started to cry softly in the cot. The older lady lifted it out and angled a bottle into its mouth. There was a gust of sea air as a big group of walkers came in, all sticks and rucksacks. She passed the baby, bottle still attached, to Anna, then went to help the girl behind the counter.

My sister held the baby on her lap, her posture tense, her face bright. It stared up at her, seemingly unconcerned by this switch from friend to stranger. I couldn't see its face but I could picture it. Milk-heavy eyes. A calm acceptance.

I pushed out my chair and Anna grinned over at me, as if to say, look what I've got! In the toilets the mirror was discoloured in that vintage style. My complexion looked darker than it was.

When I returned, the girl was holding her baby again, rubbing its back. Anna came over and sat down. 'This weather.'

Rain raced down the windowpanes. The sea was closer and the beach smaller. The schoolchildren had their hoods up, jostling each other as they hurried back to the car park.

We ran through the downpour to the car and got inside fast. 'Leonie only moved up here last week,' Anna began, as I turned the ignition. 'She's from Cornwall originally. It sounds like she travelled about a lot before she had Fleur.'

Leonie and Fleur. I kept quiet. Sometimes it was the best way to keep her talking.

'Mary is a local. She owns the café and that hostel in the village. Leonie's living in a chalet there.' Anna looked out of the side window. 'Can we stop at the shop? I want to buy some shortbread.'

I turned in and went online while she dashed through the rain. I searched for Leonie on Facebook but I couldn't find her without a last name.

On the way back along the peninsula, we met the car I'd seen above the cove. There wasn't enough space for us both and I was getting into reverse when the other driver beat me to it, his head turned back to see where he was going. I raised my hand to say thank you as we passed. He nodded in response.

'Maybe that was the hand,' Anna said. 'Or the midnight rambler.'

'Maybe.'

She said, 'Very polite though, for a potential psychopath.'

'Aren't they always very polite?'

'Polite and good-looking.'

I said, 'I was watching the road.'

'Dark eyes. Dark hair. It's a winning combination.'

'It's half the population of the world.'

'What can I say? I'm easy to please.'

I let that remark hang. I wouldn't say Anna is a slut; she's just man-orientated. It's because she doesn't like being alone and I blame growing up in a shared bedroom for that. Another way Dad's plan to keep us young and innocent backfired.

———

It rained all afternoon and evening. I lit the gas lamp and the candles and sat at the table with my journal. I was thinking about last night. I worked out that the intruder must have been here between midnight and two. The hours between Anna going to bed and my intermittent waking. It could have been the reason I woke in the first place.

'Who do you think it was last night?'

Anna looked up from her Harry Potter. 'I don't think it was anyone. It was probably a squirrel.'

'What about that man we drove past?'

'Nah.'

'Trying to scare us?'

She shook her head.

'Why are you so certain?'

She closed her book. 'Look, there's an axe under the bed. If anyone gets in here I'll start swinging it around. I'll chop his hands off, and his dick.'

'What if it's a woman?'

'It won't be. Chill out, Catherine. The door's locked. Nobody can get inside. Nobody wants to. We're fine.' She got up and took her sketchbook out of her bag, then sat across from me at the table.

'What are you doing?'

'I'm going to draw you.'

'No you're not.'

'Get a book or something and just pretend I'm not here.'

'That's impossible.'

'Write your diary. You won't even notice me.'

She didn't understand how intrusive it was, to sit there studying someone and putting it down on paper. I decided to do the same to her with words. I ignored whatever she was drawing and wrote a few sentences. *Hair like a snake sliding down her shoulder.* I studied her, wrote a few more. *Moving her quick, sharp pencil like a knife.*

She saw what I was doing and laughed. 'Are you writing about me?'

'I might be.'

'You'd better be.' Then, 'Are we going to compare afterwards?'

'No.'

She sighed. 'He nearly smiled, didn't he, when we passed him.'

'Who?' I wrote, *Always thinking about a man.*

'The guy in the car.'

'The one you want to castrate?'

'Maybe not straight away.' She added, 'He's called Callum.'

I looked up. 'How do you know that?'

'I asked Mary if there was anyone else living down here. He's her nephew.'

It was something I remembered from school; my sister knowing who everyone was. And everyone knowing her. Back there, I was 'Anna's sister' which was annoying, considering I was older than her. It was, 'Have you heard about Anna's sister?' And, 'Oh my God, *Anna's sister?*' I sometimes thought that usurping of my identity was the reason I moved away, and not the other thing at all.

She turned a page in her sketchbook. Fleur, asleep in the carrycot, eyelashes resting on full, round cheeks. Arms flexed upwards at the elbows, fists by her ears.

Wherever you went, there were babies. You couldn't avoid them. And sometimes when I saw one, I wanted to hold it and feel its soft, solid weight in my arms. The steady warmth of its skin. But I never did. I kept my hands in my pockets and kept walking and the light, ungrounded sensation passed as I got further down the street.

That happened regularly. It was normal for me.

Anna turned the page again. She said, 'What do you think?' It was her drawing of me. My face half in darkness. A pen in my hand.

'Is it finished?'

'Yes. Do you want it?'

'Not really.' I wanted to look at Fleur again. I reached for the sketchbook and turned back to her sleeping face.

'Does she remind you of anyone?' I asked, casually.

Anna looked at the drawing. 'No. Apart from Leonie. Why?'

'She looks familiar.'

'All babies look the same to me.' The candle spluttered in its pool of wax. She said, 'It's a rubbish drawing. I didn't get her right at all.' She shut the sketchbook and reached over for my journal.

'No.' I quickly took it back.

'Sorry.' She looked like she didn't know what to do with her hands. She reached for her glass of wine.

'I think I'll go to bed,' I said.

'You can't go to bed yet.'

I didn't want a debate about it, I just wanted to go to bed.

She said, 'Are there any crisps left?'

'In the cupboard. See you in the morning.'

I wasn't tired but I wanted to be alone so I could think. I changed into my pyjamas and blew out the candles in the bedroom, then got inside my sleeping bag. I tried to picture Fleur's face. Not how it was in Anna's drawing, but how it was when she'd looked at me for those long moments in the café. But without her in front of me, it was gone.

Instead, I saw Leonie turn quickly from me with Fleur against her shoulder. I saw the look she gave me when she first found me waiting at the counter. She'd said a lot in that split second before her wall went up. *I know you.* And something else. *Be careful.* Then a smile as if neither of those thoughts had crossed her mind at all.

———

The rain woke me. A sudden heavy downpour that grew in volume until it sounded like something solid not liquid hitting the roof. It woke Anna up, too. I could always tell when she was awake. Something changed in the atmosphere when I wasn't alone with my thoughts anymore. Sure enough, the bed creaked as she sat up. 'Catherine?'

'Yes?'

'Have you got any spare ear-plugs?'

I dug some out of my suitcase and passed them up to her.

'Thanks.'

I got back in bed. After a while the rain eased a little. It sounded like applause now. I imagined myself in a concert hall; rows of people clapping for the orchestra, their admiration went on and on. The musicians had played supremely well. The applause started to fade as they left the stage, and now it sounded like the radio static that hung between the lochs and forests. Barely there. Soft and softer still and I was almost asleep. Then there was a knock on the bedroom window. My eyes shot open.

Did I imagine it? Was it a dream that had started playing too soon? But why could I still hear the sound in my head? 'Anna,' I whispered.

She didn't stir. I stared at the curtain where the sound had come from.

It was quiet. Minutes passed and I started to relax a little. Then three knocks, louder this time. Knuckles rapping hard on glass. The light changed as a figure moved past the window. 'Anna,' I said urgently. 'There's somebody outside.'

I got up and shook her awake, glancing back at the window behind me.

'What's up?'

'Someone knocked on the window. Take your ear-plugs out.'

She sat up. 'Are you sure?'

'Definitely.'

We listened, barely breathing. The rain had stopped and

the room felt too quiet, too still. I whispered, 'They knocked. Then I saw their shadow.'

She whispered, 'You're freaking me out.'

'It's not *my* fault.'

'Shhhh!' She held her breath. There was a scrape outside. Footsteps. Then bang, bang, bang on the cottage door.

'Oh my God.'

I couldn't speak. My legs and arms went weak. Who was out there?

Anna said, 'The door's locked. They can't get in.'

'Who is it?'

She paused for a second then slid down to the floor and reached under the bed. She stood up with the axe that was meant for chopping firewood. She tested the blade against her fingers and snatched them away because it was sharp. She said, 'If someone's knocking on the door in the middle of the night, I'm answering it with an axe.'

Oh God. Her fight or flight response had always been set to fight, even in the most unwise situations. When someone made her afraid, it made her angry and reckless.

I said, 'Do not open that door.'

'They're trying to scare us. I'm not having it.'

She went into the living room and got the key from the hook by the door. She put it in the keyhole and listened. I shook my head at her. '*Please don't.*'

She took a breath and turned the key, flung open the door, the axe raised.

There was nobody there. The night air was cold and grey. She stepped outside and quickly looked from left to right. She waited another minute or so, then came back in and locked the door. 'I'm going back to bed.'

'But what if they're still out there?'

'As long as they don't come in here, I don't really care. I just want to go to sleep.'

'I won't get back to sleep now,' I said.

'Do you want this?' She held out the axe. I shook my head. She put it on the table next to our empty wine glasses.

It was half past two in the morning. I stayed awake all night.

4

ANNA

Tuesday. Sunrise 04.28. Sunset 22.19

I still had a few moments each morning when I wasn't sure where I was. The van? Mum and Dad's house? Our bunk bed from twenty years ago in our childhood bedroom? I heard rain blowing against the window, wind in the trees. Scotland. Oh Jesus, all that drama last night. That banging on the door like the police wanted to speak to us about something we'd done. I slid down from the bed. Catherine was sitting at the table writing in her diary, her phone face-up beside her. The axe within reach. She looked up. 'There's something wrong with the water.'

'Huh?'

She turned on the kitchen tap. Water the colour of the stream through the marsh flowed out. It filled the washing-up bowl with a murky, pond-like brown.

'What is that?'

She said, 'You tell me.'

'Have we got any bottled?'

'I think this is what they were up to last night.'

I needed coffee to deal with this. I poured bottled water into the kettle and put it on the stove. Someone had contaminated our water supply? How would they even do that? I remembered the ring binder I'd hidden during my feng shui frenzy. Somewhere in there, amongst the ramblings about where to buy fishing bait and baffling family jokes, it had mentioned issues with the water clarity. I found it partway through a paragraph about the best place to see a sea eagle.

By the way, if there are any problems with the water, there's likely something afoot at the spring where it 'springs' from.

I showed it to Catherine. 'It says they sometimes have problems with the water here. It was probably nothing to do with last night.'

She looked doubtfully at me. I looked back at the notes.

Your best bet is to go up there and be prepared to get wet. Take a spade and a sense of humour. The map shows you where it is, roughly.

Roughly? And what spade? The jaunty tone made me want to throw it across the room.

'It says we've got to go and find the spring.' I sank back into the sofa. 'Can't we just call a plumber?'

'We've no phone signal. And a plumber won't come all the way out here.'

'There's a map.' It was a hand-drawn sketch showing the cottage, the track, a stream and somewhere up the hill behind us, a circle where the spring was. 'So the water literally comes from a stream in the woods? It's like *Jean de Florette* around here. Sinister locals and blocked springs.'

Catherine didn't laugh. I sighed. 'Okay, well, I'll get dressed, then we'll go and find it.'

'We can't stay here without water.'

'We've got water. It's just a bit brown.'

'We can't drink it. I wouldn't even want to wash with it.'

'Let's not panic until we've found out what's wrong.' I went into the bedroom, leaving her frowning at me. She'd gone straight to worst-case scenario. I mean, we could buy more bottled water, couldn't we? And some yokel knocking on the window wasn't going to make me leave. In daylight it seemed even more cowardly. The kind of thing bored teenagers would do for a laugh if they had a really shit sense of humour. I popped my head around the door again. 'If somebody actually wanted to get in and hurt us, they wouldn't knock first. They'd do it with stealth.'

By the time I'd dressed, Catherine had found the spade and was smearing midge repellent on her neck and hands. I did the same and we set off in the rain, taking a path that led up through the woods behind the cottage. Catherine said she was going back to get her phone in case there was a signal higher up. She said she'd catch me up so I kept walking. The way was obvious at first but it soon became uncertain, as if perhaps this wasn't a path after all, just a trail made by deer. I ducked under oak branches and clambered around boulders, crossed the stream, crossed back again, my feet sinking into mud and moss. I was wondering how long we could stay here without a clean water supply. I could happily go feral and wash in the sea, but I doubted Catherine would. I looked back to see if I could see her. When I turned round again, there was a man standing further up the hillside, looking down at me through the trees.

I stopped. We were too far away to speak, too close for not speaking to feel natural. It was a standoff, only bearable because the rushing of the stream filled the silence.

We both started walking towards each other at the same moment. I recognised him as the man in the car. Mary's nephew, Callum. His boots gripped the steep slope as he came towards me. His legs were tanned as if he'd been wearing shorts for months. He nodded a hello, like when we'd passed him on the road.

'Hi.' I stopped just below him on the path. His face was roughened by weather and his gaze was direct and slightly disconcerting. I was blocking his way down. I said, 'I'm trying to find a spring.'

'Are you staying in that cottage down the hill?'

My eyes were level with his chin. 'Yes.'

'How's your water looking?'

'It's the colour of a very peaty whisky.'

He gave a little laugh. 'Aye, well, mine's the colour of whisky and Coke.'

The colour of your eyes. They were still fixed on me. I stepped aside in case he wanted to pass me, but he didn't move. I said, 'So. Does something need fixing?'

'Is that why you brought a spade?'

'The instructions in the cottage said bring a spade.'

'You've got instructions? What do they say?'

This didn't sound promising. 'That was it, really.'

He looked away for a moment, thinking. 'My dad would know what to do.'

I waited but he didn't expand on this line of thought. I said, 'Maybe you could call him?'

He didn't seem to hear. 'I've just been to the spring. I think the water table's risen because of the rain.'

I had no idea what that meant. 'Okay.'

'We just have to wait till it gets back to normal.' His eyes focused on something behind me. Catherine, further down the path.

I lowered my voice. 'My sister will make us leave if we haven't got clean water.'

'Get bottled water at the shop. You probably shouldn't be drinking this stuff anyway. Not without boiling it first.'

'But what if we want a bath?'

He shrugged, as if to say, I can't help you there. I wondered what his bathing plans were, but I couldn't think of a polite way to ask. He said, 'It's only peat. People would pay good money for that water in a spa.'

'Like a mineral soak?'

'Aye. Good for the skin.' The rain pattered on the trees. He fastened his jacket up over his chin. 'Are you heading down?'

I followed, wondering if I ought to go and check out this spring for myself. The stream flowing alongside us was clearer than the stuff that came out of our taps. It ran down the hillside in little waterfalls and pools. Twigs and birch leaves bobbed at the edges.

He stopped where another path led away through the woods on the other side of the stream, so faint I hadn't noticed it on the way up. He said, 'I'm heading that way.'

That way was more deep woodland and lichen-covered rocks. I said, 'Where do you live?'

'You drew a picture of it.'

I wasn't sure what to say. He smiled, looked at the ground when I didn't smile back. 'Well. Good luck.' He was about to set off back into the woods and we hadn't solved the problem of the water yet.

I said, 'Is there nothing we can do? About the spring?'

'It's just nature. Let it run its course.'

Was that it? I said thanks, and there was a hint of sympathy in his expression, like he could see I wasn't happy but he wasn't going to get involved. 'No bother. Hope you get yourself sorted.' He walked rather than jumped across the stream, not even trying to keep his feet dry.

I started down the slope. Catherine said, 'Was that that guy again? What were you talking about?'

'He said there's peat in the water because it's been raining so hard. It's nothing to do with whoever it was last night.'

'Do you believe him?'

I shrugged. 'Yeah.'

'What are we supposed to do?'

'Nothing, apparently. He said it's "just nature". And we have to let it run its course.'

She sat down on a boulder. 'How long is that going to take?'

I looked back at where he was striding off into the woods. Rain-wet hair curled against the back of his neck. He moved fast, following a route you wouldn't even know was there.

'Hours? Days? Weeks?'

He was gone. Hidden by the trees.

'Anna?'

'What?'

'What are we going to do?'

I looked at my sister. 'Wait, I guess. See what happens. We can get some water at the shop.'

The rain stopped after breakfast and the sky became streaked with blue. Catherine wanted to go to the beach again so I put my swimming costume on under my clothes. We locked up and I went to open the car door, then stopped, took a step back.

There was a scratch in the paintwork right across the passenger side. Unbroken. Deliberate. 'Catherine,' I said.

She looked over the roof of the car at me.

'Come and see this.'

She came round and saw where I was pointing. 'Oh.' She looked stunned by it, then confused. 'I don't remember scraping anything.'

She didn't seem to realise what it was. For a moment, I

considered not telling her. But they'd know at the car hire place. Joe would know if she described it to him. I said, 'It's been done on purpose. Somebody's keyed our car.' I sighed. After last night, and the water this morning, we didn't need something else to worry about.

She said, 'Somebody's done it on purpose?'

'Fuckers. We're going to lose our deposit. I haven't got that much money to spare.'

'Was it last night? It must have been.'

'I'm pretty sure it wasn't there yesterday. I'd have seen it.'

'What will we do?'

'I don't know.' I laughed, exasperated, because since when had I been the one who knew what to do when things went wrong. I looked at the line in the paintwork and felt kind of wounded, like whoever had done it had attacked me and Catherine personally, not just our car. That was the point, I guessed. It was nasty. Petty. And it would cost a load of money to fix. I said, 'I just wanted to come on holiday to relax. I didn't want dodgy water and crazy squirrels and some twat keying our hire car.'

'Maybe we should just go home?'

'We're not going home.' I got in the car and waited for her to follow.

The tide was in at the beach. I spread out the picnic blanket on the narrow strip of smooth sand between the water and the cotton-grass. Catherine took out her diary but didn't open it.

'Do you want a coffee?' she said.

'Maybe in a bit.'

'At least if it starts raining, there's somewhere we can go.'

It didn't look like it would but the skies changed from one

moment to the next. Rain then sun then rain again. Mist giving way to rainbows. One minute you were too hot, the next too cold. I must have taken my jumper on and off about twenty times already today.

I watched a mother and two young children in wetsuits run in and out of the sea, screaming and laughing about how cold it was, while the dad filmed them on his phone. An older lady – was she their grandma? – pulled an inflatable dinghy down to the water. She set it afloat, climbed in and paddled expertly out into the bay. Short, quick strokes taking her forwards. This was the kind of lady I wanted to be at that age. One who took off in a boat when the grandchildren were getting a bit raucous, while the parents watched enviously from the shore.

I thought about drawing it all, but I was happy just watching. This scene of normality was very welcome after the weird vibes in the woods. Out on the jetty a young man fished out leaves from a kayak, one arm and shoulder inside the boat, it looked like he was being swallowed by a shark. Leonie said yesterday that they were for wildlife tours. I got up and wandered over. I said hi. He mumbled hi back.

'Are there any tours today?'

He looked at me with eyes in a permanent squint from summers spent in endless daylight. 'Not today.' He reached back into the kayak. Pulled out a handful of crisp brown leaves and dumped them on a pile beside his legs. He wanted me to leave.

I said, 'Can I hire one for an hour and paddle about by myself?'

He sat up. 'You want to go in a boat?'

'Yes.'

He had the same rough brown whorly hair as Callum. The same pioneer build, but he was about ten years younger. He said, 'Do you know what you're doing?'

'I used to live in Canada. I went kayaking a lot.' Used to live. I'd never said that before. Only, I've just come back from Canada, or I've been in Canada, as if I'd reached the end of a vacation, not started a new chapter of my life.

He wiped his hands across his jeans, thinking it through. 'You can hire one for an hour for twenty pounds. But don't go out of sight.'

'Okay. Should I pay you now or after?'

'Whenever.'

I handed him the money and he put it in the back pocket of his jeans. He looked at me, literally sizing me up, then picked a life jacket from where they were drying out in the sun. 'Here.'

He turned away when I started getting undressed. Maybe I should have gone in the café to change? I pulled the life jacket over my swimming costume and tightened the straps. He tightened them further, then stepped back. 'You're good to go.'

'Can I leave my stuff here?'

'S'up to you.'

'Will you make sure nobody walks off with it?'

He nodded. I didn't trust him but there was nothing valuable in there anyway; I'd just given him all my money. I looked back at the beach where Catherine was watching us. I pointed to the canoes and gave her a thumbs-up sign. After a moment she gave one back.

He held the kayak steady while I climbed in and took the paddle. 'Stay in the bay. Don't go near those rocks. It's too shallow.' As an afterthought he said, 'There's a whistle on your life jacket if you need me.'

'Are there any strong currents?'

He glanced at the water. 'You'll be all right.' He pushed the boat away from the jetty. I let it glide then dipped the paddle in, propelling it forwards. I was heading into the wind. I hadn't even noticed it on land but out here it filled my ears and sent spray into my eyes. Within a few minutes the tops of my legs were wet but the effort of paddling kept me warm. I got a rhythm going and turned towards the open sea. There was nothing in between me and the islands.

I wanted to leave the stress of last night and this morning behind me on the shore. It had taken me ages to get back to sleep after I'd been outside with the axe. I'd been expecting a knock on the window at any moment. It was the waiting and not knowing that made it so annoying. I'd rather confront someone face-on than lie there wondering what they were going to do next. Did I scare them off when I went outside, armed? Or had they already left? I just wanted to forget all about it but that was difficult now I'd seen what they'd done to our car. We'd have to get it fixed. The car hire company would rob us blind if we gave it back looking like that.

I stopped to rest my arms when they started to ache. A blossom of pink seaweed floated alongside my kayak. It was feathery and rootless, more like a fish than a plant. I watched it drift away then paddled until my arms tired again. I stopped and let the bow drift back round. I could see Catherine writing her diary on the beach. The boy standing at the end of the jetty. He shook his head at me. He thought I'd gone too far out. I lifted a hand in acknowledgement. He put his hands on his hips in a long-distance sulk.

There was a cry from the beach that sounded like a seagull. It was Leonie's baby, Fleur. Leonie was pushing the pram along the path from the café. The kayak boy went to help her lift it up onto the jetty, then she went back the way she came, leaving him to push the crying baby up and down. Was he Fleur's dad?

On the beach, Catherine had put down her diary. She was watching Leonie walk back to the café and there was something about her stillness and posture that I didn't like. What had she said yesterday about Fleur looking familiar? 'Does she remind you of anybody?' She stood up, folded the picnic blanket, and followed Leonie inside.

The crying became louder as the boy went along the jetty, faded as he went back towards the shore. After a while, it went quiet and he pushed the pram back to the café. Baby sleeping. Job done.

When he returned, I paddled back in.

He looked down at me in the water. 'That it?'

'That's it.'

He held the kayak steady as I climbed out. 'I thought you were trying to get back to Canada when you started heading straight out to sea.'

'I was.' I took the life jacket off and put it back with the others. I said over my shoulder, 'You looked like a pro, pushing that pram along. Are you her dad?'

He started blushing like crazy. 'No. I'm not her daddy.' He picked up my bag and handed it to me. 'Here.'

'Thanks.' He was frowning, like I'd said something out of order. I said, 'I drew her yesterday. That's why I asked.' I found my sketchbook in my bag and showed him the picture of Fleur.

He looked down at it. 'What's this?'

'Oh, I'm an artist. It's just what I do. It's not finished yet.'

'She's Leonie's.'

'I know.' I wouldn't go drawing somebody's baby without asking their mother first. He rubbed his hand over the back of his neck and turned away. Maybe he was like Catherine who thought it was intrusive to draw someone's portrait.

He nodded towards the shore. 'Your sister's here.'

Catherine was waiting at the end of the jetty. She had her arms wrapped around her sides like she was cold, even though she was dressed and dry, unlike me.

'I'll go and get changed inside,' I said when I reached her.

Her eyes had a stripped bare look to them. 'I'll wait in the car.'

Catherine had gone quiet again and it wasn't a comfortable, easy silence either. She was elsewhere and every time I tried to bring her back, she flinched, like my voice was too loud or what I was saying was particularly offensive, when I was only talking at a normal volume about the weather. I asked her a question and it seemed an effort for her to answer. I just wanted to know where we were going. We were driving in the opposite direction to our cottage, following the banks of a sea loch whipped into waves by the rising wind. The first drops of rain hit the windscreen. The hills across the water were misted with grey.

I asked her again. 'Are we heading anywhere in particular?'

'We're just following this road.'

Yes, I could see that. 'Where to?'

'I don't know. I don't know where it goes. You're the one with the map.'

I looked out of the side window. I wanted to say, 'What's up?' but I was afraid of the response.

I rooted in my bag for my phone, just in case we'd reached an area with a signal. *No service.* I didn't have anyone to call anyway, not in the UK, and that thought made the hollow feeling in my chest grow. I just wanted to chat. You know, exchange pleasantries, maybe make someone laugh. I wondered whether I could go and visit Callum when we got back to the cottage or would he think that was weird when I didn't actually know him? Or perhaps, with the population being so low around here, it would be okay. Otherwise, how did they cope? You'd have to be very good at being alone. I liked my own company but I preferred to have someone to appreciate it with me. Someone responsive and smiley and interested in what I was saying. Not my sister, shut away in her own personal snow globe, still and unreachable, no matter how much you shook her world.

We crossed a stony, silver river. The wipers raced against the rain. I started to feel like I was in a snow globe with her, both of us behind glass, peering out at the world beyond. A car approached. Human life. I put my palm against the window. Who are you? How do I reach you? Don't go. It was gone.

A midge fuzzed about on the glass. I squashed it with my thumb. 'I'm getting pretty hungry.'

A few minutes later she pulled in at a lay-by and turned the car round. 'Let's go back.'

'Okay.' As if I had a say in the matter.

We parked up in the village and I dashed through the rain to the shop while Catherine checked her emails in the car. The usual lady was at the counter. She looked up from her knitting and said hello when I walked in. I bought us fruit cake, cheese, bananas, crisps, chocolate, wine, water, candles. When I went to pay, she said, 'Callum tells me you're having problems with your water.'

And I'd thought my parents' town was small. 'It was brown when we woke up this morning.'

'You'll need more than that.' She went to the shelves at the back and returned with a four-pack of bottled water. 'Have these on us.'

'Thanks. I'll pay.'

'Oh, it's nothing. Take them.'

Back at the cottage, there was more water sitting by the door. Two heavy five-litre bottles, unsealed as if they'd been refilled rather than bought new.

I said, 'The lady in the shop made me take more water as well.'

'She made you?'

'Well, you know, she gave it to me.' I unlocked the door and carried in the shopping. I put one of the unsealed bottles on the table and poured myself a glass.

'Are you sure that's drinking water?'

It was already in my mouth. Too late now. I swallowed. 'He wouldn't have left it there if it wasn't.' I was assuming Callum brought it. It tasted okay, anyway.

'We still haven't got water to wash with.'

'I'm going to disguise the colour with bubble bath. It'll be fine.'

'It's dirty. It could make you ill.'

'It's just peat. It's not poisonous.'

'I didn't say it was poisonous.'

'I didn't say you did.'

She glared at me. 'We can't stay here without water.'

I hoped she wasn't suggesting we leave again. 'We're in one of the wettest countries in the world. There's water everywhere. There's ten bottles here in this room for a start.'

'But what are we going to wash with?'

'We can wash in the sea.'

'The sea isn't clean. The beach is covered in rubbish.'

'What are you talking about? It's pristine.'

'Not that beach. The one near here.'

'Did you find a beach and not tell me?'

She sighed heavily. 'I just want to go home.'

Well. Fine. She was missing Joe. Or she was fed up with me

73

already. 'Why do you want to go home?' My voice sounded whiny and childish.

'Because things keep going wrong.'

I tried the tap again, hoping it would have cleared while we were out. It hadn't.

'I can't wash in that,' she said.

She had a point but I didn't want to admit it. 'I'm having a bath.'

I went into the tiny bathroom and turned on the taps. How had Callum made it sound enticing, like a luxury spa treatment? I poured in half a bottle of bubble bath. It looked like the run-off you'd get from washing a really muddy car. I didn't stay in it for long and there was a residue of silt when it drained away.

Catherine went to bed early again. I decided to draw the view from the front as it looked in twilight. I sat at the picnic table, using a mug to stop my paper rippling in the breeze. The view was framed by oak trees and it occurred to me that someone must have made it like this on purpose; they cleared that gap in the woods so you could sit here and watch the sun sink towards the islands and the flame-coloured sea.

I started sketching a rough outline, feeling out of my depth with this sublime scene. I'd always rejected Ade's suggestion that I draw landscapes when we were living in Banff. Too obvious, I'd said. The shops on the main street were overrun with watercolour prints of the mountains that loomed over the town, and most weren't very good. Flat and unimaginative. No sense of the spirit of the place. I looked at my own drawing and thought I could apply the same description. I needed to tune into my surroundings more. Let that weird, persistent light flow down to my hand.

I looked up. I'd heard something on the track. I squinted but everything was grainy and merged into one over there. It could have been a deer.

No, somebody was approaching through the trees, tall and soundless and swift. I stood up, emptied the ashtray onto the ground, gripped it in my hand. I took a step away from the table, eyes trained on the woods.

Callum. He was startled when he saw me standing there in the near dark. 'Jesus. What are you going to do with that?'

I was still clutching the ashtray like I was about to throw it at his head. 'Defend myself.'

He said, 'I didn't mean to scare you.'

I lowered the ashtray. 'I wasn't scared.'

'No, me neither.' He laughed. 'I guess it serves me right for coming round so late. I forget what time it is on nights like this.'

'Hmm. A lot of people seem to keep strange hours around here.'

'That's true.' He looked at my half-done drawing on the table. 'So I hear you're an artist?'

He'd been talking about me. 'Yes.'

'It's very good.'

'It's dark. You can't even see it.' I hid it under my sketchbook. 'I was just messing around. There's not a lot to do in the evenings.' I remembered the bottles left on the doorstep. 'Did you bring the water?'

He nodded. 'I was going to leave a note. But I didn't know your name.'

'Anna.'

'Callum.'

I didn't like to say I already knew. I sat down again, hoping he'd do the same.

He said, 'If you're stuck for things to do, there's a band

playing at the centre on Monday night. If you're still here then. I'm going, if you and your sister want a lift.'

'What kind of band?'

'Traditional. Pipes and fiddles, that sort of thing. The Elders, they're called. They're all about sixteen.'

'Yeah why not.'

He nodded. 'Should be a good night.'

A line of light fell onto the grass outside the bedroom window. Catherine, wondering who I was talking to. Callum sat himself down at the other end of the table, facing the sea like I was. 'How's it been going then, apart from the lack of entertainment and basic amenities?'

And the weirdos trying to scare us in the dead of night. I wondered what he knew about that. 'Fine. Well, okay.'

He read my expression. 'Yeah?'

'It's just a bit isolated.'

'It is that.'

'There could be anyone out here.'

He looked quizzically at me.

'Wandering psychopaths. Crazy axe murderers.'

His mouth was slightly open. He was half smiling, half confused. 'You're not worried I'm one, are you?'

'No.'

'Well that's good to know.'

'You haven't got an axe.'

'I forgot it. I'm not very focused on my job.'

'The one thing you needed to remember.'

He smiled.

I said, trying for normality, 'We went to the beach today.'

'I know. My cousin hired you a canoe.'

His cousin? I thought they looked alike. I said, 'He thought I was going to steal it and paddle away.' In the distance, the peaks of the island were black against the setting sun. 'What island is that?'

'Rum.'

'It looks really close sometimes and faraway at others.'

'Maybe it moves about when we're not looking.'

'Like that monster you've got up here?'

'That monster?'

'The one in the... lake.'

He looked at me out of the corner of his eye. 'You're only jealous because you haven't got one in England.'

'I'm jealous of a lot of things you've got up here. Like this view.'

'Aye, it's not bad.'

I said, 'Are you staying for a drink?'

'If you ever get round to offering me one.'

Inside, the furnace glowed red in the stove but the edges of the living room were in darkness. He pulled out a cigarette lighter and went round the room lighting the candles. I turned on the gas lamp, singeing my fingers as the flame sprang into life. I poured glasses of wine. He sat on the sofa, his hands resting on his knees.

'You're not worried for real, are you, about axe murderers? This is a very safe neighbourhood. Mainly because nobody lives here.'

I wondered how much to tell him. For all I knew, he could be the one who vandalised our car at two in the morning. I doubted it though; something told me he wasn't the type. I lowered my voice in case Catherine was listening. 'It's just... Well, on our first night, it looked like someone had been snooping around outside while we were asleep.'

Callum raised his eyebrows slightly.

I said, 'They pulled the table cover off, and threw the ashtray on the floor.'

'It was probably a pine marten looking for food.'

'And then last night, they knocked on the window and banged on the door.'

He looked at me for a moment. 'What time was this?'

'Late. Between two and three.'

He blinked. 'Are you sure you didn't dream it?'

'Yes I'm sure.'

He took a deep breath. 'But who'd do that?'

I'd had the same conversation with Catherine earlier. She'd said, someone who doesn't like us.

I said, 'Someone who doesn't like English people staying here?'

'Nah, that kind of tension doesn't exist around here.' He added, 'There aren't enough of you around.'

I took a sip of my wine.

He said, 'Seriously. This isn't an unfriendly place.'

No, not in the daytime. Not sitting here in the candle glow drinking wine with him. But in the cold, quiet mornings, and the long hours of twilight. I considered telling him about the scratch on the car but decided against it. I wasn't sure why. Maybe because this was his home and I was making it sound backwards and sinister, like the setting for a low-budget horror film.

I heard the bunk bed creak in the next room. Catherine. She came in and stared at Callum sitting back on the sofa, a wine glass in his big hands. He smiled and said hi and got the smallest possible response back.

I said, 'It was Callum who brought us the water.'

'I thought you could wash with it,' he said.

'It's not drinking water, then?' Catherine said.

I said, 'Of course it's drinking water.'

'You can drink it,' Callum replied. 'It's from the mains.' He got up and took three glasses from the draining board then filled

78

them from one of the bottles he'd brought. Catherine watched from the doorway. He said, 'It's good water. Taste it. Better than you get in a city.'

He gave me a glass, and held one out for Catherine. She took it reluctantly then put it on the table without drinking.

I quickly swallowed half of mine. 'It's nice.'

Callum sipped his in silence then put his glass in the sink. 'I better be getting back.'

She knew how to kill an atmosphere. She probably thought I was being reckless after what happened last night. Inviting strange men inside, drinking their so-called water. She poured her glass down the sink and went back into the bedroom. Callum stood by the door.

I said, 'Stay for another drink if you want.'

'No, I'll get off.' He hesitated. 'Are you worried?'

I wasn't sure what he meant. About the water? Or the noises in the night?

He said, 'If you wanted me to stay and sleep on the sofa, I can do that.'

'Um, it's okay, we'll be fine. I'll just lock the door and put my ear-plugs in so I can't hear anything.'

He smiled. 'Good plan. Well, night, then.'

'Night.'

I shut the door as he crossed the clearing, heading towards the trees. Was he being gentlemanly by offering to stay and protect us? Or something else? That steady way he'd looked at me. I had the same alert feeling I'd had when I first saw him moving through the woods, when I couldn't quite make out who he was or what he was here for.

5

———————

CATHERINE

Wednesday. Sunrise 04.28. Sunset 22.20

When I got up the next morning, Anna had left a note on the table: *Can we go home tomorrow?*

Home. Today? Yes.

Then the words reformed. *Can we go here tomorrow?* It was on top of a leaflet for a wildlife hide overlooking a loch further down the coast. A seal with black, glassy eyes peered out from the cover. On the back, a woman pushed a buggy along a walkway through woodland. The text beneath was about wheelchairs and accessible trails. It could be somewhere Leonie took Fleur on her days off. I thought of her yesterday at the beach, wheeling the pram from the café to the boy with the canoes. Fleur had been crying, distraught; I could hear her even from where I sat on the sand. I watched the boy pick up the pram in one movement and carry it up the jetty steps. Leonie looked at the ground as she went back inside.

I'd needed to call Joe from the payphone just inside the café door so I packed up my journal and blanket and followed her in.

She glanced at me when she saw me then turned back to the counter.

I dialled Joe's number and it went through to messages. I put a pound in the slot and the seconds started ticking away.

'Hi, Joe, it's me. I hope you're okay. Something's wrong with the water at the cottage. Can you call me back either on this phone now, or on my mobile later. I might not have a signal but–' Three beeps and the tone died. I put the receiver back on the hook.

Leonie was staring towards the wall at the back of the café. I said, 'It must be hard, working and looking after a baby at the same time.'

Her expression didn't change. She said, 'What can I get you?'

I asked for a slice of cake then sat down by the window. I was hoping Joe would call back on the payphone. Then the boy, Tom, came in with the pram. 'Sleeping like a baby,' he said, parking it up.

'Thanks. I couldn't get her to go off.' Leonie glanced at me and away. 'Do you want coffee?' she asked him.

Lots of women were drawn to babies. It wouldn't be strange for me to have a look. I got up, walked over, peered inside at Fleur. She was tucked up in a pastel-green crocheted blanket, her lips just touching, her nostrils quivering as she breathed. She was beautiful. Perfect, even. I smiled at her. Then Leonie was beside me. She pulled the cot hood sharply down over Fleur's face. She had stepped out from behind the counter to do it, swift and decisive.

'She'll sleep longer if it's dark.' She returned to her station by the till. 'Did you want something else?'

She had hidden the baby from me. I said, 'A cup of tea, please.'

She left the coffee she was making for Tom and filled a cup with hot water.

I said, 'Is she your first?'

She said, 'Shall I leave the bag in or take it out?'

She was waiting for a response. 'Out. Thanks.'

She hadn't heard the question. She must have heard. She wasn't listening. She was listening but deciding not to answer.

She said, 'Two pounds fifty, please.'

I gave her the money and she put it in the till, then got the pram and wheeled it into the kitchen. Tom glanced at me then followed her, the door swinging shut behind him. His drink was still sitting there half-made on the counter.

There was one of Anna's drawings under a mug on the picnic table. It showed the silhouette of the islands and light reflecting on the sea. The dew had soaked into the paper and smudged the pencil lines so that it looked like a watercolour. I brought it inside, placed it on the hearth in front of the stove and watched it dry into waves. When Anna woke up she asked what I thought about going to the wildlife hide. She had hopes of drawing an otter or a seal.

She talked about Callum as we drove down the coast. How he'd offered to stay the night and how she wasn't sure what his intentions were.

I said, 'I'm glad you said no. You only met him yesterday.'

'Of course I said no. I wonder what would have happened though, if I hadn't.'

'Don't invite him to stay, Anna.'

'I'm not going to. There's nothing worse than sharing a bunk bed with a guy, especially when there's someone in the other bed.'

It sounded like this was something she'd done before. I didn't ask who or where. We turned into a car park. I couldn't see the loch through the thick woodland but I knew from the map that it was there. We put on waterproof jackets and followed a path between oak thickets dripping with rain. It turned into a walkway over a marsh of moss and shrubs and stunted trees hung with spider webs. It was very quiet and even Anna had stopped talking, as if silenced by the trees.

The walkway led to a wooden hut built on stilts. Inside, it was gloomy and damp and you could see the undergrowth below through the spaces between the floorboards. Laminated posters showed the wildlife you might spot through the opening across the front: eagles, herons, otters. Anna sat down and pointed her binoculars towards the loch.

I said, 'Was Leonie unfriendly to you on Monday?'

'In what way?'

'She was abrupt, when I went in the café yesterday. I asked her questions and she just ignored them.'

'She was probably busy.'

Except there was only me in there until Tom came in.

Ignoring someone is awareness concealed by indifference. She wouldn't ignore a question from anyone else who went in there. She behaved differently towards me.

I picked up a logbook in a waterproof cover and flicked through the pages. People had noted their wildlife sightings inside.

Anna said, 'Any otters?'

I scanned through the most recent entries. 'No.'

'Dolphins?'

'No.'

'Whales?'

I put the book down. 'Somebody saw a sea eagle.'

'God, I'd love to see an eagle. Swooping down. Or an owl.

Oh wow! There's a heron. It's got something in its mouth. It's caught a fish!'

I looked through the gap. The heron flew steadily across the water towards the far shore of the loch.

'A seal!' Anna said.

'It's a rock.'

'It's not.' She gave me the binoculars and I scanned them over the waves. They caught on something new in the water. It ducked down then resurfaced. A round head with far-apart eyes. I said, 'It's watching us.'

'We're supposed to be hidden.'

'It can hear you talking.'

'You talking.'

We turned then because an older couple in waxed jackets and wellington boots had stepped into the hide. I gave the binoculars back to Anna. 'It's gone,' she whispered after a few seconds. We didn't mention it to the couple. I noted it in the book. They'd see it when we left.

Anna nudged me. 'Look on the island, under that rowan tree. I think I saw something otter-like.'

I focused on the shore where the tree roots grew up from the stones, scanning for something sleek and in motion. There was nothing there. I made myself comfortable. Something would appear if I watched for long enough.

———

Joe wanted us to go back to that same flat above the shop. He suggested it a few years after we were married, after another month of failing to conceive. We had been trying for over a year by then. I took the right vitamins. I rarely drank alcohol. I tracked my cycle, taking my temperature every morning and waiting for the beep to show it had been stored in the fertility tracker before I got out of bed. I watched a line zigzag across a graph on my phone each month, looking for a jump in temperature to indicate ovulation, then after a week of sex scheduled into our day like a work meeting, a sustained rise to indicate pregnancy. The first jump always came, the second came and dropped away, and my period arrived a day or so later. The big finale after twenty-three days of minute fluctuations in body temperature.

Joe's reassurances became thinner as time went on. That ambivalence he'd once had about being a parent was gone, or perhaps it had never been there in the first place. Either way, he was set on it now. I could see it in the way he spoke about friends from back home who were starting families. His eyes brightened when he looked at their Facebook pictures; young men with beards and tattoos and a baby sinking into their lap. Four hundred messages of congratulations underneath. Being a young father was cool in a way that being a young mother wasn't. Or didn't used to be, anyway. Maybe that had changed too.

We went to see our GP, together. He told us to slow down and let ourselves fully relax instead of always being on a timetable of work, work, sleep. I nodded but I left that appointment feeling more anxious than before. Diet, alcohol consumption, vitamin intake, they were all things I could control. But relaxation; it was such a vague concept and surprisingly difficult to attain. If you thought about it too much, it became another goal to work towards, another thing to feel guilty about when you failed.

This was why Joe wanted us to go somewhere familiar for our next holiday. He said it would be a real break where all we needed to do was rest. There'd be no planes to catch, no foreign languages to learn or new cities to navigate. Our trips away were usually long-haul and set to a tight itinerary of sightseeing and travel connections. We'd arrive home more tired than when we set off.

So we booked the flat above the shop again and timed it to coincide with a 'fertility window'. It was May and the beach was busy with families enjoying the first warm sunshine of spring. On our first morning we stayed in bed late, both of us waiting for the other to start the process of getting me pregnant. Later we explored the rockpools on the beach opposite our flat. We turned over stones, watched shrimps dart into the cover of kelp. Parents with young children did the same slow meander as us, eyes downwards, buckets knocking against bare legs, fishing nets on bamboo sticks searching through the seaweed.

Joe beckoned me towards him and pointed into a rockpool. A crab sat motionless on the bottom, trying to make itself invisible. It was the size of my hand and its shell was sunset colours of pink and orange. I wanted a net to fish it out, a bucket to put it in. I wanted to show one of the children who were looking so intently for a find like this. None were nearby and they were all engrossed in other pools, other underwater worlds, their parents clutching their hands to stop them from slipping in.

I said, 'Is it dead?'

'I don't think so.' Joe pulled up his sleeve and put his hand in the cold water. He touched its shell and it moved, sending up a little storm of sand. It scuttled, like crabs do, until it was tucked under a rock shelf, out of sight.

Without really discussing it, we started walking across the sands towards the tidal island we'd visited last time. But when we reached the causeway, there was a sign forbidding visitors from going any further. The island was closed to protect nesting birds during breeding season. I read it and my mood dropped. I'd been looking forward to going there again but it was more than that. I felt locked out. From the island and its skies full of wings, its hollows in the grass harbouring eggs and chicks. And from everything it represented. Life, fertility, the kind of reproduction that happens naturally without graphs and pills and ten minutes a day of meditation.

The feeling took the life out of me. I sat down on the causeway amongst the broken shells. Joe took his binoculars out of his rucksack and focused them on a flock of oystercatchers. After a few minutes, I started to cry. It took him a while to respond; his eyes were fixed on the birds on the island.

Eventually, he knelt down, his binoculars hanging round his neck. 'What's happened?'

Nothing had happened. That was the problem; nothing was happening.

He said, 'Talk to me, Catherine. Why are you crying?'

I said I was worried I'd never get pregnant. He put his arms around me. 'We'll go back to the doctor and ask him about IVF. I'll make an appointment for when we get home.'

'No, I don't want to.'

'Why?'

'Because I already know what he'll say.'

He paused, not understanding. 'What will he say?'

I shrugged. It was obvious. 'No.'

The oystercatchers rose up then settled again. Joe watched them without seeing. It was as if this outcome hadn't occurred to him at all.

He said, 'Why would they say no? There'll be a waiting list. But they won't just say no, you can't have it.'

He was so young sometimes. So naive. He lived in a bubble and at times like this I wanted to burst it and wake him up. I sighed. 'Joe.'

'What?'

'They're not going to spend all that money on helping me. Think about it. About what I did.'

He blinked. 'That won't affect it. They don't take things like that into account.'

'How do you know?'

'I don't know. But I'm positive it won't make any difference. It might even help our case. It shows you're fertile and that everything is working properly.'

'Except it isn't, is it? It's not working.'

His arm dropped from my back. There was a long pause before he answered. 'That's why we're asking for help.'

'Nobody's going to spend thousands of pounds helping me have a baby.' I got up and walked ahead of him along the causeway towards the road. When I reached it, I stopped and waited. He was a few minutes behind me, the binoculars still hanging round his neck.

'I would,' he said, when he caught up.

'You would what?'

'Spend thousands of pounds.'

'You don't have thousands of pounds.'

He kissed the top of my head and pulled me into him. It made me cry again for a few panicked moments. He held me firmly as if he was worried I was about to fall apart completely, there on the roadside. I straightened up. 'Let's go back to bed,' I said.

I went to the storm beach again when we got back from the wildlife hide. Mist drifted in from the sea and I could only just make out the village across the bay. I picked my way along the tideline. The rubbish strewn amongst the rocks appeared to be much the same. The computer. The curved length of pipe. And plastic bottles, everywhere, bobbing by the shore, caught amongst the kelp, washed as high as the footpath.

I sat down on a flat rock free of seaweed and took out my journal. I needed to make sense of yesterday. The contamination of the water. The key scraped across our car. Leonie's hostility in the café. Then there were the bottles of water Callum had left. And it was Callum we'd caught returning from the spring in the woods. He had assured Anna that the contamination was natural and Anna had accepted this as easily as she'd accepted the water he gave us instead. I remembered how he'd looked at me when I had refused to drink it. How she had looked at me.

I walked from one end of the cove to the other then turned and walked back. All this plastic. So strange how it had washed ashore here. I hadn't seen a beach this defiled anywhere else along the coast.

I heard car wheels, an engine die. On the cliff top above the cove, Callum looked down at me for a moment before he walked away.

Everyone knew everyone else around here. They talked to each other; in the shop, in the woods, at the end of the jetty where nobody could hear. Everyone knew each other and everyone knew what was going on.

Except, perhaps, Anna. She was looking the other way, wilfully I thought, while this unfolded around us. That evening she talked almost constantly; about her ex in Canada, about what had gone wrong, about how she just wanted to be on her own for a while. Then a moment later she said the isolation here was getting to her and she wanted me to drive us to the pub. At one point, she was threatening to walk there herself. She smoked a cigarette outside. She said she was going to see if Callum was home. She changed her mind and poured more wine. I felt like she was leaving no space for me to speak into. Like she was silencing me with her non-stop talk, and that it was deliberate.

Several times I tried to shift the conversation to Leonie but she always turned it away again. She began talking about the boy with the canoes: Tom. How old did I think he was? How old did I think Callum was?

I said, 'How old do you think Leonie is?'

'Early twenties. Mid-twenties.'

'She's twenty-three.'

'How do you know?'

I didn't answer. A log fell in the furnace. I could feel Anna's eyes on me.

'Did you ask her?' she said.

'No.'

She said, 'I think Tom is about twenty-one. And Callum about thirty-five? Maybe older. They look alike, don't they? Tom reminded me of Callum and I thought it was just because I had him in my head, because he's so freaking handsome. But they are actually related. I suppose that's pretty common in a small community.'

'Everyone knows everyone else.'

'Everyone is related to everyone else.' She was doodling on her sketchpad, seemingly oblivious.

I said, 'Except for Leonie. She's on her own.'

'She's got Fleur.'

'She wouldn't let me look at her.'

Anna looked up.

'She pulled the pram hood over her face so I couldn't see her.'

'When?'

'Yesterday in the café.'

Anna paused. 'Maybe the sun was in her eyes.'

'Her eyes were closed. She was asleep.'

'So she didn't want her being disturbed.'

'It wasn't that.'

Her voice softened. 'Is that why you were upset? I mean, who does she remind you of?'

She was catching up, finally. I said, 'It doesn't matter. I'm going to bed.'

She watched me get up, then picked up her pencil again, as if she wasn't that interested anyway, but I knew she was. The lead didn't touch the paper. It was suspended just above.

6

ANNA

Thursday. Sunrise 04.28. Sunset 22.20

Catherine needed to check her emails so we drove to the pub again the next morning. We sipped coffee at the same table as before and keyed in the same wi-fi code. Going online made me feel mildly anxious and I wondered why I was bothering. I didn't want to know what all my friends in Canada were up to, especially not Ade. We hadn't been in touch at all since I left and he was starting to take on an air of unreality that gave me a kind of vertigo, like when I first climbed into my bunk bed at night. What had happened to the life I'd built for myself out there? It had been so easy to erase.

Except I hadn't erased it, I'd erased myself, by leaving. On Facebook I saw that it was all still going on without me. I clicked through pictures of my friends drinking by the lake. Scanned group chats about the first barbecues of the summer. I needed to delete myself from them but I couldn't face doing it right now.

I stood up. 'I'm going for a walk.'

Catherine had been staring intently at her screen. She tuned back in and focused on me. 'It's happened again,' she said.

'What has?'

She read from her phone. '"There has been an unknown login on your account".' She took a full breath in. 'This is the third time in five months.'

'Which account?'

'My email.'

'Tell your IT department. They'll sort it.'

'It's my personal one.'

'Change your password?'

'Hmmm.' She looked back at her phone.

'See you in a bit.' Watching her sort out her email security issues wasn't how I wanted to spend the morning. It was sunny and windy and the sea was a deep blue. I crossed the road and headed towards the little harbour where the masts of sailing boats were chiming in the breeze. Then I circled back towards the playground, framing a drawing in my mind. I was already halfway there when I saw Leonie. She stopped at a bench, parked the pram next to her, facing the sea rather than the empty climbing frame and swings.

I would go and say hello. I was thinking about what Catherine said yesterday about her hiding the baby from her. It sounded like she had been a little bit too interested in Fleur, which was understandable, considering. She was broody and getting close to crunch-time. The baby question was so loaded for her. It probably followed her everywhere.

I wandered over. Fleur's eyes were fixed on the water. Leonie's too. It took her a moment to hear my hello over the breaking waves. When she did, she looked like she'd been dragged back from a daydream, like she was not quite ready for me, not quite pleased to see me.

'How's it going?' I said.

Her hair was greasy and her lips were dry. 'Okay.'

I sat down. 'Did she wake up early again?'

'Yeah. I'm hoping the sound of the waves will send her to sleep.' She glanced in at Fleur then quickly looked away from her, as if avoiding eye contact. 'Any water sound. Rain. The tap running. They all calm her down.'

'When was she born? Maybe she's a water sign?'

She paused for a moment. Was she so tired she couldn't remember her birthday? She looked at me. 'Twenty-fourth of February.'

'She's a Pisces. Makes sense.'

'A Pisces.'

I said, 'I'm a fire sign. Aries. I'm all about the sun.'

'You don't get much of that in Manchester.'

'Not a lot. More than here.'

'Nobody comes to Scotland for the weather.'

The waves in the bay rose and fell like Fleur's chest beneath the blanket. When I peered in at her, she had a zoned-out expression, as if she'd be asleep soon. I felt myself relaxing too. I said, 'People come to Scotland to escape.'

'Is that why you're here?'

'I came to put off the inevitable.'

'What's that?'

'Putting my life back together. Starting again from scratch, again.'

Her eyes twitched with tiredness behind her fringe. 'You're lucky. I'll never have an empty page like that with this one.'

'It must be worth it though?'

She didn't respond.

'But hard,' I said. 'Bringing up a baby on your own.'

'Yeah.' Her voice was flat. 'And lonely.' She squinted as sunlight bounced off the sea. She turned to me. 'But I couldn't be without her. I knew that from the moment I saw her. I wouldn't let anyone take her from me, not for one minute.'

Did she mean literally, in the maternity ward? Or in general? I couldn't tell and I felt like she'd flipped the conversation on me. She was looking at me as if she expected me to argue. She said, 'I feel bad every time I have to leave her. Even when I'm with her, I feel like I'm not "present" enough.'

'Mother's guilt.' It was something I'd heard people say.

'That's right. Mother's guilt.' Her tone was hard to read. Our eyes met for the first time. 'But what I don't understand is, if you feel guilty all the time anyway, what is there to stop you from doing something really bad?'

I looked back at the sea, unsure what to say. For a while there was just the steady sound of waves breaking against the shore.

She leaned over to look in at Fleur. 'She always sleeps by the sea.'

I stood up. A self-conscious movement. 'I better go. Catherine's waiting for me in the pub.'

'She's in there, is she?'

I nodded. I wanted to get away from her.

'See you later,' she said.

I didn't mention any of this to Catherine. I wasn't sure why. It just seemed easier not to, somehow. We drove back to the cottage and ate lunch. Catherine sat at the table, writing in her diary, her arm hiding it from view. The sun fell through the window onto her wrist.

I said, 'You've been bitten.'

'Where?'

'On your arms.'

SARAH TIERNEY

Red pinprick marks. When she pushed up her sleeves, there were more. She'd been scratching them without noticing she was doing it. 'They're all over me.'

She went into the bathroom. When she came out the groove between her eyes had deepened. 'They're on my legs and back. It's from the water. I washed with it yesterday.'

'But I had a bath in it and I'm all right.'

She was scratching her collarbone, the tops of her arms. 'Why has it affected me and not you?'

'It's not a rash, they're insect bites. I'll get you an antihistamine.'

'I don't take pills.'

'Why?'

'I just don't.'

'Not even paracetamol?'

'No.'

I found them in the side pocket of my big rucksack. 'Don't you feel pain?'

'What do you mean by that?'

'Nothing, it was a joke. Stop scratching. Here.'

She wouldn't take them. I checked my own arms. I had a couple of bites but nothing like the amount she had. I took an antihistamine anyway, just in case. She watched me do it, withholding comment, as if I was swallowing something much more exciting than a hay fever tablet.

I said, 'Let's make some plans for the rest of the week.' I got the OS map out and spread it across the table. An intricate coastline of islands and peninsulas. Tightly packed contour lines of mountains.

'Where are we?'

'Here.' Catherine pointed to a blank space that had been worn away by other people pointing at the same spot.

I found the empty cottages further along the headland: a

few tiny squares in a dot-to-dot horseshoe. The path between us was a broken line. My eyes followed the track back along the peninsula towards the steady certain yellow of the coast road. Another yellow road led away from it into a vast area of forest. It went on and on until it went off the map, passing no villages in between.

'I wonder where this leads to. We could drive up it and find out? Take a picnic maybe?' There were little pink tables stamped at intervals along the way.

'It probably doesn't lead anywhere.'

I turned away, spied the wine on the kitchen counter. My cigarettes beside it. 'Well, won't that be cool? Reaching the end of the road?'

I poured myself a glass and took it outside. I sat in the sun watching the light changing on the sea. After a while, I got a blanket from the bedroom and lay down to sleep in the grass. When I woke the sun had barely moved in the sky even though a few hours had passed. I felt a dullness in my head from the wine. Holiday drinking. It wasn't as much fun on your own.

Catherine was still writing her diary at the table and I wondered what there was to record; we'd done nothing all day. Her arm shielded it as though she thought I might try to read what it said. She was as furtive about it now as she had been as a teenager. I'd never managed to read it, though I'd tried to pick the lock a few times. I remembered the fear of her walking in and catching me. Before lights out at night, I'd squint through the gap between the bunk bed and the wall when I could hear her scribbling away. She'd somehow know and shift to the other side of the bed. Not that I could see anything anyway.

'What are you writing about?' I said, refilling my wine and sitting down on the sofa.

'Don't ask me that.'

'Why?'

'It's like asking what someone's thinking.'

'What *are* you thinking?' I laughed. 'Yeah, that is pretty annoying. I hate it when people ask me that. Like they're my therapist or expecting something deep.'

Catherine looked up. 'Have you got a therapist?'

'No. Have you?'

She shook her head.

I said, 'Your journal is your therapy.'

She closed it shut. 'And what's yours?'

I shrugged. 'Prosecco? I think Mum's got that on a fridge magnet.' I took a sip of wine. 'I actually don't think I need therapy. I'm not unhappy.'

Catherine got up and started putting her boots on. 'I'm just heading out for a bit. To clear my head.'

Translation: don't come with me. Fine. When she'd gone I poured the rest of the wine and opened another bottle. Then I looked around for her diary but she must have taken it with her. I remembered the relief I'd always felt as a child when I couldn't pick the lock. I wasn't afraid of getting caught but of reading what was inside.

It was a while later when I heard it. A bassline low and steady like a heartbeat, coming from the direction of the sea. I went outside into the clearing but it had stopped. Had I imagined it? Was I losing it in the jungle? Would I be running through these woods barefoot with the axe before the end of the week?

No, there it was, beneath the rush of the wind in the treetops. I swigged down my wine and locked up, liking the idea that Catherine might come back and find me gone. I was tired of sitting around waiting for her next appearance or disappearance. I felt like I'd lost control of my life again by just drifting aimlessly along with her plans. With anyone's plans. A night out, a holiday, distant music winding through the woods. I thought of Ade saying, exasperated, when I told him I was moving back to the UK: 'Decide which country you want to live in, and just fucking stay there, *for fuck's sake.*' This from a man whose house had wheels. Who was he to talk about roots and stability?

I took a path I'd not noticed before, the dff-dff-dff getting louder with each turn. There was a car, turned towards the sea, house music pounded through closed windows. Inside, Callum tapped his finger on the steering wheel. He grinned when he saw me and I laughed.

He leaned across to push open the passenger door. There were empty beer cans in the footwell. An open one on the dashboard next to a puzzle book. He turned the music down to a more reasonable volume.

I said, 'Are you having a party?'

'Just watching the sunset. Listening to some tunes.' He reached for a can of beer from the back seat and handed it to me.

'Thanks.'

'No bother.' He stared at me for a moment as if he wasn't quite sure what I was doing there.

I said, 'I could hear the music from the cottage.'

'I never thought I'd get complaints from the neighbours out here.'

'I'm not complaining. I was getting cabin fever. I thought I was hearing things.'

'I know that feeling. You start imagining all sorts when you've not spoken to anyone for a few days. So how's it been going? Any more strange noises in the night?'

'That wasn't imaginary.'

'I know. I'm not saying–'

'It's been quiet since Monday.'

'That's good.'

'The water's still brown though.'

'Same at mine. That'll sort itself out.' The way he said it made me think he'd sorted out the noises at night. Did he know who it was, or at least have an idea?

I said, 'Do you know Leonie?'

He paused. 'A bit, through Tom.'

'I was chatting to her today. She looked like she'd had about two hours' sleep.'

He didn't reply. I had the impression he didn't want to talk about Leonie. I picked up the puzzle book on the dashboard. *Killer Sudoku*. 'Is this how you stop yourself going crazy?'

'That's my Dad's. It's way too hard for me.'

'Does he live around here?'

'He did. He died.'

'Of sudoku?' I said it without thinking. Oh God, I was drunk. 'Sorry, I didn't–'

'Of sudoku?' His confused expression turned into a laugh. 'No. It was cancer.' His eyes met mine for a second then fixed on the sea.

'Oh.' I didn't know what to say. 'When?'

'February.'

'This February?'

'Yeah.'

He was still looking straight ahead. I thought of something I'd heard about how people find it easier to talk in cars because they don't have to look at each other. I said, 'I'm sorry.'

'Not your fault.' He started skipping through the tracks on the CD, focusing hard as if it was taking up all his concentration.

I said, 'I'm bringing you down. Should I leave you alone?'

'Nope. Stay.' He turned the volume up a little. 'You're the best thing that's happened at this party.'

'I'm the only thing that's happened.'

'Not true. Your sister was here earlier.'

'Sitting in your car?'

'Nah, she went down to the beach.'

'What beach?'

'The one down there.' He lifted his finger to point across the clearing. There was the start of a path at the top of the cliff.

'I didn't know there was a beach so close by. Nobody tells me anything.'

'It's not a pretty beach. It's full of junk. Wreck Cove, it's called.'

'Is she still down there?'

'Well she's not come back up. So unless she swam away…'

Was that her hiding place? She'd had them as a child. A hollow beneath a hawthorn tree at the back of our garden. A gap between the sofa and the radiator where she sat with a stack of books.

I said, 'I'd better check she's all right.' I was about to get out when he lifted off the handbrake and rolled us towards the edge of the cliff. 'Whoah! What are you doing?'

He stopped a few metres before the drop. 'Getting closer so you can see her. There she is.' We could see the beach below us now. Catherine was standing amongst the thick orange seaweed, staring up at us. I waved but she probably couldn't see. What was she doing down there?

I said, 'Maybe I should go down. Except she probably wants to be on her own as well. Why is everyone so solitary around here?'

'I'm not solitary.'

'You live in a deserted village.'

'That's circumstance not choice. I've got a flat in Glasgow. Friends. A life. You'd be surprised.'

'More than me then. I did have a life. I left it in Canada when I moved back.'

He looked across at me. 'Here we go. I'm bringing you down now.'

'You're not. I like building things up and tearing them down. It's how I fill my time.' I sighed. The sky was pink and gold. 'Is that sun ever going to set?' It hovered over the islands, just sitting there, looking spectacular.

'Yeah, in August.'

I turned to face him. He looked at me through the corner of his eyes. I said, 'I don't think I can wait that long.'

He smiled, holding my gaze, then looked back at the sea. 'It'll set but it stays just below the horizon. That's why it doesn't get fully dark.'

'What a rip-off.' Our voices had dropped along with the music, which kept building up and backing away, teasing us, like the slow-setting sun. Protracted and kind of infuriating.

He said lightly, 'I never thought of it like that.'

I moved my drink into my other hand so that the hand closest to his was empty. I brushed it against his in the space between the seats and left it close enough for him to take. But he moved his hand away, onto the steering wheel, his arm like a barrier between us. I shifted away slightly, embarrassed, and sat there not knowing what to say. He nodded along to the music as if nothing had happened. Hadn't he asked to stay the night the last time we met? Didn't he kind of ask me out? What had changed?

It was the sudoku comment. Or the fact I hadn't washed for two days. Either way, he was giving me 'no thanks' vibes. Fine. I was about to make my excuses and leave when the music cut out.

'Battery's gone.' He tried starting the car but it died. 'I thought it'd last longer than that.'

'Hmmm.'

'I may need to borrow yours to jump-start it.'

'Yep.' Catherine was at the top of the path. I got out, glad for the interruption. 'It's me.'

'I know.'

Callum got out too. 'Anything interesting on the beach?'

Catherine studied him. 'Should there be?'

He said, 'I found half a dolphin down there once.'

Catherine stared at him.

I said, 'Which half?'

'The head. Cut clean across the middle of its body.'

She was looking at us as though we were talking in a different language. Her face was shadowy in the fading light. She said, 'What happened to its tail?'

'Who knows? Could have got caught up in a ship's propeller.' His voice was matter-of-fact. 'I'll walk you two back. I'll sort the car tomorrow.'

We took the path through the woods. To fill the silence, I asked Callum about the whalebone on his wall. He said it was probably from an orca. He found it on a beach on the north coast then accidently left it on the train on the way home. It had been handed in at lost property and he'd had a thirty-mile trip to get it back.

'When I rang them, they said, can you describe it to us, so we know it's yours? Like they had folks ringing up all the time asking for a lost whalebone. I gave it to my dad – he put it up at the hut. He said it was meant to be lucky.'

I said, 'Do you ever see whales around here?'

'Now and then.'

'What about the northern lights?'

'Sometimes. Not in summer.'

He left us once we got in sight of our cottage. When he said bye he didn't meet my eyes like he did the other night. He looked away, like his mind was on something else. His dad perhaps and the bone he'd nailed to his wall to ward off bad luck.

When we got inside, I drank a full pint of water then went straight to bed. It was the only sensible thing to do after all the wine and beer and rejection. I closed my eyes. I could smell the smoke from the extinguished candles as Catherine opened and closed the bedroom door. I pushed myself up onto my elbow so I could see her. She was getting changed into her pyjamas by torchlight.

I said, 'Callum is giving me mixed signals. Usually I can tell when someone likes me. I mean, it's obvious, isn't it? But either he likes me and is pretending not to, or he just doesn't like me.' I lay back down. 'What do you think?'

Catherine clicked off her torch and got into her bunk. I heard her shifting to get comfortable in her sleeping bag.

'Anna?'

'Yes?'

'There's something I need to talk to you about.'

'About Callum?'

'No, not about Callum. Forget about Callum for a minute.'

But that's who we'd been talking about, wasn't it? Who I'd been talking about, anyway. She must have had a whole other conversation going on in her head.

She said, 'I've been thinking about how much to tell you.'

It sounded like she'd planned this sentence in advance. I opened my mouth to say, about what, then shut it again.

She said, 'You may have noticed that Leonie has been acting a bit odd towards us.'

Leonie again. I hadn't told her about running into her this morning. Some instinct had stopped me. I'd been avoiding thinking about why all day.

She said, 'I know the reason for it. And I think you know too.'

I paused, trying to catch up. 'Know what?'

'Why Leonie looks like me. Why she's behaving so strangely around me.'

'What are you saying?'

'You *know* what.'

I said, 'I don't.'

But it wasn't true. I knew exactly what she was saying. I just didn't want to say it out loud. I sat up then slid down to the floor so I could see her face.

'Leonie?'

She nodded.

'You think she's...'

'Yes.'

I stared at her. I didn't know what to say. It was a real what-the-fuck moment. Only topped by the original what-the-fuck moment when my sister, the sensible one, the one who'd never had a boyfriend, got pregnant at fifteen years old.

Catherine didn't tell me, Mum did. I walked in on them talking. 'How many weeks?' Mum was saying and I gormlessly interrupted with 'How many weeks till what?' Neither replied but when Catherine had gone, Mum ushered me into the bathroom, the only room in our house with a lock on it. I think I laughed when she said it. I think I said, 'As if.'

Mum's voice was low and urgent. 'You mustn't tell any of your friends. Not one. Are you listening?'

I felt suddenly sick. I sat on the edge of the bath, working a towel between my fingers. 'Catherine can't be pregnant.' She was too clever to let something like that happen. She was predicted an A for Biology, for God's sake.

Mum continued, 'I need you to be out this evening while I tell your dad. I've given Catherine money for McDonald's. She'll meet you at the bus stop at home time.'

I tried to think what Catherine was wearing when she left. Her school uniform of course, the jumper long and baggy, but that was the fashion so it didn't seem unusual.

I said, 'But she hasn't got a boyfriend.'

'It was a French boy she met at a party. She won't tell me his name.'

'An exchange student?' They'd been here in the spring, wearing Benetton jumpers and carrying their rucksacks on both shoulders. Nobody talked to them much. Not because we didn't want to, we just didn't know how to say anything beyond 'Où est la plage?' or, more useful in our landlocked town, 'Il pleut'. Then Janine Shimwell in Year Eleven had a party and invited them all, and I remembered Catherine was sick the day after. I didn't even know she'd been there. She didn't usually get invited to parties. And she'd told me she'd gone to Rachel's for pizza and a video. She'd snapped at me when I'd asked her whether she thought Johnny Depp was still fit as Edward Scissorhands.

Mum said, 'Did you hear what I said about not telling anyone?'

'I won't. But people will notice that she's having a baby.' I felt a cold panic forming. I'd have to change school. We'd have to move house.

'She's not having a baby.'

I looked at her. 'You just said she was.'

106

'I said she's pregnant. She's not having a baby.'

Mum took the towel out of my hands and put it back on the radiator. She said, 'You'd better go or you'll miss the bus.'

I rarely spoke to Catherine at school. Sometimes we'd pass each other in the corridor and not even say hello. It wasn't that we weren't friends, it was just that sharing a room had made us bored with the sight of each other. So my friends were surprised when she met me at home time and I said I'd see them tomorrow.

'Where are you going?' Lindsey asked.

'McDonald's.'

'Why?'

'*Why?*'

'Can we go now?' Catherine walked away and somehow stayed a few steps ahead of me all the way there. I got what I always did: cheeseburger, small fries, strawberry milkshake. It bothered me that Catherine only got fries. And that she left them in their cardboard pouch, untouched.

I said, 'I don't think Mum's making us tea tonight. We're supposed to eat here.'

She picked up a floppy French fry then put it down again. 'I'm vegetarian. I shouldn't even be in here.' She took a fountain pen out of her school bag and started sketching devil's horns on the cartoon of Ronald McDonald on the tray cover.

I watched her trying to draw a three-pronged pitchfork coming out of his hand. She was getting it all wrong. I resisted the urge to take the pen and do it for her. I checked no one was at the table behind us and said quietly, almost whispering, 'Um, Mum told me.'

She stopped drawing but didn't look up. 'I told her not to.'

'Why?'

'Because it's none of your business.'

'She probably thought I'd guess and tell someone if she

didn't tell me not to. As if.' I looked down at my food. I said, 'It's not like anyone needs to know about it. Ever.'

Catherine looked up. 'They're going to notice eventually. Maybe not before the summer holidays, but by September, definitely.'

'But won't it be gone, by September?' Was there a waiting list or something? I thought you could just have it done straight away.

'I'm not having an abortion.'

I wanted to shush her. She shouldn't be saying things like that out loud. 'Mum said–'

'It's not her decision. Or Dad's.' The ink had stopped flowing in her pen. It scraped across the paper. 'I'm having it adopted.'

'What do you mean?'

'What I said.'

Yes, of course she would. Adoption was Catherine all over. It was the right thing to do, and she always did the right thing. Adoption wasn't like killing someone, like abortion, and it wasn't going to ruin the rest of your life, like keeping it. It was the thing everyone said they'd do, if they got pregnant. It was what I'd said I'd do when we were talking about it that time at Lindsey's sleepover. But I'd said it knowing I wasn't pregnant. Catherine was saying it knowing she was.

'You're actually going to be pregnant? So people can see?'

She shrugged, focusing too hard on her picture. 'That's how it usually works.'

'What about school?'

'What about it?'

'You can't go if you're pregnant.'

'I'm not staying at home for nine months. Eight months. No, seven and a half.'

She frowned then and for the first time, looked a little bit scared. I looked away. I was upset too. And angry. I wanted to know how she could have been so stupid to get pregnant. I wanted to know who the French boy was, and how come she'd started having sex all of a sudden when she was supposed to be such a square. And I wanted to say to her, do you know how awful it'll be when people find out?

I didn't say any of it, knowing it wasn't the response I should give, but something must have shown on my face.

Catherine said, 'Mum said I'd have someone to talk to about it if she told you.' She got up abruptly and started putting on her coat. I looked at her middle. I couldn't see any difference. She said, 'What a joke that was. You don't care what I'm going through. All you care about is what your stupid friends will say.'

She left me sitting there, knowing she was right.

What can I say? I was self-obsessed and insecure. But I don't think that's unusual in an eleven-year-old girl. I read somewhere that the part of the brain that creates empathy doesn't fully develop until you're in your twenties. For me, that was about right, but Catherine was the opposite. She was saving whales before she'd even left primary school.

She spent her weekends planting trees, volunteering on the recycling round, playing Vera Lynn songs on her cornet at the old folks' home. She saw all the world's problems and thought it was her job to fix them. She handed round petitions against the industrial chimney that polluted the air over our town. She wrote letters for Amnesty International, raised money for the WWF. Meat was murder. Abortion was unthinkable. But adoption. She could do that. There were couples who desperately wanted a baby but couldn't have one. She could help. She could change their life.

This was what she was telling Mum when I sloped home that evening. Catherine's arm was wrapped round her stomach, her face pale. Mum was sitting beside her, looking very tired.

Dad wasn't there but I heard him coming downstairs as I took off my coat and placed it on a dining-room chair. Me and Mum turned towards the doorway. Catherine looked at the TV. It was switched off.

Dad stood just inside the room. 'Just get rid of it,' he said, once he'd realised Catherine wasn't going to look at him. 'It's a handful of cells. It's not a person.'

Catherine kept staring at the blank screen.

He said, 'This could all be sorted out by the end of next week.'

Still no reply.

He said, 'You're young and naive and you have no idea what it's like to be pregnant.'

She couldn't resist the obvious answer. 'And you do?'

'I do,' Mum said. 'And I don't want you to go through it at your age.'

'Millions of women do it.'

'You're a child, not a woman.' Mum seemed to be the only one with a grip on the situation.

'I'm fifteen. I know what I'm doing.'

Mum's voice was quiet. 'No, you don't. You don't know what it will be like to have a baby and then give it away. You don't know how that will make you feel.'

Catherine's face was still, like she couldn't hear what Mum was trying to tell her. Or she didn't want to. She'd made her decision. She wouldn't change her mind now.

———

'Leonie is my baby.' Catherine's words hung in the darkness like a light that burns on your eyes even after it's gone out.

'You think Leonie is your daughter, grown up?'

'I'm about ninety-eight per cent sure of it.'

Catherine was Leonie's mother? Leonie was Catherine's daughter? That hunched up, red-faced baby was stretched out and fully grown, with a baby of her own? I peered down at her. 'But that's insane.'

She looked at me for a second then abruptly turned to face the wall.

'Catherine?'

She turned onto her back. 'It's not insane. It's who she is. She's my daughter. She found me online.'

'When did this happen?'

'A while ago. Through Facebook.'

I stared at her. I'd seen a TV programme about exactly this: adopted children using social media to find their birth parents. They did a search and sent them a message and arranged to meet up, and the social workers and adopted parents knew nothing about it. I'd watched it thinking, that could happen to Catherine, and now it had.

She spoke again. 'She doesn't know where I live because I'm very careful not to put that information online. But I didn't think about that when I emailed you about this place. She read it and saw where we were staying. That's why she's here.'

'You think she hacked your emails?'

Catherine paused. 'Yes.'

'But how would she do that?'

'My password is her date of birth.'

'Right.' I was finding it hard to take all this in. 'Hang on. I can't see properly.' I found the torch and turned it on. But then I didn't know where to aim it. Not at her. Not at me. 'Let me get the lamp.'

I brought it in and lit it with a match. A flare of flame then the hissing, moonlike glow. It made more shadows than light.

I said, 'So... this is good news, isn't it?'

She shifted in her bed. 'I don't know. I mean, why has she

followed me? Why not just message me and ask to meet? And vandalising our car and banging on the door. She seems to want to scare me.'

'We don't know that was her.'

'It must have been.'

'Why? What has she said?'

'Nothing. Yet.'

I thought for a moment. 'I spoke to her today.'

'When?'

'When you were in the pub.'

'Why didn't you say anything?'

I tucked my legs under me. 'I don't know. I just didn't.'

'What did she say?'

I tried to recall the gist of our conversation but all I could think of was how uneasy she'd made me feel. 'I can't remember.'

'Think.'

I tried. 'Something about there not being much sunshine in Manchester. And that Fleur always sleeps by the sea.'

'What else?' She was interrogating me.

I paused. 'She said she wouldn't let anyone take Fleur away from her.'

Catherine's face fell, like the muscles in it had stopped working.

'And that she couldn't let someone else bring her up.'

'She was talking about me. She was judging me.'

I didn't know what to say. 'Maybe. I don't know.' I had to admit, it sounded that way. Catherine's breathing was shallow. Her face tense. I said, 'So Fleur is your granddaughter?'

'Yes.'

I got my sketchbook from the other room and brought it back into the pool of light around the lamp. I turned to the drawing of Fleur and studied it closely. I felt something flare up and die down in me. An echo of an echo of a face I'd seen before.

Catherine said, 'She looks like Leonie did when she was a baby.'

I said, 'I can't remember what she looked like.'

Catherine's expression made me wish back my words. It was callous to tell your sister you couldn't remember her daughter's face. I said, 'Maybe there's something familiar about her eyes.'

'Yes. It's her eyes.'

Catherine's baby had blue eyes, I remembered that. Had I looked into them, just this morning, on that park bench? Had Leonie turned to me and seen a reflection of herself? I'd had a really strong urge to get away from her, and the first time Catherine met her, she'd gone pale and said she felt sick. It was as though we'd both recognised ourselves in her on some unconscious level. How weird that our bodies knew before we did.

Catherine touched the face in the drawing. 'Eyes don't age. They're the one part that stays the same all your life.'

'They change colour. All babies have blue eyes when they're born.'

Catherine's eyes were grey. They shrank when she scrutinised you. 'Do they?'

'I think so.'

'But they could have stayed blue,' she said.

I thought of the hours-old baby wrapped in blankets in that hospital cot, her eyes searching the bright, new world above her. And I thought of Leonie, sitting by the sea, tired and jaded. The same girl, twenty-three years later, still looking for her mum.

7

CATHERINE

Friday. Sunrise 04.28. Sunset 22.21

I have been trying to ignore my daughter's reappearance for some time now. At first it was easy enough. She made no contact, I made no contact. We were aware of each other but neither took a step closer. We stayed on the very edges of each other's lives and I became accustomed to it, in a way, her presence in the corner of the room. I knew she was watching me online. There are so many places to find a person on there nowadays. But also so many ways to hide, which is what I did, and I thought I had done it well. But it only took one careless email, and there she was, befriending my sister, knocking on my bedroom window, making me question what she would do next. 'It's stalking,' I told Anna, when she eventually woke up the next morning. 'She is stalking me.'

Anna took a sip of her coffee before answering. 'Can you stalk your own mother? I mean, don't all children follow their parents around? It's how they stay safe.'

I didn't see what she was getting at. 'Young children, you mean?'

'Yeah.'

'She's twenty-three. She doesn't need me to feed and clothe and protect her. There's nothing I can give her that she can't get herself.'

'Maybe she feels unloved.'

'She is unloved. By me, anyway.'

'Catherine, you're so harsh.'

I put my drink down and pushed out my chair. I needed to get dressed. 'I have to be.'

'Tough love.'

I turned. 'It's not love.'

'Well it's something.'

I closed the bedroom door behind me. The gas lamp was still on the floor by the bed. Talking had been easier last night, cocooned in darkness. Discussing this in daylight made me feel exposed and on edge. And Anna wouldn't let the subject go. When I went back through, she said, 'It makes sense that she'd start thinking about you now she's got a baby of her own.'

I hadn't considered that. Had she looked at Fleur and thought, how could she do it? How could she leave me to be brought up by strangers?

She'd want to understand why and the want would turn into a need. She'd say to her friends or her therapist, I'm going to find my mum. And they'd say, yes, if that's what you need to do.

Except she'd found me but she hadn't asked me why. She hadn't said a word in fact. And that was what worried me, because it suggested she wasn't interested in my side of the story. She didn't want to understand, she wanted something else, and I didn't know what it was.

Joe didn't have thousands of pounds to spend on IVF. But he had enough to pay for some therapy. We were getting ready to go out for a walk along the canal, moving around each other in the bedroom, experts at sharing the small space of my flat.

'What kind of therapy?' I said. I was imagining something medical. Vitamin injections. Hormone replacement. Something to boost my biological ability to conceive. Because it was my fault, apparently. Not his words, obviously, but implied when he did a sperm test a few months after the holiday in Scotland and the results came back as normal.

'Psychotherapy.'

I turned from the mirror. 'Psychotherapy?' The word seemed longer when I said it.

'To help you process what you went through.'

'You think it's my brain that's stopping me from getting pregnant?'

'No, of course not.' He was on the other side of the bed. He came round to where I was standing. 'But you've been through trauma and your body is holding on to it.'

'Trauma.'

'Yes. And you've buried it. I think it could really help to talk to someone about it.'

I moved away. 'I talk to you.'

'It took you years to tell me what happened. You let me think your scar was from having your appendix out.'

'Because I wasn't ready to talk about it.'

'But you've never talked about how you felt. It's totally understandable, I know I'd be the same.' He took a deep breath. 'A therapist could help. They know how to get these things up into the light.'

'I deal with things on my own. I'm not a talker. That's not who I am.'

'Everyone has the opportunity to grow and change, Catherine. It's what life is all about.'

'According to who?'

He pursed his lips. He wasn't going to reveal his sources but there was a stack of books on his bedside table that I could refer to if I wanted to find out. *Emotional Intelligence. The Chimp Paradox. The Power of Now.* When I'd called them self-help, he'd jokingly said he preferred the term self-improvement. I'd said you don't need improvement, in my opinion, and he'd looked quietly pleased. He'd said, 'Are you saying I'm perfect?'

'Nobody is perfect. I'm saying I love and accept your imperfections.'

'I don't want to know what my imperfections are.'

'Good, because I don't have a list.'

He'd said it was part of his job as a copywriter to be interested in how people think and what motivates them to make certain decisions. It made sense to me and I accepted it as that. I didn't foresee that he would apply his pop psychology to me. That I would be the one who required self-improvement.

I told him no. I didn't need therapy.

'You don't need it but it could help. It might make you happier.'

'I'm already happy.' Wasn't that obvious? Our happiness together?

'It might heal the pain you've buried that could be affecting how your body works. Our emotions and our physical health are deeply connected. You can't treat them like two separate things. If you feel like you aren't worthy of having a child, that will affect your ability to conceive. I truly believe that.' He reached out to put his hand on my arm.

I backed away from him. 'I don't.'

'It's a fact.'

'It's not a fact! And I've never said I don't feel "worthy". Of course I'm worthy.'

He sat down on the edge of the bed. 'I know but you've got all this guilt inside you. I'm not saying you should feel guilty but you do. You don't deserve to carry that around with you all your life.'

Listening to that made me feel guilty about feeling guilty. And about not being aware that I felt guilty. This conversation, argument, whatever it was, culminated in me crying and him putting his arms around me, saying it was okay. He said it's understandable, and this is why we need to talk to a professional about it. Someone outside the situation who can guide me through it. He said, I'll come with you, if you want. We'll go as a couple. And I thought, absolutely not.

He'd said I was unhappy when being married to him was the happiest I'd been in my entire life. He'd said he wanted me to grow and change which meant that the way I was now somehow wasn't good enough. That was why I was crying. It wasn't buried emotions coming to the surface. It wasn't 'guilt'. I didn't make this clear and I should have, because the next day he made an appointment at a therapist. I was bone-tired and didn't want to fire up the argument again so I didn't protest. It's for us both, he said, but clearly it was for me.

Callum turned up as we were finishing breakfast. The sun was out so we were sitting outside at the picnic table. He needed to use our car to jump-start his, apparently. Anna seemed to know all about it.

I put down my tea and went to get the car keys off the hook. 'It's all right, I'll go,' she said.

'You're not insured.'

'It's two minutes away.'

'And you're in your pyjamas.'

'It won't take a moment.' She got the key, slipped on her flip-flops and skipped across the wet grass in her sleep-creased shorts and T-shirt. Callum shrugged at me, then followed her over to the car. He stopped when he saw the scratch on its side. 'What happened there?'

Anna glanced back at me before she spoke. 'Someone did that. The same night there was banging on the windows.'

'Jesus.'

'It's a hire car.'

'Have you reported it?'

'No. We didn't even think about that.'

He knelt down to study it more closely. 'It's not that deep. I know someone who might be able to sort it.' He stood up, still frowning at the long line across the paintwork. Was he angry? Shocked? Guilty? It was difficult to tell.

Anna returned an hour later on her own. When I asked what they'd been doing all this time she said, 'Talking.' She added, 'We drove to the village to get a phone signal. We can take the car to his mate's garage in Mallaig this afternoon. He might be able to fix the scratch.'

'Today?'

'Yeah. We could do that then go and talk to Leonie when we get back.'

'No, I don't want to talk to her.'

'We need to do something. I can talk to her if you want.'

'No.' I turned away and took a few deep breaths. 'Let's get

the car sorted. Then we can decide what to do about Leonie later.'

'Okay.'

I said, 'Is Callum coming with us?'

She nodded. 'Uh-huh. I better get dressed before he comes back.'

'Did you go to the village in your pyjamas?'

'Yes but I stayed in the car.' She started pulling clothes from her rucksack. 'I need something clean to wear.'

I sighed and left her staring at a mound of crumpled T-shirts and jeans. At least he had deflected her attention away from me.

———

Callum's friend folded himself out of a hatchback that looked too small for him, like a clown's car. He was tall and gangly in overalls and heavy work boots and he looked like he wasn't long out of school. He shook Callum's hand and gave us a nod across the oil-stained forecourt. Pop music blasted from a radio somewhere. A phone rang from a shipping container made into an office. Someone out of sight picked it up and had a muffled conversation. Callum pointed down at the scratch. His friend looked at it without speaking.

Anna said, 'We think someone did it with a key.'

He didn't comment, just knelt down and ran his finger across it. When he stood up, he said, 'It's not gone through.'

Callum said, 'Can you sort it?'

'Maybe. I'll have a go.'

'How much will it cost?' I asked.

He glanced from Callum to me. 'It's a favour. Don't worry about it.' His eyes moved to something behind me. Tom, standing in the doorway of the shipping container, a mobile phone in his hand.

Anna said to him, 'You work here as well?'

He nodded.

Callum said, 'He's a man of many talents. Many jobs, anyway.'

I turned back to his friend. 'Tell me how much it is. We'll pay.' I didn't want to be indebted to them.

Callum shook his head. 'Let's get out of here before he takes your money,' he said. To his friend he said, 'Give me a call when you know what's what.'

'Will do.'

The garage was on a side street not far from the harbour. The smell of petrol followed us all the way to the quayside where lines of cars waited to board a ferry. We stood against the railings, high above the murky water, and watched it slowly reverse towards the dock.

'Where's it come from?' Anna asked.

Callum squinted at the name on the side of the hull. 'Skye.'

She sighed. 'I'm getting that feeling you have when you drop someone off at an airport.'

'What's that? Jealousy?'

'Like I want to go somewhere new.'

He glanced at her. 'Do you want to go and see a castle?'

'Always.'

I hadn't heard of a castle in Mallaig. 'Is there one near here?'

'Pretty near.' He pushed himself away from the railings. 'Wait here. I'll be back in a minute.'

When he was out of earshot, Anna said, 'He's being really nice, isn't he, helping us with the car?'

'What does he want in return, though?'

'I don't know. Me?' She added, 'Hopefully?'

It was the obvious explanation; that all this was an attempt to impress Anna. It was working, if it was. We could see our reflections in the water; Anna's hair and face shimmered in a rainbow on the oily surface.

Over on the ferry, the cars started driving out in turn. Callum came striding back along the quayside, the sun on the side of his face, his hands in his pockets. 'Okay, sorted. Let's go.'

He started walking back the way he came. 'What's happening?' Anna asked at his side.

'We're going to Skye.'

'On the boat?'

He grinned. 'Yeah.' He handed us our tickets. Day return. Passenger only. 'It's only a half-hour trip.'

Anna was smiling right across her face.

I said, 'I thought we were going to see a castle?'

'That's where it is.'

Anna laughed. 'This is awesome.' She was like a child, she was that excited.

I wasn't sure about this sudden change of plan. 'What about the car? Maybe I should stay here?'

He said, 'Don't be daft, we're all going. We'll be back before he closes.'

Anna took my arm and dragged me forwards. I pulled myself free and followed them reluctantly. I supposed it would be okay if it was just half an hour's journey. The crowds became busier as we got further along the quay. We got caught up amongst a group of teenage girls carrying huge rucksacks, with flasks and sleeping bags and rolled-up mats tied to the straps. We were squeezing round them to get into the queue for the gangplank when Callum stopped abruptly.

'Leonie,' he said. We'd nearly walked straight into her.

'Hi.' She had Fleur strapped to her front. Her hair blew over her face.

Anna and I exchanged looks.

'Did you get off the ferry?' Callum asked, frowning.

'No, we were just watching.'

'Oh.' His eyes were searching her face. 'We're going to Armadale.'

She nodded. 'Oh right.'

'Come with us if you want,' he said, but he didn't sound like he meant it.

'No, I've got some shopping to do before Tom finishes at the garage.'

'Okay.'

'Have fun,' she said. 'See you later.' The last comment was addressed to us all. It was the first time she'd looked at me and Anna in the whole exchange.

I crossed the gangplank in a daze. I had a tight, nauseous feeling in my chest. We were mother and daughter but we acted like strangers.

In front of me, Callum put his hand on Anna's back, just above her waist. She slowed down, bringing him closer to her and he said something into her ear. On deck, passengers milled about, looking for the best places to sit. There was the sound of seagulls and safety announcements, the smell of petrol and seawater.

'Inside or out?' Callum said.

'Out,' Anna said.

'I'll sit in,' I said. 'I'll come and find you.'

I headed into a lounge and sat down at an empty table. The way she'd blanked me until the last moment before she walked away. Had she known we'd be here? I needed to think it through. I needed to process what had just happened. I reached in my bag for my journal but it wasn't there.

I checked again. I pulled everything out onto the table. Purse, phone, umbrella, pen, but no journal. My bag had been on the back seat of the car, next to Callum. It must have fallen out when I'd picked it up before leaving the garage.

I had to go back and get it. I headed for the exit doors but there was a change in the vibration of the engine below and I felt the ferry start to move. The buildings on the quayside slipped from window to window. We'd set sail.

But my journal. Tom would see it. Leonie would read it. The thought made my stomach lurch. I closed my eyes. How had this happened? I always had it with me. Always. I'd never lost it before in my life.

I could see Leonie reading it right now. The slant of sea and mountain through the window was disorientating. I needed fresh air.

On deck, the wind was strong and I tasted salt on my lips. I saw Callum and Anna, standing at the very back of the ferry, their shoulders touching, looking at the wake of churned-up water. Some plan was unfolding here. And Callum was almost certainly a part of it. I waved when they turned and saw me, as if I'd just been taking in the view.

I intended to stay on the ferry and go straight back to Mallaig but it wasn't possible; everyone had to disembark. The next crossing was in another forty minutes.

On the dockside people got into waiting taxis. A tour group gathered around a lady with a red umbrella. The backpackers stood in a huddle, looking at a phone screen. Callum turned to us. 'I've got a confession to make.'

I said, 'What?'

'The castle. It's not really a castle. It's more like a ruined house.'

'You brought us to see a fake castle?' Anna said.

'A fake, fallen-down castle,' he replied.

She said, 'I feel like I've been lied to.'

He laughed. 'Get back on the ferry if you want.'

I said, 'I'm going to get the next one back.'

Anna gave me a look. 'I was only joking. I still want to see it.'

'I know. It's not the castle.'

'What's up?'

I breathed in. 'I left my journal in the car.'

'So just write in it later.'

I said, pointedly, 'Anyone could pick it up and read it.'

Anna shrugged. 'Is it really that exciting?'

Was she deliberately not understanding? 'It's not "exciting". It's personal.'

Callum said, 'Do you want me to ring the garage and ask them to put it somewhere safe?'

'No.'

Anna frowned. 'It'll be fine. Just forget about it until we get back.'

From a distance, the 'castle' was everything it ought to be: ivy-covered turrets, a commanding view over the sea. But when we got closer, the illusion fell flat. The outer walls were intact but there was nothing behind them. I saw sky through the lancet windows and brambles behind the archways. It was a film set, a façade.

Anna loved it, anyway. She took photographs with it as the backdrop. Me and her. Me and her and Callum. Her and Callum. Callum's phone rang in his hand as he was holding it up to take one of Anna.

'Tom,' he said, turning away. 'We're in Armadale. What time are you closing up? Yeah we'll be back by then. How's it looking?' He waited, nodding. 'Grand. I'll let them know. Put their minds at rest.' He clicked off the call. 'The scratch is gone. Tom says you can't see a thing.'

'Thank God.'

'So I said we'll be back for five. So we need to get the four o'clock ferry.' He checked his phone. 'We've got time to go round the garden if you like.'

I said I'd meet them back here in half an hour.

Anna thought I was being tactful by leaving them alone together. But I just wanted to sit and think for a moment, on my own.

There was a research centre next to the castle's café. A silver-haired lady saw me hovering in the doorway and came over. 'Can I help?'

'I don't think so.'

'Are you here to trace your ancestors?'

'My ancestors?'

'Your family history? A lot of people come here to look at our archives. We go right back to the seventeen hundreds.'

'I'm not Scottish.'

'Ah, you might be surprised. What's your surname?'

'Bradley.'

She typed it into a computer on one of the desks. I waited. I was feeling unsteady, like I was still on the ferry, trying to stop myself from lurching with the swelling of the waves. I had a bad feeling about this whole excursion and I needed to put the pieces together, figure out why.

'Ah no, we don't have any of those. Never mind, worth a look.'

I gave her Callum's surname instead and her eyes brightened. 'Oh well, there's plenty of them around.' She tapped it out on the keyboard. Records filled the screen. His connections were everywhere, going back hundreds of years.

'You've got family here, then?' she said.

'Yes.' I added, 'I met one of them for the first time this week, actually.'

'Really? Well isn't that wonderful.'

I smiled.

'A distant cousin?'

'No. My daughter.'

'Oh.' She paused and looked back at the computer. I thanked her for her time and left. I needed to talk to Anna; get her opinion on all this. In the gardens, the path zigzagged through high rhododendrons and azaleas. It was like a maze and I passed the same fountain three times before I saw them on the other side of the lawn. I could just see their backs; they were sitting on a bench, facing away from me. Callum was showing Anna something on his phone. She was leaning towards him, legs touching, laughing.

'Hi.'

He quickly clicked off his screen before I could see what was on there.

'You made me jump,' Anna said. I'd made them both jump. She got up. 'Had we better start heading back to the ferry?'

'Yep.' Callum stood up too. I saw him glance at his phone again before he slipped it in his back pocket.

I found it hard not to hurry when we finally docked at Mallaig. I ended up ahead of Anna and Callum, who were dawdling along the quayside, sipping the tea they'd bought onboard. At the garage, there was nobody on the forecourt and our car had been moved to a different place at the back. I went over and looked through the passenger window onto the back seat. My journal wasn't there.

Tom appeared behind me. 'You're back.'

I said, 'Yes. Have you got the car key?'

'Yeah, sure.' He took it out of his pocket. I unlocked the passenger door and searched under the seats with my hands. It wasn't there.

'Have you lost something?'

'My journal.'

'There was nothing in the car.'

I tried to read the expression on his face but I wasn't sure what he was thinking. He shrugged and turned away. Callum and Anna arrived.

'Let's have a look then,' Callum said. They crouched down where the scratch had been.

'You can't see it at all! Thanks, Tom.' Anna looked like she was about to hug him. 'You must have saved us about two hundred quid.'

Tom mumbled, 'It's no bother.'

Callum said, 'I'll buy you a pint sometime.'

I said, 'So where's Leonie?'

They all turned to me. Tom answered after a moment. 'Having a brew at a friend's.'

Had she taken my journal with her? Or had Tom put it somewhere in the office? I looked over at the shipping container. I couldn't think of a reason to go inside.

'Your diary must be at the cottage,' Anna said, as we were pulling out onto the main road. In the back seat, Callum didn't say anything. He looked out of the window as if he wasn't listening.

Anna turned back to talk to him a few times as we drove down the coast. He pointed out his old high school and the best place to watch the steam train that was in the Harry Potter films. She tried to get him into a conversation about the books but he hadn't read them and couldn't remember which of the films he'd seen.

'Boarding schools and wizards? It's not my thing.'

'You're missing out.'

'I'll live.'

We dropped him off at the gate by the cattle grid. 'Don't get too attached,' I said when he'd gone.

'I'm not.'

'What were you talking to him about?'

'When?'

'Today.'

'Loads of things.'

'You didn't talk to him about Leonie, did you?'

'No, of course not.'

When we got inside, we searched the whole place but my journal wasn't there. It wasn't under my pillow, or on the table, or on the sofa. I knew it wouldn't be. It had fallen out in the car. Tom had found it and given it to Leonie.

'It must be around somewhere,' Anna said.

'It's not. It was in the car. I think Leonie's got it.'

She rubbed her eyes as if she had a headache starting. 'So what's in it that's so important?'

I didn't want to think about what was in it. Every time I did, I felt sick like I had on the boat. 'It's private.'

'This is why I've never kept a diary.'

'No, you just take naked pictures of yourself instead,' I snapped.

She blinked. 'I didn't take them myself.' As if that made all the difference. 'And how is that the same anyway?'

'Because it's personal. Because it's not something you would want other people to see.'

'I'm going for a smoke,' she muttered. She sat outside,

sheltering her cigarette from the breeze with a cupped hand, trying to get it lit. I followed her out and sat opposite her. She gave me a weary look. She took a drag and put the lighter down between us.

My eyes caught on the picture on the side. I picked it up.

'Now what?' Anna said.

'Where in Cornwall is Leonie from?'

'I don't know.'

On the lighter, underneath a picture of a surfboard was the word, *Newquay*.

I pointed to it. 'She's from Newquay. This belongs to her.'

'I found it under the sofa.'

An image came into my head: the key to the cottage sitting in the cup holder between the front seats of the hire car.

Anna said, 'What's wrong, Catherine?'

'I left the key to the cottage in the car. She's been here while we were out.'

'What?'

She came here while we were on the island, knowing there was no danger of us returning until much later. She let herself in. Looked through our belongings. Wondered which were mine. Her lighter fell out of her bag as she stood up to leave. Or she dropped it on purpose, knowing we'd find it when we got back.

I said, 'She scratched our car, tried to terrify us at night, and now she's been in our cottage.' I breathed in and got a lungful of cigarette smoke. I couldn't get enough air.

Anna said, 'This whole situation is freaking me out.'

I said, 'It's not you she's trying to scare.'

'We need to talk to her, sort it out.'

I nodded. I let a second or two pass. 'The right thing to do is report it to the police.'

'Report Leonie to the police?'

'Report the vandalism and the theft.'

She stared into the clearing, thinking this over. She got out another cigarette and picked up the lighter but she didn't put the two together, as though she wasn't sure how they were supposed to connect.

8

ANNA

Saturday. Sunrise 04.28. Sunset 22.21

I couldn't sleep that night. Every slight noise made my eyes spring open, and the woods are not a quiet place when the sun has set. Aside from the wind in the trees, which sounded a lot like a car approaching, and the squalls of rain against the window, there were weird animal calls that were somewhere between a baby crying and a wolf separated from its pack.

I lay awake for hours. I was thinking about Callum. How he'd put his hand on the small of my back to steer me through the crowds on the ferry. And I was thinking about Leonie. How she'd gone from creeping around at night to scratching our car to breaking into our home.

Were there things Catherine hadn't told me? Had she done something to make Leonie turn against her? Had she pushed her away when she'd tried to make contact? Or said something thoughtless and cruel, like telling her she was unloved? It wasn't beyond her.

Or did it all stem from the original insult; the fact that

Catherine gave her away. Maybe Leonie thought her diary would help her understand why. Or tell her who her father was? Was that what Catherine was so worried about her reading? It was a story she'd never shared with anyone, probably not even Joe.

All I knew about that party was that the girl who'd held it had an indoor swimming pool, and that she was charging people to go, two things unheard of in our town. She lived in this old manor house on its own in the hills, surrounded by thick rhododendrons and woods. I went there myself, a few years after Catherine had left home. The girl who held it had a brother my age and we all ended up back at his after the pub one night. We were all madly jealous of his living arrangements because he had his own lounge and bathroom and kitchen, all in this converted, high-ceilinged 'billiards room', separated from the main house where his parents and sister lived. It was freezing cold in there. We wrapped ourselves in blankets to keep warm. At the time I'd wondered if that icy room was where Catherine slept with the exchange student. One reason it was so cold was because part of the ceiling was made of glass. It was a teenager's version of romance; a French boy and a view of the stars from the bed.

And now here we were, two decades later, and the baby they'd made had found its way back to her. I thought of Leonie talking about guilt and loneliness and how she'd never leave her baby, not for a second. Her words had been hard and cold over the gently lapping waves.

But, I wanted to tell her, you're not fifteen; you're twenty-three. What would she have said if I had? Would she have spilled out her anger at Catherine right there on that bench? Or would she have walked away, waiting for a better way to make her feelings known?

It was almost eleven by the time I finally dragged myself out of bed. Catherine wasn't around. She'd left a note to say she'd gone to the beach. Wreck Cove, Callum said it was called, where the sea pushed all the passing debris and driftwood back onto the land.

In the living room the furnace was low and the log basket was empty. I went out to the wood pile to refill it. I was nearly back at the cottage when my bare foot slipped on something squidgy and sharp. I dropped the basket, looked down. In the grass, by my foot, there was a smear of flesh and pulsing pink skin. I screamed and frantically wiped my foot across the ground. What the fuck was that? It was mangled but it was moving. I backed away from it, my heart racing.

Catherine came rushing up the track. She must have heard me cry out. 'Anna?'

'There's something alive. It was on my foot.'

She edged closer to where I was pointing and looked with interest rather than disgust. 'It's a baby bird. It's dead.'

'But it moved.'

She knelt down beside it. 'There's maggots in it. That's what's moving.'

I shuddered. I could still feel the wet sensation on my foot. Maggots? 'Did I kill it?'

'No. It was already dead.'

I got a bit closer. A creature half-formed and smaller than a baby's fist. There was a sliver of beak, eyes that had never opened. I could see a stubby white worm squirming beneath the featherless skin.

'I stood on it, I thought it was an embryo.' I was horrified, words spilling out.

'I'll move it into the woods. Go and wash your feet.'

In the bathroom, I used a flannel to rub at my heel. It had looked like a tiny, unborn baby, like you see on a hospital scan. Like Dad's 'handful of cells' had come to life and I'd crushed it, smothering it. I scrubbed harder then let the mucky water drain away. Even when my feet were dry in socks and shoes, I could still sense where it had touched my skin.

Back outside, Catherine was at the spot in the clearing where the bird had been. She said, 'I don't understand how it ended up here.' She had a shattered eggshell in the palm of her hand. It was sand-coloured with speckles, and looked light enough to blow away in the slightest breeze. 'It can't have fallen out of a nest. There aren't any trees close enough.'

The edge of the woods was about ten metres away. The chick had been between the door and the woodpile, only a few steps from the table.

'Maybe the nest was on the ground.'

'Then where is it?' She took a photograph of the eggshell on her phone and carefully wrapped the broken pieces in kitchen towel. 'Are you ready to go?'

We were heading to Mallaig to report the break-in and the scratched car to the police. We also needed a locksmith. When we got a signal I found one online and called the number on his website but he didn't answer.

In Mallaig we parked outside the police station, a low, white building opposite the train station. Catherine turned off the engine and took a new notebook out of her bag. 'I need to read through this before we go in,' she said.

'What is it?'

'What we're going to say.'

'Shall I have a look too?'

'No, I'll do the talking.'

She was wearing black trousers and a cream blouse under her summer jacket. I was in jeans and a hoodie. It looked like I'd been called in for questioning and she was my solicitor.

In the police station an older man in a screened-off office was talking on the phone. When he put it down he came over to the counter where we were waiting. 'Can I help?'

Catherine cleared her throat. 'Yes. I need to report a crime.'

He asked what it was, and where it had taken place. Criminal damage, Catherine said, and theft, and intimidation. She knew all the terminology.

He looked up at the last one. 'Intimidation of what kind?'

'Threats. Stalking. A break-in.'

'Okay.' He tapped it all into a computer. 'And your address?'

'We're on holiday here. Do you want the address of where we're staying?'

'Yes please.'

I didn't have a clue what our address here was, but Catherine had it all ready in her head. She was acting like she knew what she was doing but I could tell she was nervous. It was in her breathing: the deep intakes of air. And in her restlessness: the fast movements of her head. Her nerves made me nervous. I'd never even been in a police station before today.

The man took Catherine's name and date of birth, then said, 'Let me see if someone's available to talk to you.'

I'd expected an officer in uniform but the lady who came to meet us was casually dressed in jeans and a chunky cardigan. She had a mug of tea in one hand and a notebook in the other. 'Let's have a seat in here,' she said, leading us into a room with a computer on a desk and a few plastic chairs. She put her tea down. 'The last two went cold before I had a sip. Third time lucky.'

She nudged the mouse pad on the computer to bring it to life then turned to face us. She was a similar age to Catherine, maybe a bit older. She read Catherine's home address and date of birth back to her, then she shifted her chair across so that there was no desk between us and turned to a fresh page of her notebook. 'What is it you want to tell me about?'

'On Tuesday the 15th of June, between one and two in the morning, our car was vandalised, outside the cottage where we're staying. Then on Friday the 18th of June, sometime between 1pm and 5pm, the cottage was broken into. I suspect the front door key was stolen from the harbour garage here in Mallaig. We took the car there to be fixed earlier that day.'

'What was taken from the cottage?'

'A diary.'

'Anything else?'

'Not that we can see.'

'Any CCTV?'

'No.'

'Any damage?'

'No.'

She frowned. 'And no forced entry. So how do you know there was a break-in? Oh, because of the missing diary. Right, got it.' She looked down at her notebook which was still blank. When she looked back up, she said, 'Let's go back to the vandalised car. Talk me through what happened.'

Catherine checked her notes. 'It was around half past one in the morning. Somebody knocked on our bedroom window and then banged, very aggressively, on the door.'

'Did you see who it was?'

'No, it was dark. But in the morning, the car had been scratched, right across one side, about thirty centimetres long. I've got a photograph of it here.' She took out her phone, still talking. 'There was also an incident on either Sunday the 13th or Monday the 14th of June, during the night. Somebody threw some items from a table outside onto the ground. I have photographs.'

'Can I see them?'

Catherine handed over her phone. The officer swiped slowly through the images, her expression unchanging. 'It looks like somebody's run a key across that car,' she said.

'Yes.'

She gave the phone back to Catherine. 'Could it have happened earlier in the day without you realising it?'

'No.'

'You're sure?'

'Yes.'

'Okay. I can give you a crime number for that. You'll need it if you claim on insurance.'

'We've already got it fixed.'

'I'll record it anyway.' We waited as she tapped something into the computer. When she'd finished typing, she said, 'The other things you've told me about; the table, and the missing diary. You've given me a lot of detail with times and dates but I can't see any evidence of a crime there.'

Catherine blinked. 'But what about the break-in?'

'There's no forced entry, and nothing missing apart from a diary that could be mislaid in the house.'

'But there was a cigarette lighter, left on the floor. It wasn't ours. Somebody had definitely been inside.'

'It could belong to a previous occupant. This is a holiday home, isn't it?'

'Yes, but it wasn't there before. We'd have seen it. And then this morning, there was a dead bird left outside our door. It's intimidation. And I know who's doing it.'

The officer nodded very slightly. 'Who?'

'Leonie Woodward. Tom Creel. Callum Anderson.'

I said, 'Catherine, we don't know that for sure.'

The officer focused on me for the first time. I had no idea what she was thinking. She turned back to Catherine. 'Has anything like this happened to you before?'

Catherine seemed surprised by the question. 'No.'

'Have you discussed your concerns with anyone else?'

'Like who? No.'

'Just your sister.'

'Yes.'

The officer glanced quickly at me. I thought she was about to say something else but she didn't. She clicked her pen nib back in. 'I'll report the car vandalism as a crime. That kind of damage is usually kids messing around. We've had some similar incidents recently. You'll be sent a letter to your home address with a crime number and a contact for Victim Support. It should arrive within the next fourteen days.'

'Aren't you going to do anything?'

'I'm not going to do anything more at this stage. I appreciate you coming to talk to me.' She stood up. I did the same, and a moment later, Catherine followed. In the reception area, the police officer smiled. 'Try and put it behind you and enjoy the rest of your holiday.'

I said we will, and thanks for your time, because Catherine had stopped speaking. It was only when we were out of the building and crossing the road that her frozen expression snapped back into life.

'Why did you say that about Leonie and Tom and Callum?' Her voice was accusatory.

'What did I say?'

'That you didn't believe me.'

We stopped on the pavement that ran alongside the train tracks. 'I didn't say that.'

'You said we couldn't be sure who it was.'

'Because I didn't want you to report Callum to the police. It was like you wanted to get him arrested.'

'No, just questioned.'

'How's that going to make me look?'

'How you look isn't the priority here, Anna.' Like something Dad would say when I was thirteen. She added, 'Can't you focus on someone other than yourself for a while?'

'Someone like you, you mean.'

'You didn't back me up at all in there.'

'You said you wanted to do the talking.'

'But it would have been nice to have some support. That woman didn't listen to a word I said.'

That wasn't true. She had been listening intently. Her eyes barely left Catherine's face and she didn't touch her cup of tea.

Just then, there was a long, high whistle and the wheezing sound of a steam train. I leaned over the fence to see down the track. A big black engine and ruby red carriages. 'It's the Harry Potter train!' I turned to Catherine. 'I can't believe it.'

She said, 'Can you please come back to reality, just for a minute.'

'This is reality.' It was a big fuck-off steam train, I wasn't imagining it. On the platform across the tracks, people held up their phones to film its slow arrival. As it got closer, a little girl waved out of a carriage window. I waved back and she bounced up and down in her seat.

'Let's go and have a look.'

Catherine snapped, 'I need you to focus on what we're talking about.'

'I will. In a minute.' The passengers were milling out of the station. I weaved through them and on to the platform. White steam and black smoke and the smell of burning coal. I looked inside at the plush seats and polished wood. Through the carriage windows I could see Catherine glaring at me from the other side of the track.

She went to bed early again. I stayed up, drinking wine, reading, feeding the fire every half hour or so just to keep that cosy glow alive in the furnace. I wondered what Callum was doing with his Saturday night? If this was normal life, I'd be checking my phone right now. Composing a casual message in my head. And it was kind of a relief that none of that was possible out here. I could send a smoke signal. Use telepathy. I had a thought and opened the door, straining my ears for the sound of a bassline. That was how he drew me in the other night; distant music playing in the woods. But it was quiet. Just the shaky bleating of a lamb, which has to be one of the loneliest sounds in the world, especially at dusk, and especially when there's no response.

I shut the door and locked it then got ready for bed. I was tired after lying awake for most of last night. Tonight, I'd make sure I had my ear-plugs in and eye mask on to block out all possible disruptions. If Leonie's plan was to freak us out with sudden noises, I'd thwart her efforts by staying soundly asleep.

Except I couldn't find my eye mask. I pulled back the sleeping bag, searched inside it, looked under my pillows, lifted the flimsy mattress to see if it was under there. It was. And so was Catherine's diary. Tucked under, near the ladder. How had it got in there?

Catherine was asleep on her front, her arms wrapped round her pillow like she was clinging to wreckage in the sea. I watched her for a minute or two. She didn't stir. I went into the living room and quietly closed the bedroom door. I sat on the floor by the stove where the embers still glowed in the furnace. Her diary had a blue cover and in the right-hand corner, in little gold letters, were her name and the year. This year. It was a present from Joe. It said so on the first page.

1 January

New year, new journal. That's what Joe said when I unwrapped this. He's been using variations of that phrase all morning. New year, new bin bag. New year, new bottle of milk. When I asked him what he was talking about, he seemed surprised that I needed an explanation. New year, new you, he said. It's on every magazine cover every January. New year, same headline.

New year, new me. Is that what he's hoping for? I will need to keep this hidden. There is no point in keeping a journal that other people can read. He said I can use it for planning, goals, to set intentions for the day. It's a bullet journal, he said. I had to google to find out what that meant. Lists, basically, and stickers. One article said it's a way to put the chaos of your life into a coherent order.

I usually write my lists on the notes app on my phone. That is probably why he bought me this; because he doesn't like me staring at a screen all the time. It looks expensive. Two shades of blue, aquamarine at the top, midnight at the bottom, like the sea or the sky at dusk. He's had it personalised with the year and my name in small gold lettering.

I'm writing this in the spare room, sitting on the single bed that runs alongside the window. The box room, we call it, because it's small and square, and it's where we keep everything we haven't unpacked yet. It has pastel-yellow walls and a view over the back gardens. I can see the lady from next door taking out her recycling bin. She has to cross our garden and two more to get to the ginnel that leads to the front of the terrace. Whoever designed these houses didn't give much thought to privacy. The sheds used to be outside toilets. Next door's conversations can be heard word for word if you sit close to the fireplace. The old man on the other side could probably hear my pen on the paper if he put his ear to the wall. I know he isn't doing that. I can see him in his backyard, pouring hot water into a stone bird bath to crack the ice.

I know Joe wants me to use this journal to look forward not back with his talk of plans and goals but that's not what I want to do. He's changed his philosophy in that sense. It's funny how we've both reversed our positions. He spent years trying to get me to talk about the past, but now when I want to revisit certain incidents and decisions with him, he changes the subject or goes in another room. He doesn't want to talk about the past, which is fine. I'll write about it instead.

I know the exact date it started because it was the same day as my first (and last) therapy appointment. Thursday 22 October, two years ago now, just over.

I'd met her a few weeks earlier, but that was the first time we sat down and talked. I don't know why it happened on that particular day. Perhaps I wanted to distract myself from dwelling on the appointment that evening. Or perhaps I was simply feeling guilty that I hadn't given her much of my time, and that it wasn't fair, considering the internship was supposed to be a learning experience for her.

She'd been spending her days reading a series of reports we'd produced about the use of isolation booths in educational settings, in between helping the researchers with the most menial aspects of their jobs. I'd been buried in a funding application for weeks with barely any time to come up for air. When I did and had finally cleared my backlog of emails, I turned my attention to the various demands from my team. She was the only one who didn't have any, it seemed. Yet I couldn't help noticing how she looked up every time I came in or stood up or spoke, as if I was the main point of interest in the room.

I registered these quick glances, and realised I knew almost nothing about her: her career goals, her degree subject. I wasn't even certain of her name until I checked the email from HR. Sophie. I messaged her to suggest we head downstairs for a coffee and a catch-up. I said we could plan her work for the next few months to make sure she was meeting the objectives of her placement. I saw her eyes light up as she read it, and I thought, I really ought to have done this three weeks ago and not left her floundering on her own for so long.

In the lift down, her reflection in the mirror looked at mine. Her appearance was very 'together', and I wondered whether she had developed this look especially for this role, or whether she always looked this self-assured. She had short boyish hair, dyed white-blonde. Strong eye make-up. Cranberry-coloured lips. She wore black, navy and sand and comfortable flat shoes. She looked more at home in this place than I did, in my tailored suit and blouse.

I apologised for how busy I'd been. She apologised for not pushing herself forwards more. That's what you're supposed to do, isn't it, she said. Yes, I agreed. But it helps if you have some encouragement too.

We had recently moved into a new building in Central London which housed lots of SMEs on short-term rental agreements. There were several tech firms, a few HR consultancies and creative agencies. We were the only non-profit, as far as I could see. The fish-bowl offices were connected by communal break-out spaces and corridors lined with quirky ornaments and insightful quotes that I silently argued with every time I walked past. One claimed that if you didn't like your reality, you could change it simply by changing your perspective on it. Tell that to the children who go without lunch in the school holidays, I thought. Or the women trapped in abusive relationships. Or anyone suffering injustice, in any way. It's not the world that's wrong, it's your perspective on it that's the problem. It was the motivational equivalent of 'I'm sorry you feel that way'.

I digress. The offices were centred on a co-working space with an always-clean kitchen, and armchairs around coffee tables. There were one-person booths where you could work on your laptop, headphones on, and soundproof cubicles for phone conversations. We chose a long, empty table with a couple of miniature cacti in the centre. Sophie sat down while I got cappuccinos from the machine in the kitchen.

She told me she was halfway through a degree in international development at Cambridge and she was happy to discover I'd studied there too. And that we were both from the north west. Two Oxbridge-educated northerners in London. Our shared history made us both relax a little. We knew where each other was coming from, literally.

It was towards the end of the day and not long after we'd sat down, we were asked to move because they wanted to set up for an event taking place after work. We duly shifted to the armchairs and as we talked I could see Sophie's eyes diverting to whatever was happening behind me. I turned to look. The table where we'd sat with our laptops and coffee was now covered in wild flowers and foliage.

This building felt like a young, urban branch of the WI at times, with all the cake sales and craft sessions and speakers they invited in each week. I didn't get involved but some of my team went to yin yoga on Wednesdays. Tonight they were holding a flower crown workshop. The girl leading it had long, centre-parted hair, pinned at the back with real roses. She wore a crochet dress over a Goa tan, like she'd just floated in from a boutique festival in Wiltshire. When she saw us looking, she smiled and asked if we'd be joining?

Sophie said, I will. I said I was meeting someone. I intended to work late then go straight to the appointment. But later I found myself wandering over to the group gathered around the flower table. There were apricot roses and lavender stems and baby's breath and pale-pink peonies, and it was so much more appealing than looking at a computer screen. I took a seat next to Sophie and we spent an hour snipping stems and taping them into place on the wire crowns. It was surprisingly relaxing, weaving the flowers into a circle until the frame was hidden. We got engrossed, and by the end of the workshop, we all had crowns of peonies and roses.

I didn't know what to do with mine. I couldn't take it with me; the therapist might read into it. Sophie was going to a party the next night so I said she could have it.

'Give it to one of your friends,' I said, 'then you won't be the only one wearing a crown.' I placed it on her head. She looked like one of the Flower Fairies. She asked me to take a photo on her phone and she tagged me in it on Instagram later that evening. I saw it on the way home from the appointment and thought of how that hour of weaving flowers into a circle had made me feel significantly better than the time I'd just spent staring at a square box of tissues and wondering whether the fig plant in the corner was real or fake.

The therapist had recorded our conversation. Long silences would fill most of the tape. Would she listen back to it? Or just skip through to the part where I said I didn't think it was working and perhaps therapy wasn't the right thing for me at that time. She'd nodded and said, 'I can see you're reluctant to talk. That's something we could look at.'

She said she believed that painful emotions lost some of their power when they were spoken out loud. It was unclear which emotions she was referring to. I touched a leaf on the fig plant as I left. Plastic. Very convincing though, from a distance.

I didn't tell Joe that I'd cancelled the sessions. He'd looked so hopeful when I'd said the first one had gone 'okay' that I didn't add 'but I won't be going again' to the end of the sentence. It had been a long day. I couldn't face his disappointment. I intended to tell him over the weekend but somehow I didn't and then it was Thursday again and I couldn't go home without him asking why I wasn't at therapy.

My plan was to work late instead, but there was another craft session in the communal area and it filled the time perfectly. A girl with a head-tie and thick-rimmed glasses showed us how to make a macramé plant holder. Knotting and weaving together those lengths of rope was my own form of therapy. One I'd chosen rather than had forced on me. I liked working with my hands after a day of report-writing and meetings. I liked creating something you could touch and see. Sophie said she felt the same way.

These 'maker sessions' were popular. They started

holding them every Thursday. We painted glass, moulded candles, printed designs on T-shirts. I kept my creations at work or gave them to Sophie. Joe still thought my Thursday evenings were spent confronting painful emotions from my past.

So when it finally happened, a late period, two blue lines on a pregnancy test, I could tell he felt silently vindicated. He thought I'd talked my infertility away. That I'd got it out of my system by telling a stranger all my secrets. I didn't correct him because what was the point, now we'd got the result we wanted? I was just glad the spotlight wasn't on me anymore.

I had a strategy ready for this pregnancy, based on my experience from my first one. I would retreat from the world again, but this time, it would be by choice. I wanted to give the baby all my strength to help it grow. No more ten-hour days and weekend working. I was leaving that busy-busy lifestyle behind. And I wanted to make a home out of our flat, for the three of us. All the crafts I'd been making on Thursdays, I gradually dotted them about each room. I still went to the maker sessions. I enjoyed them so why not? But one week, the noticeboard said it would be a gin-tasting class, which obviously I couldn't participate in. I hadn't told work yet that I was pregnant, so when Sophie asked why I hadn't put my name on the list, I made up an excuse on the spot; Joe was taking me out for dinner at a new Lebanese restaurant near our flat.

I suggested the restaurant to him when I got home that night. He said, yes, of course we should. It wasn't a celebration as such. Just an acknowledgement that we'd reached a certain milestone. Six weeks pregnant. It would have a heartbeat. My first scan was booked in next month. It was finally happening.

I knew that most miscarriages occur during those early weeks but I also knew that once an embryo is growing inside you, it takes on a life of its own, whether you want it to or not. I'd felt that life force when I was fifteen. How tenacious it was, how focused on its goal. How it was always busy tightening its grip on existence and expanding its space in the world. It wasn't going to just slip away into nothing. Babies didn't do that, and I should know.

I was on the train to work when I felt something leak out of me. I sat very still until we reached the station, then made sure I was the first onto the platform and through the ticket barriers. In the toilets, I saw the wetness was blood and it kept coming back every time I wiped it away. At the taxi rank I gave the driver the name of the maternity hospital where I would be having the scan. He wanted a postcode and this simple request made me cry. I got in the taxi behind instead.

I don't know what I thought I'd achieve by rushing to the hospital like that. It was a handful of cells; they weren't going to operate and bring it back to life. There was nothing they could do other than say yes or no. Babies existed whether you wanted them to or not and the reverse was true as well. No heartbeat. The blood tests confirmed it.

I texted Joe to tell him, which in hindsight wasn't the right thing to do. I didn't want to have to say the words but I should have forced them out. I typed, It's gone. I'm sorry. And he called me immediately. He said he'd come to the hospital but I didn't want to wait around for him to arrive. You can't avoid babies but you can usually avoid pregnant people, but not in a maternity hospital. I said I'd meet him at home.

That night we had very little to say to each other. The words that usually flowed between us seemed to have

149

stopped along with the heartbeat. I went to bed. He watched TV. He said he'd cancel dinner for Thursday, and I said why?

'I didn't think you'd want to,' he said.

I thought, well I can go to the gin-tasting now. It was the only thing from 'before' that I could make sense of in my mind. Everything else felt like someone else's life. Hazy. Not really relevant anymore.

The gin-tasting was a place marker for where to restart after this detour into motherhood, this dead end. The host was a Camden micro-distillery set up by two history graduates who'd met working in a bar. Their gins had a Mediterranean feel in their flavours and garnishes. They were inspired by 1920s archaeology digs in Italy and Egypt. It was a very specific brand but ultimately gin is gin and it all does the same thing. That workshop wasn't about creating, just consuming. A different kind of distraction, the usual kind.

They began with a talk about gin's origins and history. I stopped listening when they started talking about why it was known as mother's ruin. I looked at the drink they'd handed us before we sat down and saw my glass was already empty. I got another from the spares by the door. The man was talking about knitting needles and hot baths. I focused on the quotes on the walls instead. The best way to change your situation is to change your perspective on it. But facts were facts, weren't they? You couldn't change things simply by looking at them differently. That was just gaslighting yourself.

I didn't believe in positive thinking; I believed in reality. And the reality was, I'd lost my baby. And I would like very much to change that situation but whichever perspective I saw it from, I couldn't.

Sophie nudged me. The introduction was over. We were moving on to the tasting part of the night. We edged along the sampling table, trying different flavours of gin combined with different tonics and garnishes. We were supposed to be discussing what each gin reminded us of. Pine needles and Refreshers, Sophie said, frowning.

'Surely it's about how it makes you feel rather than how it tastes,' I said.

'How does it make you feel?' asked one of the distiller-historian-barmen.

It was like being at therapy again. 'Drunk.'

He turned to the next person. My perspective on this was all wrong.

We sat down with our drinks. Sophie said, 'I don't think I like gin. I'd rather be drinking tea and knitting.'

'The youth of today.'

'I want to be an old lady already. Or at least middle-aged.'

'When you're middle-aged you'll wish you were young again.'

'I won't.'

Was she unhappy? She tucked her hair behind her ear and looked directly at me. 'You remind me of someone,' she said.

'Who?'

She thought for a moment, squinting her eyes. Then opened them, surprised. 'I think it might be me.'

We both started laughing and I found it hard to stop, even when the hosts started the next part of their talk. I took myself into the kitchen to wipe my eyes and regain my composure. Sophie followed. 'Shall we go somewhere else?'

'For another drink?'

'What about Starbucks?'

'Okay.'

The combination of gin and caffeine suited us and we

got into a good conversation about a TV series we were both watching. Joe called to say he was near my office so I told him to join us. When he arrived he laughed in a bemused sort of way. 'What happened to the gin-tasting?'

'We prefer cake.' I introduced him to Sophie. 'She thinks I remind her of her,' I said.

He thought I meant in appearance. He looked at us in turn, both holding those giant mugs, sitting on those giant sofas. 'There is a similarity,' he said. 'But it's hard to say what.'

Sophie and I smiled across the table at each other.

'It might be that you've both been drinking gin,' he said.

'We're not drunk,' we said at the same time, and started laughing again.

Thursday nights became our night. Mine and Sophie's. And Joe sometimes came along later if he was in the area. We did the makers session, then went for tea and cake. Sophie had moved into a different team by then so I wasn't her manager anymore. We became friends rather than colleagues, and the age gap didn't matter. We just got along. A few times I met her at a café at the weekend. She was the first friend I'd made in years. Since I'd met Joe, in fact.

Then her internship came to an end, and she moved back to Cambridge to complete her degree. I knew she would be leaving, but it still surprised me, somehow, when she wasn't around anymore. There was a definite gap in my life. I described it to Joe as a 'Sophie-shaped hole on Thursdays and Saturdays'. And he said, 'Are you sure it's Sophie you're missing?'

I looked at him. Where was this going?

'She's about the same age as your daughter.'

'My daughter?' I thought of the still heartbeat, then of

the relinquished baby. Neither fitted the description of 'daughter', or of 'Sophie' for that matter.

Joe said, 'Your grown-up daughter.'

'I don't have a grown-up daughter. I gave her away.'

'She's still yours biologically. It's feasible that you might be missing her on a cellular level.'

What was he talking about? A cellular level? 'I don't think about her at all.'

'Never?'

'No.' Rarely, anyway. Back then, a grown-up daughter was a concept I couldn't visualise in my mind.

He said, 'Have you ever considered getting in touch with her?'

I shook my head.

'I've looked into it. You'd need to apply to the Adoption Contact Register. There's a form on their website.'

'No.'

'It might help.'

'I said I don't want to.'

He didn't listen to me. He never listened. I said it was a bad idea. He responded by sending me a link to the form. I ignored it, sitting there in my inbox, until it got bumped down the screen and out of view.

At work, I found the CV that HR had emailed me before Sophie started her internship. There was no date of birth. Not unusual, nowadays. I tried to remember whether she'd ever brought in cakes to the office – standard practice when it was your birthday – but she hadn't, at least not when I'd been there. I recalled what she'd told me about her family. Her parents were older than most, elderly even, her mother had a cancer scare the year before. She had no siblings; she described herself as a 'lonely only' which had made me laugh because she seemed to go out every evening to book readings, or yoga, or friends' houses. She wasn't lonely in the slightest.

But the thing I kept coming back to was when she said that I reminded her of herself. How had she said it? Suddenly, out of the blue. It had seemed spontaneous at the time, but perhaps that had been an act. Perhaps she'd been working up to it. To see what reaction I'd have.

I'd fallen into a fit of laughter even though it wasn't remotely funny. We'd both giggled uncontrollably as if we were sharing a secret, a private joke that no one understood, and at the time, even I didn't know what it meant.

I messaged her to suggest I visit her one weekend in Cambridge. It was something we'd talked about before she left but we hadn't made any definite plans. I caught the train there and she met me at the station and we spent the day walking around the town, revisiting the college where I'd studied, the halls where I'd lived. I couldn't stop myself from scrutinising her. I was aware of how we mirrored each other's movements, of how our thoughts followed similar patterns. It was almost as if the connection between us didn't need to be spoken out loud. It existed whether we acknowledged it or not.

That was the truth I ought to have held on to; that we didn't need to bring who we were to each other out into the open. I should have known that we couldn't suddenly shine a light on something that had been in the dark for so long without it causing a flinch, an involuntary recoil.

I was clumsy. I didn't know how to bring it up. In the end I put it in a long, multi-paragraph message which I have since deleted from my account. In it, I asked her directly if she was my daughter. A short while later, it was marked as 'Seen'.

But she never replied. Not a yes and not a no. I followed it up with a longer explanation of why I had asked. This one, she didn't open. Or if she opened it, she didn't want me to know.

Unseen. She was hiding from me. I didn't understand why at the time because I didn't consider it properly, from her point of view. I thought she had come in peace, without malice. The alternative didn't occur to me at all.

It was six days after I sent the unseen message that things started happening at work. A flash meeting with my manager about progress. Emails I should have been copied into that got 'lost in the system'. Passwords that no longer worked. It was seven weeks later that I was called into the meeting with HR.

Joe says we left all that behind when we moved out of London but I disagree. Once you've opened up the box, you can't just shove everything back inside.

9

CATHERINE

Sunday. Sunrise 04.28. Sunset 22.21

It was light but it was always light here; it didn't mean it was morning. I dressed in the living room and went outside and it was as though I had walked into a cloud. The woods and sea were hidden in mist and the world seemed smaller than yesterday. I went to where the dead chick had been left on the ground. There was a pine cone lying in the exact same spot, even though the nearest pine tree must have been at least ten metres away. I picked it up. The scales were closed, not open. Its significance was lost on me.

I got the OS map from inside and opened it out across the picnic table. I traced the track that led from the road to where our cottage ought to have been. It was a blank space amongst the green. At some point, by someone, it had been erased.

Closed not open. Ashes, flowers and flame.

Anna came out, wearing a hoodie over her pyjamas, bare feet in walking boots.

'I can't get back to sleep.' She sat down then stood up again because the bench was wet with dew. 'I'm so tired. What time is it?'

'I haven't looked.'

She took out a cigarette and smoked it, leaning against the cottage wall. It was strange for her to be up this early. And she didn't normally have her first cigarette until much later in the day.

She said, 'There definitely was somebody that night, wasn't there? We both heard them.'

Why was she asking me that? 'That police officer knew more than she was letting on.'

Anna nodded vaguely then wandered away, dropping ash into the grass. I watched her smoking at the tree-line, her outline smudged by the mist. When she came back she said too brightly, 'Maybe we could drive to that picnic spot in the forest today?' Then, out of nowhere, 'There's a band playing in the pub tomorrow night. Callum said he'll give us a lift if we want to go.'

I'd been wondering what would happen next. 'Will Leonie be there?'

'Maybe? You don't have to come.'

'I'm not hiding from her.'

'She probably won't be there.'

'I'll come.'

'Okay.' She picked up the pine cone and rolled it against her palm, absent-mindedly, as if she wasn't really aware of what she had in her hand.

The mist wasn't shifting. If anything it had become thicker and lower. It folded over the trees and hid the end of the track. You could walk into it as if you were walking into a dream.

Anna said, 'Isn't it eerie out here? I feel like we're in one of your snow globes. Cut off from the world.'

Why was she talking about my snow globes? 'I've not seen them in years.'

'They're in the wardrobe in your old room.'

'They've kept them all this time?'

'What kind of person would throw away a collection of snow globes?'

'Er, Dad.'

'Callum's dad died in March.'

Callum's dad?

'He had cancer.' She got up when she heard the kettle whistling. It had been a bizarre change of subject. I couldn't work it out.

I checked the fuel gauge before we set off. It was still at the halfway point where it had been hovering for days. We drove away from the coast across heathland that gradually rose upwards before descending into a valley of dense pine plantations. We passed forestry tracks where trucks had sunk their wheels into clay. A river with water so clear I could see the stones on the bottom as we crossed the bridge. They were silver-blue and grey and an iron-rich red.

I thought of the cloudy water that flowed from the taps in the cottage and felt my skin prickle on my back where the rash was strongest. I had not spoken about the contamination to the police officer. I'd lacked concrete proof and this had stopped me from addressing the issue. Which was exactly what they had intended. I turned to Anna. 'What do you think she's playing at, with the water?'

Her pause stretched as far as the next bend. 'Playing at?'

Like Joe. *Tell her what?* 'With the water.'

She said, carefully, 'You make it sound like the water going wrong is some kind of game.'

I laughed because she didn't know how right she was. That was it; a game, or more accurately, a long, convoluted joke. I'd heard it before though. I knew the punchline.

I said, 'So you think it's just a coincidence?' The road began to climb in sharp switchbacks. I lowered the gear and put my foot down to maintain my speed. 'And all those things she keeps leaving outside the cottage?'

'What things?'

'The flowers and ashes. The dead bird. The pine cone.'

I looked over to see her response. She said, 'You're driving too fast.'

'When we got here, the water was fine. Then I saw Leonie hiding by the cottage and the next morning, it was contaminated. Then Callum tried to make me drink the water he brought. And that woman in the shop. Did you see Callum's face when he realised that I know? That I know what they're trying to do?'

Anna was looking straight ahead. 'What are they trying to do?'

'Poison me.'

No response.

I said, 'They're playing with me. They're playing a joke on me.'

'Poisoning you is a joke?'

'No, that's not the joke. The joke is a cover for that.'

The joke was all the other small, sly actions designed to make me doubt my perceptions and convince other people I was imagining things. Burning the candles while we were out. Messing about with the fuel in the car so I'd think it wasn't getting any less.

'Slow down, Catherine.'

Erasing the place on the map where our cottage should be. Moving the axe ever so slightly under the bed so you could see the blade glint as you crossed the floor. And of course, that first, not-so-subtle sign: placing those flowers and ashes together in the dirt.

I said, 'They're gaslighting me. And they think I don't know it.' I took a corner badly but corrected it before any harm was done.

'Can you stop the car, please. Now. *Now*, Catherine. Pull in here.'

I turned into a lay-by and braked. 'They must think I'm stupid.'

Anna swallowed, giving herself time to think. 'Are you saying that you think Leonie poisoned our water supply?'

'Yes.'

'Why?'

'For the same reason she damaged our car and stole my journal. It's a campaign of intimidation.'

'No, I mean why do you think the water's been poisoned? It's just peat. It's natural. It's not poison.'

'That's what they want you to think.'

Her voice was quiet. 'Who is they?'

'Leonie. Tom. Callum. Mary. There's probably others involved too, but I'm not sure who yet.'

'Nobody is trying to poison us.'

I laughed and shook my head. When I turned to look at her, her face was crumpled. She said, 'Catherine, you're reading into things. *You're not thinking right.*'

I laughed because there it was: the punchline. Delivered perfectly by my very own sister. The punchline is, there is no joke. The punchline is, you're paranoid.

I said, 'I wonder where I've heard that before.'

She took a deep, sudden breath in. 'I need air.' She got out of the car, shut the door, and walked away across the car park, her hands hiding her face from view. I put the car into gear. In the rear-view mirror, I saw her spin round as she realised I was leaving. Then the road turned a corner and she was gone.

I kept on driving, the switchbacks becoming tighter and steeper. Eventually the road stopped at another car park. I'd reached a dead end, apart from the view, which went on for miles. The forest, the sea, the islands. The bay where the village was. The café by the beach. Even, I was sure of it, the white walls of our cottage in the woods. The whole scene was set out clearly before me and I felt none of the confusion I'd had at sea level, when I was uncertain whether I was looking at the mainland or an island, an inlet or loch. From here I could even see the weather before it reached me. A patch of rain out at sea. Wind moving across the trees. The shadow of clouds on the mountainsides.

I took out my notebook and read through my list. Leonie. Tom. Callum. Mary. I was missing someone. There was an empty seat at the table, some key player I hadn't yet identified. I went over it all again in my head. Every incident and remark, from the flowers on the ground, to the police interview, to Anna's refusal to see what was staring her in the face.

I began the drive back when it started to rain. Was it here I'd left her? Yes, there was a map on a board. I remembered her walking towards it, hands over her face. But she wasn't there now. I drove on. She may have set off on her own rather than wait for my return. I reached the bottom of the valley and crossed the bridge over the river. She couldn't have walked this far. Had she taken a detour through the forest? Or there was another explanation. That her disappearance was a form of maneuvering I hadn't foreseen.

I had always believed that Anna felt sympathy for me, due

to what had happened. When I was pregnant she seemed genuinely concerned for my well-being. She helped me put on my shoes when I couldn't bend to reach them. She brought me drinks and biscuits when I couldn't manage the stairs. And there was a moment in the hospital when she put her hand on my arm, presumably assuming I wanted some form of comfort or reassurance.

But perhaps I was mistaken about this. Perhaps her initial reaction to my pregnancy – anger and shame – were what remained from that time.

She cared what people said about her, and by extension, about me. Her popularity at school turned into second-hand notoriety. She had always worked hard to blend in by doing everything exactly as you were meant to. She was careful in her choice of clothes and music. In the way she spoke and the vocabulary she used. And I'd ruined that meticulously executed conformity overnight. For her, it was nothing short of a tragedy.

Or was it that she was judging me for relinquishing a baby? If so, she wasn't alone there. And the difficulty for me was that I didn't know, upon meeting someone, whether they were aware of my past or not. I didn't know who my daughter had spoken to. Who she had befriended or connected with on social media. Which friends or colleagues or relations had been sent her whispering DMs.

Back at the cottage, the door was locked. I surveyed each room for a sign Anna had returned but it appeared to be just as we'd left it this morning.

That night when she'd met with Callum in his car above the cove. What had they been talking about? What plans had they made? They'd been waiting for me and I didn't understand why. It wasn't light enough for me to see the expressions on their faces.

She'd said that he lived in an empty village further along the peninsula. I found it on the map, locked the door behind me, and followed the track until it turned into a path through woods. I reached a wall with a stile. A low stone building on the other side. Below were five or six small, squat cottages. Only one looked as though it was lived in.

Fog drifted in from the sea as I walked down the hill. When I looked back at where I'd come from, it was obscured by grey. The house was at the end of a walkway. A bone hung on the wall by the door. I knocked.

'Catherine.' As if he was surprised to see me.

I looked past him. 'Is Anna here?'

'No, she's not here.' There was confusion or was it amusement in his eyes? 'Have you lost her?'

He led me into a living room with a lit fire in the grate, a glass of beer on the floor, a crime novel resting on a sofa arm. He said, 'Did she say she was coming over?'

'Not to me.'

He rubbed the side of his head. 'So, you just thought she might be here?'

I said, 'Well she must be close by.' I watched his face. It was on pause. I said, 'Can I have a glass of water, please?'

'Yeah, sure.' We went into a kitchen where there were the remains of a meal by the sink and two chairs at a table, pushed in tight. Callum filled a glass from a plastic bottle. I took it but didn't drink it. Was Anna in another room? Were they all in another room, sitting silently, looking at each other, straining to hear our conversation?

I said, 'Can I use the bathroom?'

'Sure. It's just through there.'

He wasn't easy to read. Beyond the kitchen, there was a bedroom, and another room opposite it. I looked in. Piles of men's clothes on the floor and bed: waterproofs, thick jumpers, heavy boots. In the other, Callum's laptop and phone and a set of weights in the corner. In the bathroom I waited, listening, but I couldn't hear anything except the steady rain on the roof and a shushing sound which could have been the sea. The whole house was very still.

Callum was waiting in the living room. He said, 'Did she head out for a walk? Maybe she'll be back by now?'

'Yes, I expect she will.' He'd ushered her out of the back door when I arrived. She was probably racing back up the hill as we spoke. I said, 'Sorry to disturb you.'

He said, 'No bother. I'll come back up with you. Just in case we need to send out a search party.'

We stepped out into the rain. He pulled up his hood and shut the door behind us.

I said, 'Are you leaving it unlocked?'

'Everyone does around here.' He meant everyone but you. 'So what time did she go out?'

'We went on the forest drive to where that picnic spot is. She got out halfway.' He already knew this.

He stopped. 'Is that when you last saw her?'

'Yes.'

His face was motionless. 'So how would she have got back here? It's too far to walk.'

'She would have got a lift.'

He nodded, thinking. 'Who from?'

Good question. It could have been any number of people but I wasn't sure which one. 'I don't know.'

'But she wasn't at the cottage when you got back?'

'No.'

'So she could still be out in the forest somewhere?'

He was a good actor, I'd give him that.

He studied my face. 'You really don't know where she is?'

He was staring at me. I stared right back. He turned and set a fast pace up the hill, over the stile, and through the woods. He was hard to keep up with. I was out of breath when we reached the clearing where his car was. 'I'll drive us,' he said. He reversed until we hit the main track, then drove fast to our cottage. He got out and tried the door but it was still locked. I got out too. I was primed to hear her voice, coming from the direction of his house. Callum was standing silently as if he was waiting too.

He turned to me. 'Does she have warm clothes?'

'What?'

'What was she wearing?'

'I can't remember.'

His hand went to his neck. 'Let's head up to where you last saw her. Go inside and find something warm for yourself and Anna, and a torch. And some food and water.'

'Is this really necessary?'

'We don't know where she is.' He almost laughed. 'Aren't you worried about her?'

'Should I be?'

He turned away, looked at the track towards his house, turned back again. 'Unlock the door. I'll help you get what we need.' After a moment he said, 'Give me the key.'

I handed it to him. Inside he started quizzing me about what exact time I had left her and where, what she had with her. I didn't know what his intention was with all this but it felt like he was trying to scare me. He got biscuits and chocolate from the cupboard, pulled our waterproofs from the hooks by the door, took the blanket off the sofa. 'Come on, let's go.'

He drove us to the main road, saying nothing all the way. The rain turned into a downpour. The wipers couldn't clear it.

We were in daylight as we crossed the moor. In the forest it was almost night.

He said, 'Are we near where you left her?'

I said it was on the other side of the valley.

'But she could have walked this far since then. I don't know why you didn't see her, though, on your way back. Perhaps you just missed her.'

I said I didn't know.

He said, 'She could have got a lift from someone. But then, why not go back to your cottage?'

I didn't know.

I saw the lay-by ahead. 'It was here.'

He pulled in sharply and stopped, leaving the headlights on. They lit closely packed tree trunks, a carpet of dead pine needles, a path. We got out and he called her name into the forest. Called again. Nothing came back.

A memory surfaced that I hadn't thought of in years. Returning home from hospital after the birth and being filled with a sudden, strong panic. The kind that blanks out everything else in the room. I remembered saying, 'Do you think she'll be okay?' I must have been referring to the baby. I don't know who I was talking to, or what they said in response.

I went down the path into the trees, beyond the headlight beam. I couldn't see more than a few metres ahead of me. 'Anna?'

She'd been wearing jeans and a T-shirt. She'd left her coat on the back seat of the car. I called her name again.

Callum's hand was on my shoulder. 'Let's go to the village. She might be there.'

I shook him off. 'No, we need to keep looking.'

He got in front of me. 'We won't find her in the dark.'

'We have to.'

'No. We'll go to the village. See if someone gave her a lift. If

she's not there, we'll phone the police. It's the best thing to do.'
He took a deep breath. 'Come on, get back in the car.'

As we drove away I felt so tired I thought I might fall asleep.
Callum was talking. Telling me not to worry and that nothing
bad could have happened to her. Wherever she was, she'd be
safe, if a little cold and wet. People don't just go missing around
here, he said. Not like that, not out of nowhere. Everything he
said was a lie.

At the village, he parked up outside the pub. 'Someone will
know if she's been around today.'

'What if nobody's seen her?'

He didn't answer, just got out of the car. I followed him
inside, the warmth and light disorientated me for a moment. I
scanned the old men by the bar, the teenagers playing pool, the
families eating in the other room. Then I heard her laugh.

She was sitting in the corner with Tom, leaning into his
shoulder, her hand under his on the table. He was laughing too.
He nudged her when he saw us standing by the door.

She looked across the room at us with that unfocused,
unsteady expression she wore when drunk.

'There you go.' Callum's voice sounded flat. Fake. Like he'd
known she was here all along.

'Catherine! You're back! Thank God.' Anna got up and
stood too close to me, not quite steady on her feet. 'What you
having to drink?'

I said, 'I don't want a drink.'

'Are you upset?'

'Was that the point of today? To make me upset?'

She ran her hand through her hair. Callum said nothing.

167

She said, 'You left me in the middle of nowhere. I had to get a lift with some random Americans.'

'You met someone you know from America?'

'I didn't know them. They were strangers.'

'Who were they?'

'I don't know. I mean, it's not relevant.' She shook her head and went to sit down again with Tom, a frown on her face. After a moment she looked hopefully at Callum. 'Are you having a drink?'

'Someone will need to drive you two back.'

'You can have one. For the road.'

'I'd need more than one.' He sat down at the next table and took out his phone.

Tom turned to me. 'Did you find your journal?' He had a half smile on his face.

'No. I've reported the theft to the police.'

Tom sat back a little. 'What theft?'

Anna said, 'It wasn't stolen.'

'What wasn't?' Tom said.

'Her diary.' She looked at me. 'I found it in the cottage. It was under the mattress all along.'

'You took it?'

She said, 'No, I found it.'

'Did you read it?'

'No.'

'You're lying.'

'I'm not.'

'I know that you are.' I said, 'You're in on this too.'

She said nothing. Her eyes were wet as though she was about to cry.

Tom said, 'Anna doesn't know anything–'

'Shut up, Tom.' Callum stared at him. Tom looked away.

I said, 'You're all part of it. I mean, I knew about you two.'

Callum and Tom kept their expressions blank. 'But I didn't know *you* were involved.' I pointed at Anna and she flinched back. 'My own sister. Did you plan the whole thing? Was it you who led her to me in the first place?'

Anna started to say something then stopped. She went to put her hand to her head and somehow knocked over her glass in the process. Whisky pooled across the table and started dripping down onto her jeans.

10

ANNA

Monday. Sunrise 04.28. Sunset 22.21

There was a crack in the wall, not far from my face. Something thin and delicate and the palest brown stuck out. A spider's leg. It quivered as if it felt my eyes on it then withdrew. I pictured its soft, small body shrinking further inside the wall.

I was afraid of spiders. I turned on my other side and closed my eyes. I would sleep and when I woke, it would be gone, and the headache and nausea would have eased, and everything from yesterday that I was trying not to think about would seem less frightening and less strange. I would sleep until the world was back in place. I felt too sick to do anything else.

The next time I woke, I was too warm inside my sleeping bag and the daylight was too bright in the room. The spider wasn't there. Was it on me? I lay very still and watched yesterday's slow-developing nightmare take shape in my mind. The hangover was the least of it.

I'd laughed when Catherine drove away, leaving me stranded in the forest without a coat or a clue where I was. But it was the humourless kind of laugh that she did, then my throat ached as if I was about to cry. I'd pushed the feeling down into my chest, and it lodged there, hard and painful, as I watched her car disappear around the side of the hill.

The lay-by had just a map on a board which told me nothing useful. A blue path led to a waterfall. A yellow path to a viewpoint. Neither led to civilisation. All I had on me was my cashcard. My phone was in the car.

The midges found my neck first. They feasted while I stood there, with no plan, just a shaky hope she'd come back calmer and maybe even a little embarrassed about the state she'd got herself in. Though when was Catherine ever embarrassed? When did she ever change her mind? She'd been adamant all her life and I'd always given in to the force of her certainty. But this was different because this time she was surely, alarmingly, wrong.

I knew it when I read her diary. I'd wanted to stop but I kept turning the pages even though it was making me feel anxious and ill because, well, Leonie had a predecessor. A girl called Sophie who thought Catherine reminded her of herself. They couldn't both be her daughter. Was Catherine wrong then but right now? Or had she mistaken both girls for somebody they weren't?

Should I have doubted her more? Had I been following along without thinking, as usual?

The midges were swarming around my nose and eyes. I walked fast across the car park but they followed. I batted at them but it had no effect.

The thing was, it wasn't Catherine who had made me

believe Leonie was her daughter; it was Leonie herself. That barely hidden bitterness and the weird atmosphere when they first met. They were like magnets drawn together then flipped over so they sprang apart. There were unseen forces at play between them; I'd felt them as clearly as I could feel the bites on my neck.

But I just couldn't believe that Leonie had poisoned our water supply. And that a whole bunch of other people were part of 'the joke'. What joke? What was she talking about? It didn't even make sense.

These thoughts were crowding my head when I heard a car approaching. Not Catherine. A Range Rover. It turned in and parked. There was a man and a woman with two little girls in the back. The parents looked like they were arguing until they started laughing. They got out, the girls dazed and slow-moving like they'd just woken up. Straggled strawberry blonde hair, big teeth, blue eyes. The older one pulled her hood up and stuck her hands in the pockets of her raincoat. The younger one had binoculars hanging round her neck. It was the same girl that I'd waved to on the Harry Potter train.

The mother smiled over at me. She gave the older girl a map in a plastic case, saying in a chirpy American accent, 'Let's go see what we can find in the woods.'

She was dressed in the kind of clothes you would sensibly choose for a forest in Scotland in summertime. Columbia jacket, hiking boots, Gore-Tex trousers. I was in my Converse, ripped jeans, and a knock-off Led Zep T-shirt. I tried changing my stance to make it look like I belonged there but the midges were eating me alive and I couldn't help covering my head with my arms to stop them.

The dad said, 'They're at their most bitey in the car parks.'

The mum rummaged in her rucksack, and handed me a bottle of insect repellent. 'Here, take some of this, please.'

'Thanks. I forgot to put some on this morning.' I smeared it on my arms, the front and back of my neck, my face, my ankles, my knees where they were visible through the holes in my jeans.

She said, 'Are you waiting for someone?'

'My sister. She should be back soon.'

Binoculars girl looked suspiciously at me. 'Where's your car?'

'My sister's got it.'

She tucked her thumbs inside the binoculars cord. 'Do you want to come and see a waterfall with us?'

'I would but she won't know where I've gone.'

'Write her a message and put it under a stone. My mom has a pen in her backpack.'

The dad was kneeling down to double-knot the other girl's walking boots. He looked up with an apologetic smile. 'I think she wants to wait here, Nora honey.'

Nora didn't look convinced. As they set off down the path, she said, 'We're going this way. Shout if you need us.'

The dad took the hand of the quieter sister while Nora ran on in front. Their voices faded as they went further into the forest. I felt better knowing they'd be coming back. Catherine would too, but that thought was somehow less reassuring. I was dreading her return almost as much as I wanted it and it was a tender, bruised feeling; the kind that could make you hate someone, if they weren't family, and weren't so obviously in need of help. What was it she'd said? *They're gaslighting me?* Who were 'they'? Oh Jesus, these bastard, biting, swarming insects. It was like Lord-of-the-fucking-Flies out here. I just needed to get indoors, away from them, so I could *think.*

When the family came back, I was sitting on the ground by the map board, my knees up to my chest, my head hunched down to try to protect myself.

They stopped, all looking down at me.

'You're still waiting?' The mother's mix of sympathy and concern made me feel even more exposed.

'Yep.'

The dad said, 'You can't stay here.'

'I'm all right,' I said. I wasn't, and it was obvious. I'd seen no cars, no people, and I couldn't stand to watch them drive away. I asked if I could have a lift.

'She needs a ride, Mom.' Nora bounced on her tiptoes. 'You can sit in the back with me and Marnie.'

The dad said, 'Sure you can. Where are we taking you?'

I named the village with the pub. 'But just to the main road would be okay.'

'We'll take you to the village. It's no problem. What about your sister?'

I paused. 'She'll find me.' She'd be worried when she got here and found me gone. It'd serve her right for leaving me. Part of me wanted to scare her and part of me was just avoiding her. I couldn't face seeing her again in that same, strange mood.

I waited while they changed out of their muddy boots and loaded rucksacks into the car. Both girls were carrying sticks they'd found in the forest. Nora didn't want to leave hers behind.

'It will be lonely,' she said.

'There's two of them,' her mum replied.

'Sticks don't have feelings, Nora.' The other sister, Marnie, flung hers towards the trees. 'They're not alive.'

'Mine has feelings. It's incredibly sad.'

Her mum sighed. 'Nora, do you want to leave the stick by the car or by the map for somebody else to use?'

'By the map.' She ran over and leant it against the board. 'Somebody will pick it up and take it back to the waterfall.'

Catherine would see it when she came back. She'd think it meant something. She'd think it was a sign.

I climbed in between their booster seats. Nora said, 'My name's Nora. I'm six. This is Marnie, she's eight. This is Tara. She's thirty-seven. And this is Jake. He's, um, how old are you, Dad?'

Marnie said, 'You don't ask adults their age, Nora.'

Nora took this in. 'It's only Dad.'

He said, 'I'm thirty-five.'

Nora said, 'What's your name?'

'I'm Anna.' I added, 'I'm thirty-four.'

It started to rain as we pulled out of the car park and onto the road. Tara twisted back to look at me. 'Are you sure your sister won't be worried about you? Maybe we should have left her a note.'

We probably should have but I didn't want to make them turn back. 'It's fine. She'll figure out what's happened.'

'Where did she go?' asked Jake.

'I don't know. She was just going to follow this road.'

'You want me to turn round and see if we can find her?'

'No, she could be miles away. She loses track of time.'

The rain was getting heavier. Nora leaned forward to speak to her mum. 'Do you think my stick will be okay?'

'I'm sure it's doing just fine.'

Marnie said, 'I bet it fell over in the mud and can't get up.'

'Mom, Marnie's being mean.'

'Okay. Music. Whose choice is it? Mine?'

'Nobody wants to listen to Celine Dion, Mom,' Marnie mumbled.

'It's Anna's turn,' said Nora.

They all waited. 'Er, what have you got?'

Jake grinned through the rear-view mirror. 'I didn't bring my Led Zep. These guys would never allow it.'

Nora called out, 'Put Adele on!'

I said, 'I like Adele.'

He slotted in a CD. The opening bars of 'Hello'. Nora said, 'I know every single word to this song.' She started singing, badly out of key.

Tara said, 'Do you have children, Anna?'

'No.' On the other side of me, Marnie started tunelessly singing along too.

'Bet you're glad about that right now.' Tara made an effort to talk to me over the crescendo of the chorus. We asked all the easy questions. Where are you from? How long are you here for? They lived in Texas and had come to Scotland because Tara had Scottish ancestry.

'I want the girls to have a sense of their history. To know where they came from. They have a hint of Celtic red in their hair. Isn't it amazing how these genes skip generations and then reappear?'

Tara said they'd researched their family tree before the trip and now they were visiting the Highland towns and villages connected with their name. She handed me a folder containing all her research and I looked through it politely as we drove out of the forest and over the moor. There were printed lists of names and dates, a rubbing of a gravestone, black-and-white photographs of families, the children in big coats, their faces almost hidden by their hats and scarves.

When we got to the village, I asked if they would drop me off by the hostel where Leonie lived. The White Sands Stay was easy to spot with its rainbow-painted sign and streams of prayer flags blowing between the trees.

'Is this where you're based?' Tara asked.

'No. I've got a friend who lives here.'

'I hope they're home.' She looked doubtfully at the hostel. Its windows were dark and the front door was shut.

'So do I.' Though a part of me hoped she wasn't. Was Leonie a friend, or was she family, or neither? I thanked them for the lift and got out. Nora waved through the back window as they drove away.

The chalets were at the back of the hostel: three small wooden huts, built a little too close together, with mildewed curtains in rotting window frames. Rickety steps led up to the doors. I knocked on the first one. No answer and when I looked through the window, there was no sign of anyone living there. I tried the next one. Nobody home. It was hers though; I could see Fleur's pram folded up against a wall and a Moses basket on a stand next to a single bed. There were Babygros drying on the radiators, packets of wet wipes and nappies on the sofa, soft toys scattered about the floor. She looked like she'd gone out in a hurry. To work, maybe? Breakfast dishes and baby bottles were stacked up by the sink.

I thought about leaving her a note but what would I say?

Hi Leonie. It's Anna. I thought Catherine was your mum, and I was your aunt, and that you wanted revenge for her giving you away as a baby. But now it looks like Catherine imagined it all and I'm not sure which scenario is worse. I just wanted to run through it with you and get your opinion...

I walked slowly back along the seafront to the bench where I'd sat with her a few days before. I knew now what she'd have done if I'd said, 'You're not fifteen. You're twenty-three.' She would have looked at me blankly. She would have had no idea what I was talking about.

Tom came into the pub not long after I sat down. He chatted to the landlord for a while before he wandered over to my table. 'How's the car looking?' he said.

'Good. Thanks for doing that.'

'It's all right.' He hesitated for a moment. 'Do you mind if I join you?'

'No, go ahead.'

He pulled out the chair opposite mine. Broad shoulders. Long legs. I had to shift my knees to avoid them touching his under the table. He said, 'It's my day off.'

'From the kayaks?'

'The kayaks. The garage. The café. The pub if they're short-staffed.'

'How many jobs does one man need?'

He smiled. 'I was saving up to go travelling.'

'Was?'

'I'm not so set on it now.'

'What's changed?'

He shrugged. 'I'm just seeing how things go here.'

I said without thinking, 'With Leonie?'

He looked at the table, blushing. He was that weird mix of confident and awkward you see in boys that age. 'Aye. I didn't think she'd be back this year.'

'She's been here before then?'

'She works the summer season. This is her third year. Didn't you know that?'

'No.' Her third year? She'd never said. She hadn't followed us; this out-of-the-way village was her regular summer base. I wanted Catherine to walk in right now so I could tell her and lay her fears to rest. It would put everything back to normal. She would see how confused she'd become.

Tom was looking curiously at me; my worries were probably visible on my face. He shook his head as if clearing something from his mind, then looked out of the window at the sea and sky. 'It's the longest day.'

'You're telling me.'

'No, it is the longest day. Eighteen hours of daylight.'

178

'It's the solstice?'

'Aye.' He added with a hesitant smile, 'So we definitely have time for another drink.'

He went to the bar and brought back two pints. We talked about my life in Canada, his life here, the boredom in the winter when the tourists disappeared and the days ended at 3pm. I didn't tell him about Catherine and how she'd left me in the forest. It felt like a secret. Like I'd done something wrong. Why did I feel guilty? I didn't know but I knew I wasn't ready to talk to anyone about it.

We moved from beer to whisky and our conversations got faster and funnier. I was having a good time. That stopped when Catherine and Callum walked in. And that sense of shame I'd had about her abandoning me returned. I wanted to say, it's not me who's in the wrong here. But my words were slurred and putting them into coherent sentences was a challenge. I decided not to speak unless absolutely necessary. Callum was ignoring me but that was nothing compared to Catherine and her tight, knowing smile. 'You're in on it,' she'd said. She had accused me of something. She had made me part of her 'they'. And I was too drunk to put her right.

———

When I finally dragged myself out of bed, she was sitting at the table, writing in her diary. I'd shown her where I'd found it when we got home last night. She'd accused me of hiding it. Stealing it. I'd got into bed and put my head under the pillow. She gave up trying to talk to me and I fell asleep, or passed out, one of the two.

'I feel grim,' I said, watching her pen move smoothly across the page.

'You look it.' Without looking at me.

'I'm making coffee. Do you want some?'

She hesitated. 'Yes but use the water from the sealed bottles you bought at the shop.'

'I'm boiling it. It makes no difference which bottles we use.'

'Forget it, I'll make my own.'

I sighed, filled the pot from one of the sealed bottles, packed coffee into the filter, and screwed it together tight. The whole process was a huge effort. I slumped down on the sofa. I said, 'I don't think anyone is trying to poison you.'

'I know you don't.' She'd stopped writing but she didn't turn round.

But I thought she thought I knew all about it.

She said, 'They haven't told you about that part of the plan.'

The plan. They. Where was this stuff coming from? When I didn't reply she moved her chair round so she could see me. She was scrutinising me and it was freaking me out.

I tried to focus on what I needed to tell her. 'Leonie comes here every summer. Tom said this is her third year of working here.'

A slight jerk of her head, as if pushing that information up into her brain. What was she doing with it in there? What strange conclusions was she reaching? I said, 'So she didn't follow you here. She was coming anyway.'

'Okay, you're right. It's all just a coincidence.'

I took a deep breath. 'Everything you think is happening, it just isn't happening.'

She reached for my sketchpad and turned to the drawing of Fleur. She got up and held it over me. 'This is my grandchild.'

She was standing and I was sitting. I had to look up to talk to her and I felt briefly intimidated. Then her expression shifted into anxiety. She was scared too.

I said, 'I don't think she is.'

Her hand dropped. She turned away.

I said, 'And the other stuff, about Callum and Tom, and the lady in the shop. You seem really confused.'

'I'm not confused. I know exactly what's going on.'

'What's going on?'

'They're judging me,' she snapped. 'I can see it in the way they look at me. In the way they smile.'

In the way they smile?

'And all those clever little signs left outside. Ashes and flowers. They're planning my funeral.'

I didn't understand. 'But I picked the flowers.'

'I know you did.'

She looked at me like she didn't know me. Like we hadn't grown up together and slept in the same room for ten years. Suspicion moved across her face and I swear it was actually visible, like the shadow of a cloud on the sea. She turned away. She felt seen and she didn't like it. She went in the bedroom and shut the door.

Steam was shooting out of the coffee pot. My hand was shaking when I took it off the stove. I couldn't leave things like this. I opened the bedroom door.

'Do you want coffee?'

She was sitting in the gloom of the lower bunk. 'Stop following me around.'

'This is my room too.'

To make my point I climbed up to my bed. Then I saw the spider. With its legs stretched out, it was the size of a tennis ball. And just a few centimetres from my face. I jumped back in shock, then slid down to the floor, not bothering with the ladder.

'Spider.'

'So?'

'So get it!'

Catherine didn't mind spiders. It was her job to get rid of them if one came in our room when we were children.

She sighed heavily, then took her time getting up to see where it was. She said tonelessly, 'I need a plate and a cup.'

I got them from the kitchen. 'Don't let it get away.'

She climbed onto the top bunk. I backed against the window when she came down the ladder holding the cup over the plate, feet searching for the steps.

We both knew the routine. I opened the front door. She carried the spider, still trapped, outside. 'Take it a long way away,' I said. 'Like right over there in the trees.' I watched from the doorway as she walked to the edge of the clearing and shook it off the plate. When she returned I said, 'So shall I make us breakfast?' I added, 'I made coffee. I used the bottled water.'

She paused. She wanted it but she couldn't risk it. She said, 'You have it,' then went back into the bedroom.

I sat on the sofa and pulled a blanket over me. I could have cried but I didn't want to, so I didn't. My sketchbook was lying open next to me at the drawing of Fleur. Why had I felt that jolt of recognition? I must have only been seeing what Catherine wanted me to see. I tried to recall her baby from the one time I'd seen her but it was so long ago, I couldn't picture her face in my mind. I could only see Catherine from that time. How she'd looked at us as we closed the curtains around the hospital bed and walked away down the ward.

Catherine had woke Mum up just before midnight to say she thought it might have started. They dressed in the clothes they'd had ready for weeks and took the bag that was already packed in the hallway. Catherine didn't look like she was in pain but I could see she was scared. Too scared to speak or eat or do anything other than follow along with Mum's instructions. I stood and watched on the doorstep as she awkwardly lowered herself into the passenger seat while Mum checked the directions to the hospital that she'd stuck to the dashboard. Catherine was struggling to reach the seat belt so I went out to help her. She pulled it under the bump and across her chest and winced in pain, her breath catching in her throat.

'Are you ready, Mum?' she said urgently as I closed the car door.

I got to the phone first when Mum rang from the hospital the next morning. 'A girl,' she said. 'A healthy baby girl.'

'Are you bringing her home?'

'Who? Catherine?'

'The baby?'

'No. She's going straight to her foster family.'

I said, 'So I won't see her?'

'She's not going to be part of our family, Anna. You know that.'

'I know but...'

'Where's your dad? Can you put him on?'

I left the phone on the stand and went upstairs to my room, shutting the door behind me. I had this sudden surge of energy that made me want to break something, but quietly so Dad wouldn't hear. I got my school cardigan in my teeth and tried to rip it in two. It stretched then tore down the shoulder. I was thinking about the baby going off into the world on its own when it was less than a day old. And how if I didn't see her today, I never would. And how she wasn't getting the attention she deserved on her first birthday; the day of her actual birth.

I went downstairs. Dad had just come off the phone. 'Well, that's that then.'

'Yep.'

I told him I was meeting my friends to go shopping, then set off to the hospital on my own.

———————

They were separated. That was the first thing I saw when I found them at the end of a long, overheated ward of mothers and babies and harassed-looking nurses. Separate beds. Separate worlds. It took a moment to get used to after all the months of Catherine and the baby being one person, and I just stood there, not sure what to say.

Nobody spoke for a moment, in fact. It was like the three of us (four of us?) couldn't quite believe what we were looking at. I was supposed to be at home with Dad, not hovering between the cubicle curtains that enclosed the hospital bed.

'Anna.' Mum was the first to speak.

Catherine squinted at me. 'Why are you here?'

Mum stood up from her chair. 'Is Dad with you?'

'No. I got the train and a taxi.'

'On your own?' She closed the curtain behind me.

'Yes.' There was a clear glass box like a fish tank by the bed. The baby was asleep inside, lying on its back in a white onesie and a tiny white hat. Its face was pinky-red and seemed to be all eyes and mouth. Its chest was rising and falling too fast, like a bird or someone who'd just finished running a race.

'Is she okay?' I asked, looking in at her.

'Does Dad know where you are?'

'He thinks I've gone to look round the shops.' The baby was lying on a bed of towels. There was a hand-knitted teddy in there with her, as big as she was. I said, 'She's breathing really fast.'

'That's what babies do.' Mum shook her head, blinking with tiredness. 'I can't believe you came all this way on your own.'

The baby's eyes were scrunched tight. Maybe she was dreaming about running. Except babies probably didn't know about running. Swimming then. She was a fish in a tank; a different species in a different element. I lowered my fingers in, as if dipping them in water, and very lightly touched her hand. It was cold.

'Does she need her mittens?' They'd been part of the set of baby clothes that were packed in the bag in the hallway. I'd sneaked a look in there when everyone was out.

Mum stood next to me. 'Babies always have cold hands and feet. You had cold hands when you were a newborn.'

'You're an expert on this,' I said.

'On what?'

'Babies.'

'Well, I have had two of them.'

Catherine sighed. 'Can you both stop staring at her? Just let her sleep.'

Mum sat back down in the chair and let out a deep breath. I sat on the end of Catherine's bed because there wasn't anywhere else. We were quiet for a while. Then there were raised voices further down the ward. A nurse was telling a man that he needed to take his children home with him, not leave them here with his wife who'd just given birth a few hours before. No, not for two hours. Not for one hour. 'You need to take them to work with you,' she said.

'I want to go home,' Catherine said.

'Just one more night,' Mum said.

'When are they coming for the baby?' I asked.

Mum said, 'Not until tomorrow now.'

'Why?'

Catherine sniffed. 'They probably think the longer I have with her, the more likely it is I'll change my mind.'

They didn't know Catherine, then. She wasn't going to change her mind and we all knew it.

Mum went to get us some drinks. When she was out of earshot Catherine said, 'I think she's getting attached to the baby. She keeps picking her up when she thinks I'm asleep.'

'I think that's just what you're supposed to do with babies.'

'I can't pick her up,' Catherine said. 'They cut me open. I can't get out of bed.'

'I could pass her to you.'

She shook her head. 'Don't disturb her.'

A nurse came in to take Catherine's temperature and give her some painkillers. Mum came back with a cup of tea and two cartons of Ribena. The baby woke up and started crying. It was a low, soft bleat, kind of sad-sounding.

'Somebody's hungry,' Mum said. She picked her up carefully and lowered her onto Catherine's lap, like she was a cake that was falling apart as you took it out of the tin. Catherine blinked and tensed her shoulders. She pulled her T-shirt up and lifted the baby so that its head was next to her breast. It started to stretch its arms and legs, and move its head from side to side. Catherine looked at Mum. 'She doesn't want it.'

'Give her a moment.'

The baby's cries became louder and rawer. Catherine held her away from her in a panic. 'What am I supposed to do? She doesn't want it.'

Mum took the baby silently and laid her back down in the fish tank. She opened a little plastic bottle of baby milk that was on the bedside table and screwed something to the top.

'Do you want to feed her?' she asked Catherine.

Catherine shook her head. Mum carried the baby and the bottle over to the chair. Catherine closed her eyes and turned her head away.

The baby was quiet now she had the bottle in her mouth. When she let it go, Mum lay her back down on the towels and she stared up at us. Deep blue eyes in a blotchy pink face. A wisp of dark hair escaping from her hat. I smiled at her. Her expression didn't change. Who knew what she was thinking?

Catherine fell asleep. Mum said she'd taken strong painkillers. She whispered that she could be in here for a few days while she recovered. The baby slept too. Her face was Catherine through rippled water; the similarity was clear then blurred then clear again. Did she look more like her dad? He didn't even know he had a daughter. Catherine had never told anyone his name.

When Catherine woke up a while later, it was almost the end of visiting hours.

'Me and Anna will have to go soon,' Mum said, once she was fully awake.

'Can't you stay?'

'We're not allowed. But I'll be back first thing in the morning.'

There were tears falling down Catherine's face as we got up to leave but I wouldn't say she was crying, exactly. It was more like water running off a rock as the tide went out. I put my hand on her shoulder but it felt awkward so I took it away. I thought it'd be difficult to say goodbye to the baby but it was leaving Catherine that was the hardest part.

She came home a few days later. Just Catherine, no baby. And after a month or so, she was back at school. I saw her at break times and lunch, sitting on her own. Her friends didn't seem to be her friends anymore and I wasn't sure what had happened. They all spent their lunch hours in the library but Catherine sat in a different part to them, on a single table tucked away between the shelves in the fiction section. I could see her in there from the third-floor window of our form room, where a few of us had somehow got permission to use the big TV to watch En Vogue videos on repeat. She had this huge heavy book she read every lunchtime but never brought home. I assumed it was a textbook but when I went in there once to get some books for a science project, I saw it was actually a novel. *Tales of the City. Six Complete Novels*. No wonder it was so big.

'What's that about?' I asked her, standing over her table.

'Gay people in San Francisco.'

'Why are you reading about that?'

'Because I like it.' She added, 'Probably because it's the complete opposite of this place.' She looked back at the page.

I said, 'I can't find the book I need.'

'Ask the librarian.'

'She's not there.'

Catherine shut her book with a sigh, saving her place with her fountain pen. She helped me find the book I needed, studiously ignoring the former members of the Chicken Crew who were gathered in the science section, writing bullet-point lists on index cards. They raised their eyes when we went over but nobody said anything. I wished she was with them, revising for her exams like she was meant to be doing, not sitting on her own reading six novels about gay people.

'Don't you speak to them anymore?' I whispered when we'd moved away.

'Who?'

'Your friends.'

'Can you stop interrogating me?'

Then one day I was looking down from our form room when I saw a boy in the year above me mouthing something to Catherine through the library window. She moved her chair round so she couldn't see him. He grinned and went inside, heading in the direction of the library. The next thing I heard, Catherine had been suspended for whacking him in the face with that giant book. The librarian had had to pull her away. The boy had a massive purple bruise across his cheekbone where the solid hardback spine had landed.

Mum and Dad were called in. Apparently, he'd called her a slag and asked where her baby was, so she'd whacked him one. Catherine said she was glad she was suspended. Exams started in a few weeks anyway and she'd learnt it all already.

She didn't go back to school after that and our house had this heavy atmosphere of tension and misery which made me keep pressing snooze on my radio alarm clock every morning. I was always late for registration and I never seemed to have the right books in my bag. In the evenings I could hear Catherine listening to crackly French radio in her bedroom. I wondered whether she was practising for her listening exam, or thinking about the exchange student.

She ended up with an A in French, and in everything else, except for music, where she got a B. We went out for a meal at Firenze to celebrate but a girl from her year was the waitress and Catherine spoke even less than she did at home.

It was an awful time all round but I thought it was just something we had to get through, and then Catherine would go back to normal. And on the surface at least, she did. She enrolled at a sixth form college in Manchester, and shifted her life away from our town, spending all her time with her new friends in the city. Then she left for university and it was like she was back on track, crisis over.

Except it wasn't over, just buried, and not very well. I mean, if you're going to hide something that big, you need to do it properly. You need a very deep hole, concrete poured on top, an immovable boulder on top of that, and perhaps some kind of insurmountable wall around the outside. Because hidden things change when they're kept in the dark and not for the better. They get twisted and confused, groping around without daylight, and by the time they reach the surface, you've got something weird and broken; a warped version of the thing you originally buried.

I studied the drawing of Fleur in the sketchbook. It wasn't Catherine's focus on her that I found disturbing; I thought that was understandable. I mean, wasn't everyone a replacement for someone else, someone lost? What disturbed me was all the other stuff that had surfaced with it. The paranoia and fear and the dark path her thoughts followed. When I remembered what she'd said about flowers and ashes I felt sick. I wanted to call my mum. Though what words would I use to tell her this? Hearing your adult daughter was losing the plot was up there with hearing your teenage daughter was pregnant. I couldn't do it over the phone.

It was Joe I needed to talk to. I would slip away and call him from the village tonight. That's if Callum still wanted to take us, after last night. He probably thought we were both nuts.

There was one bottle of wine left. I would leave it on his doorstep with a 'thank you' note. Or should it be a 'sorry for all the trouble' note? I wasn't sure. I'd work it out on the way.

When I got there, it seemed a little rude to just leave the wine and run. Kind of wimpy and ashamed. I would at least try knocking on the door, quietly, so he might not hear. I wasn't quiet enough though, and he opened it with a look rather than a hello.

I said, 'I bought you this. To say sorry about the drama

yesterday.' I half held out the bottle of wine. There was a second's pause before he took it.

'Thanks. You didn't have to.'

'Anyway, that was it, really. I'll leave you in peace.'

'That's it?'

'Yes. Sorry and thank you.'

'Are you coming in?'

'Okay.'

I followed him through to a kitchen with a wood-burning range like ours. There was a table in the middle, a sofa along one wall. I wondered which of the belongings scattered about were his and which were his father's. The sudoku books and the stack of unopened medicine boxes, his father's. The iPhone and the running shoes, his. Then there were a few things that could have belonged to either: a Swiss Army knife, a bird identification book.

He put a kettle on the stove. 'I don't mind a bit of drama. I was just pissed off last night because we'd been driving around looking for you, thinking you were lost in the forest in the dark. And there you were in the pub, getting hammered on whisky with my cousin.'

'In my defence, Catherine should have known to check the nearest bar first.'

'Aye well, next time I'll do that.' He turned to face me. 'So what happened? How did you get separated?'

I was too tired for this conversation. 'We had a disagreement. Sister stuff, you know.'

'Yeah, me and my sister used to argue. But she never abandoned me in a forest miles from home.'

'Catherine's just like that, sometimes.'

'So that's normal for her?'

I looked away. I was thinking about all the other times she'd disappeared on this holiday, leaving me without a phone signal or a way back to civilisation. And of how she left home at eighteen for university and never came back, not even in that first term for Christmas. We'd not been expecting her to leave so completely. We'd thought she'd move back home in the holidays, like all the other students.

And I was thinking, cruelly perhaps, of the other abandonment. The one that started all this trouble in the first place.

Callum said, 'She seems a little bit...' He thought for a moment. I could finish his sentence for him easily enough. Paranoid. Crazy. Delusional. He said, 'Confused.'

I didn't know whether it was the sympathetic way he was looking at me, or just the exhaustion after yesterday, but I had to turn away because otherwise, I was going to cry. I went to the window to get myself together. I heard him pouring the tea. Putting mugs on the table. I focused on the walkway across the marsh, the little cottages on the other side, the hills behind them. The sea was just out of sight. I said, 'Does anyone else live down here?'

He came and stood beside me. 'Not just now. That cottage over there is a holiday home but it doesn't get many bookings. And they usually leave early.'

'Why?'

'It's an acquired taste, living here.'

'How did you acquire it?'

'Had to, I guess. My dad was set on staying here rather than being stuck in hospital having chemo.'

'But wouldn't it have helped him?'

'It could have given him a few more months. They caught it too late to stop it.' His face was calm but his voice had dropped a little deeper. 'He said he wanted to die where he was happy. He thought you can't ask for more than that.'

The steam from our tea misted the windowpane in front of

us. Two little ghosts rising up out of the mugs. I said, 'So it was just you and him? Even when he was really ill?'

'We had a few visitors. Tom. My dad's pals from the pub. But yeah, it was mainly just us. My sister's got little ones and my mum hadn't spoken to him in thirty years.'

I thought of them cut off out here on those winter nights. The furnace flickering and his dad drifting in and out of sleep. No telephone, no neighbours. Miles of sea and woods between here and the village. And Callum waking up on a dark February morning to find the loneliness suddenly so much sharper.

I said, 'It must have been really hard.'

'The quiet, you mean?'

I paused. 'Kind of.'

'I grew up here, didn't I? This is my natural volume level. Seabirds and waves.'

'I guess it's therapeutic, living out in the wilderness, when you've lost something.'

He didn't answer. He was standing very still. The ghosts on the windowsill were shrinking at the edges. He said, 'I guess it doesn't matter where you are. The rest of the world doesn't get a look-in when you feel like that. Sunsets, northern lights, whatever.'

I didn't know what to say. I'd never lost anyone close to me. Just grandparents and their deaths hadn't hit me hard. So I couldn't relate, like I couldn't relate to Catherine and her crazy certainties, or Leonie and her sleep-starved loneliness. I saw her staring at the sea, talking about how hard it was to be a mother on your own.

All these missing people: Catherine's baby, Callum's dad, Fleur's daddy, whoever he was. Everyone around here had a huge, gaping chasm in the middle of their life and I needed to be careful I didn't fall in. People with parts missing were like black holes, sucking in all matter for miles around and still staying empty inside. But surely we all lost people as we got older? Was this just how life was, then, and I'd never noticed it before?

This was why I shouldn't drink for five nights in a row.

Callum said, 'Do you mind if I put the football on?'

I was back in the room again. 'No, go ahead.'

He turned on a little radio and we took our drinks over to the sofa. The commentary flipped between matches, updates were coming in from all over Scotland. I was tired and the room was warm. I fell asleep listening to the names of unfamiliar football teams, picturing the players standing around in the rain. When I woke, Callum was still sitting beside me.

He said, 'You missed a goal. Five goals, would you believe it.'

'Who won?'

'Not us.'

'Who's us?'

'Rangers.'

I said, 'I don't think I can get up from this sofa.'

'Why would you want to do that?'

'I have to go and check my sister is okay.' Perhaps I shouldn't have left her at all? Was I her carer now, like Callum and his dad?

'You're worried about her?'

I thought of Catherine saying 'They're planning my funeral' and nearly laughed. Nerves. Tiredness. It was all too much. I pushed myself up to standing. 'Yeah. I'll see you later though?'

On the doorstep, he said, 'It'll be all right, you know.'

I didn't see how it could be. But hearing him say it made me feel slightly better anyway. It was funny how you could take comfort from words you knew weren't true.

I would call Joe this evening and he would drive up tomorrow and we would figure out what to do together. I felt better with a plan in my head. But even so, I had this clenched-up feeling when I pushed open the cottage door. Catherine was sitting at the table, still writing. I didn't want to start a conversation with her in case she said something crazy. I really wished we had a TV or even just a radio, like Callum. Something to change the atmosphere, to shift the focus away from us.

She said out of nowhere, 'She'd need to get a babysitter. Maybe she won't be there.'

She was talking about Leonie, as usual. 'Maybe.'

'Do you think I should stay here?' she said.

'Why?'

'To keep an eye on things.'

I wanted her with me so I could keep an eye on her. If she stayed at the cottage, I'd be worrying about what she was doing all night.

I said, 'I think we'd better stick together.' I was going along with her paranoid scenario, using it for my own ends, and I knew it was wrong but I didn't have the energy to keep battling my reality against hers. We were in different worlds and we were both convinced that ours was the real one.

I'd always thought reality was subjective, that there was no definitive version of it, and everyone saw the world differently, and that was fine. But that theory just didn't work here. There was real and there was not-real, and Catherine was living in the realm of the not-real. I just needed her to come back into my world for a moment, so that she could look back and see that she'd gone wrong.

The way she thought; those leaps and connections. She reminded me of an artist I'd met in Canada who saw signs in everything that happened. He painted a picture of a raven then a raven appeared in the sky. He dreamt of a friend from way back, then a friend of that friend sent him an email. He called it synchronicity; he used the word a lot. He thought the universe was watching and providing and helping him on his way.

The artist was happy in his world without coincidences where everything was connected and everything was centred on him. But it was arrogant like Catherine was arrogant; to see yourself as centre-stage when you aren't even part of the play. Nobody here was interested enough in her life to want to ruin it. They had babies to feed, jobs to go to. They didn't have time in their day to leave hidden messages in signs and codes. It just wasn't how people communicated, unless they were a spy, and I doubted even spies used pine cones and scattered cigarette stubs as threats.

I changed into a dress and shoes I'd not worn since getting here. Catherine stayed in the clothes she was wearing. When I heard Callum driving up the track, I had this sense of relief. We locked up the cottage and hurried out to his car, being bitten and rained on in the five-second dash.

Callum glanced at my feet as I got in beside him. 'I see you've got your dancing shoes on.'

'Will there be dancing?' I'd thought it was just sitting and listening.

'Oh yeah. It's a ceilidh.'

'A ceilidh? You kept that quiet. What if I don't know the moves?'

'It's not *Strictly*. You just follow your partner. It's pretty simple.'

I said, 'I'm not that into organised dancing.'

He took a corner twice as fast as I would. 'I wouldn't call it organised. Especially by the end of the night.'

'But you all have to do the same thing?'

'Well, yeah. That's the idea. What, are you planning on spinning off into your own little solo or something?'

'I'm planning on just watching.'

'We'll see about that.'

'I went to a ceilidh once,' Catherine said from the back seat.

We paused, waiting for her next words.

'I enjoyed it,' she said.

'Good lass. See, Catherine's going to dance.'

I glanced at her in the rear-view mirror. She was an unknown quantity now. I didn't know what she might do or say next.

The ceilidh was at a community centre that overlooked the bay. We went into a foyer where groups of women chatted and laughed as they took off waterproof jackets and fleeces, revealing patterned blouses and silver jewellery underneath. Their husbands were dressed casually in comparison. There were a few groups of teenagers looking completely at home, even though their parents were probably here too. We bought drinks from a serving hatch set up as a bar and made our way through to the main hall. Tables around the edges, a clear space in the middle. On the stage at the far end a girl with fine Nordic features and flicky blonde hair lowered a microphone stand to her height.

I was taking all this in, not really looking where we were heading, when Tom called to us from across the room.

'Grand. We've got a table.' Callum started heading over there. I didn't look at Catherine. I followed him hoping she would follow me in turn.

Tom grinned as I sat down. 'My new drinking buddy.'

'I hope you felt as bad as I did today.'

Callum shook his head. 'The state of you both.'

'I didn't get up till twelve. And that was only because I'd said I'd collect this one from the station.' He stood up and pulled out a chair for Leonie. She must have come in behind us. She'd tied her hair back and drawn a line of sparkly gold along the lids of her eyes, which somehow made her actual eyes look even more dead tired than when I'd seen her at the park. She had the pram with her, its hood pulled up and over. A changing bag hung on the handles along with her coat and handbag.

Catherine pulled out the only seat left at the table: opposite Leonie and next to the pram. Everyone stopped talking. In the gap in conversation I thought I could hear the sound of waves crashing against the beach but surely that was impossible in here?

I said, 'Is this Fleur's first ceilidh?' It was the only thing I could think of. Fleur wasn't even awake.

Leonie nodded. 'And mine.'

'And mine,' I said.

Tom said, 'It'll be carnage out there with you English lassies weaving around all over the place.'

Callum was smiling at me. I said, 'You told me it was easy.'

'Aye, if you've got a partner who knows what they're doing.'

'Not you then,' Tom said. 'It's a pity we've not got another man here. You three will have to share us.'

'Someone needs to stay and look after Fleur.' Catherine's voice was cold.

I said quickly, 'So, who's the band?'

Leonie said, 'She's got the whole village looking after her in here. And she's asleep.'

Catherine took a sip of her drink and looked at the stage. The lights dimmed and the musicians walked out and people began to applaud.

Four boys in plaid shirts and jeans. The elfin-faced girl in a midnight-blue dress. They picked up their instruments: violin, double bass, guitar, pipes and a flute, then began to play with no introduction. Within moments a steadily building foot-tapping had spread across the room. It was that kind of music: fast, absorbing, hard to stay still to.

The tune ended and the girl said hello to the audience who responded with hellos back. 'I'll give you a song from Lewis.' She put her pipe down and began singing in Gaelic. It was clear and bright and it stilled the room. I wanted to ask Callum if he understood the words but he was turned away from me, his face in profile. He seemed to be the only person at the table who was listening. Catherine's eyes flicked to Leonie who was somehow too focused on the band. Tom was fidgety, drinking too fast, his pint glass already empty.

I needed to call Joe but I couldn't do it sitting here. At the end of the song I got up and went out into the car park. I had no idea what to say to him. Sometimes it was better to just let the story spill out unrehearsed. But I would have to be quick so they wouldn't wonder where I'd gone.

I'd keep it simple. I'd say she's ill and you need to come up here. Then I'd explain it fully when he arrived. Face to face was better than over the phone.

It was ringing. He answered. 'Hi.'

'Hiya. It's Anna.'

No response. Was there a satellite gap? I said, 'Catherine's sister, Anna.'

'Hi.'

'How are you?'

'Okay.'

He seemed further away than the four hundred miles between us. I said, 'I'm calling because I'm worried about Catherine.'

A pause. 'Right.'

The line crackled. I wasn't sure what to say. He was making me do all the work. Perhaps he couldn't hear me properly. I said, 'She's not herself.' How could I explain it? I tried again. 'Some of the things she's been saying. They're not right. It's like, she's not right. In the head.' I winced at the clumsiness of my words.

'I mean, I'm sure it's just that she's stressed or tired or something. She doesn't seem to get any sleep.'

There was another silence that set my anxiety spinning. 'Joe? Are you there?'

He said, 'Try not to get into a conversation with her about it.' He took a breath. 'And don't let her involve you in her world. It makes it worse.'

I had a sick feeling high in my chest. 'What's wrong with her?'

He didn't answer. I knew he was still there, I could hear him breathing. I said, 'You need to drive up here.'

'I can't.'

'You have to.'

'I've got things to do here.'

'Well, when you've done them.'

I could only just hear his answer. 'No.'

'She needs help. We need to get her to a doctor.'

'Good luck with that.'

What did that mean? I said, 'But–'

'I'm sorry, Anna. I need a break from this.'

'From what?'

No answer, and this time he wasn't just speaking quietly, he'd gone.

Maybe I hadn't explained it to him properly. It was hard over the phone, with a dodgy signal, maybe he hadn't fully understood.

Except it wasn't that he hadn't grasped what was happening; it was that he already knew. He hadn't tried to reassure me, or tell me it was just how she was sometimes. He knew she was ill, and he wasn't coming up here to help.

I walked back to the community centre and stopped at the bar. A lady poured whisky into a plastic cup and I said I'd have two, thinking I'd give one to Catherine, knowing I'd drink them both myself.

The hall had filled with dancers and she was in amongst them, with Callum. He had hold of her hands. She was spinning and stepping in time to the music. She was good. She took salsa lessons with Joe on Tuesday nights. They'd been going for years.

I downed the first cup. Tom grinned as he passed me. He was dancing with one of the older women. She led him rather than the other way round. Leonie was still in her seat, her hand on the pram as if it was her dance partner and they were just sitting this one out. As if there was a danger someone would whisk Fleur away from her and into the sea of people swirling around the room.

The song ended and Tom was standing in front of me. I gulped down the other whisky and took his hand. The music started up again and dancing with him made me imagine tumbling down the waterfalls in the stream behind the cottage. I was swept under, pushed out to the side, pulled back to the surface and into the flow. When it ended, we were both bent double laughing. He took my hand and steered me back to the table. The room wasn't quite still, the floor not quite steady.

Catherine sipped her wine and said nothing. Leonie ignored us. I sat down, getting my breath back and Tom went off to the bar. Underneath the music, so nobody else could hear, Callum said, 'What are you doing with my cousin?'

I met his eyes. He was jealous and not bothering to hide it. I said, 'We can dance, if you want.'

'Do you want to?'

'No, not really.' I couldn't stand to be that close to him and not kiss him.

'Don't spare my feelings, will you?'

The music was loud. Nobody but him could hear what I was saying. 'Maybe we could just go to bed instead?'

He didn't blink. 'We could do that.'

'When?'

'Whenever you want.'

I thought, tonight. I thought, someone else can take Catherine home, and we can just leave now. Except something was happening with her and Leonie at the far end of the table. Catherine was staring at her, while Leonie determinedly focused on the stage, even though the song had ended and the band were putting down their instruments. The applause thinned out and stopped.

Catherine said something and I couldn't hear what it was but there was a flicker of movement on Leonie's face. Did she look like Catherine? No, but they both had that tight, held-in air. That I'm-not-going-to-reveal-anything look. The one that revealed everything about how much they had to hide. It wasn't familial resemblance, more mutual distrust. Oh God, I couldn't deal with it. Could I just go now with Callum? We could fuck in the car park. Or in the woods. It wasn't cold out. Then there was another drink in front of me and Tom was offering me a cigarette.

Leonie said, 'I'll have one.' She looked at the pram as if unsure what to do with it. She said to Callum, 'Could you watch Fleur for me?'

'Am I invisible?' Catherine said.

Leonie paused. 'I can't leave my baby with someone I don't know.'

'I'm not "someone you don't know".'

Leonie got up, ignoring her, and pushed in her chair.

'I know you,' Catherine said.

Leonie stopped. 'Well, I don't know you.'

Catherine said, 'Leonie Jane Woodward. You live in

Newquay with your parents. You work in a restaurant opposite the station. You voted Green at the last election and made sure all your friends knew about it. You paint seascapes and sometimes you post pictures of them online. But you don't ever post pictures of Fleur. Not even when she was born. Didn't you take any? Is it because nobody took any of you?'

Leonie blinked. 'What are you talking about?'

'The day you were born.'

Tom put his hand on Leonie's arm and said, 'Come on away,' but she didn't seem to notice. She just stood there, hands holding the back of her chair. In the sudden quiet, I heard the sea again. Waves dragging on the shore. It was coming from the pram, and everyone's eyes moved onto Fleur's sleeping body. Leonie reached into the blankets tucked over her, and pulled out her phone. She pressed a button and the sound of the waves stopped.

Catherine said, 'Do you want your lighter?' She took it from her bag and put it on the table. The surfboard and beach and *Newquay* printed across it.

Leonie looked at it. She didn't speak.

Catherine said, 'You left it in our cottage.'

Leonie's face didn't move. She kicked off the brake on the pram and pushed it straight across the hall, people cleared out of her path as she approached. Tom tried to catch her up. Catherine stayed where she was, a tight smile on her face.

I went after them. I needed to explain to Leonie that Catherine was ill and that it made her say strange things. I needed to tell her that she didn't need to take any of it personally. They were just outside the door, cigarette ends glowing. Neither of them said anything when I went over.

I said, 'Catherine's not thinking right.' Like my sister was senile or simple in the head.

Leonie took a quick drag with a shaking hand but didn't reply. My phone vibrated in my pocket.

It was Joe. I clicked answer. 'I'll call you back in a minute.'

He said, 'I'm driving up tomorrow.'

I turned away because Tom and Leonie were staring at me and I needed to concentrate. 'You're coming up here?'

'Yes.'

'Thank God. But what shall I tell Catherine?'

'I don't know.'

'I might not tell her.'

'It's up to you.'

When I put my phone away, they were both still looking at me, as if waiting for an explanation. I said, 'Sorry. It was Catherine's husband.'

'Joe.' Tom laughed, looking past me. 'When's he coming then?'

'Tomorrow.' What was that laugh about? I tried to remember what I'd wanted to say to Leonie about Catherine but she was leaving. She bumped the pram down the steps and across the car park. Fleur gave a little cry out. Leonie stopped, switched on the sea sound on her phone, and dropped it back in the blankets.

Tom shook his head, stubbed his cigarette out on the floor. 'She's always got that thing on. Florrie probably thinks they live in a lighthouse.' He turned to me. 'Another one who's not got a clue what's going on.'

11

CATHERINE

Tuesday. Sunrise 04.29. Sunset 22.21

L ast night she'd said, 'I don't know you' and I'd thought, why not just be honest about who we are? But I see now that she *was* being honest. What she'd meant was, I don't know you now, *as an adult.* I don't know what you're like as a person.

She felt like she didn't know me, which was understandable considering how long we had been apart. It was how I felt sometimes when I had to work hard to figure out what she was really thinking underneath that shell. It was difficult at times to see that how she behaved; cold, indifferent, was the opposite to how she felt.

I knew she hated me, I had no doubt about that. Sometimes the only way out of love is hate. That's what we had between us, love forced into hate. Could it be wrenched back to its original form? There would always be marks and distortions. It would never be as smooth and straight as it once was, but it would be beautiful in its own crooked way.

I wanted her to understand this. It is what I ought to have

said to her last night but instead I went on the attack. It was the way she turned from me. She had refused to look at my face. In the moment, I saw it as rejection, but it wasn't that at all. She was a child so angry it cannot ask for the love it needs.

I remember the one night I spent with her. It was the night after the birth, or rather, the removal, because in the end they had cut me open and lifted her out. An emergency caesarean. I don't remember why. I remember that it left me unable to sit up without help, and that there was a time in the middle of the night when she was crying in the cot alongside my hospital bed. She wanted to be fed and I couldn't get out of bed to pick her up because my abdomen pulled and burned where they'd stitched me up. I pressed the button for a nurse but no one came. Her cries got louder. I pushed myself onto my side, then sank onto my front. The burn across my middle blanked out everything and made me gasp. I slid my feet to the floor, pressed my hands into the bed and that way reached standing. In the cot, she was crying like she was in just as much pain as I was. Like she was so hungry her insides hurt. I slid my hands under her back, her Babygro was warm and clammy against my palms. I lifted her out, I thought I was going to be sick, and now I couldn't see how to get us into a position where I could feed her. My T-shirt was in the way and once I'd got her close to me, she wouldn't put her mouth in the right place. She didn't know how this worked any more than I did. She kept turning away. I stood there frozen with her against my chest. I couldn't walk, couldn't sit down, couldn't feed her and the noise she was making; it was as if her world was about to end.

When the nurse came she didn't understand why I was crying too. I said, why didn't you come before? She said, we've got a ward of thirty ill women to look after. She smelled of cigarette smoke. She said, 'Hasn't anyone shown you how to work the bed?'

There was a button to raise the headboard and take you from lying to sitting. I didn't know. She said, 'We'll look after baby tonight so you can get some sleep.' And she took her away to the nurses' station to bottle-feed her.

When she'd gone, I lowered myself back onto the bed. But I didn't go to sleep. I had failed at the most basic element of motherhood; feeding the baby. It confirmed to me once more that I had made the right decision. I wasn't going to be her mother, I wasn't meant to be her mother, so it was right that I couldn't feed her. I felt relief that she was no longer beside me, relief that the curtains were closed and it was just me once more, and that the next day, I would sign the papers and she would be taken away for good.

I got up to make a hot drink but we'd used the last of the kindling so I had no way to light the stove. I tried with newspaper and firelighters and it flared briefly into life then was ashes a moment later.

I would take a bag into the woods and fill it with sticks. It was better than lying awake in that coffin bed listening to Anna breathing above me. I dressed quietly in the bedroom. She didn't stir. She lay under her sleeping bag rather than in it. Last night she'd complained she couldn't find the way in before suddenly falling into a deep, drunken sleep. She would probably still be in that same, passed-out position when I got back.

I followed a deer path up into the woods. I collected twigs and pine cones and filled the bag within minutes. But I didn't want to go back yet; I wanted to keep walking, keep moving; staying still felt risky somehow and I wasn't sure if I was running from my thoughts or from something more concrete. I was hiding in the woods but who was I hiding from? Leonie, Tom, Callum, Mary, Anna.

Anna said she wasn't part of it but I knew otherwise. I'd

watched her last night, whispering, plotting, sneaking off outside to talk on her phone. She was up to something. I had to be careful around her. It was why I hadn't been able to sleep. My brain wouldn't switch off even though my eyes were dry with tiredness. I had to stay alert to stay safe.

I stopped. I'd glimpsed something red between the trees a little further up the hillside. I got closer and saw it was a ball hanging from a rope. No, a buoy, like you'd see floating in a harbour but this one was hanging in mid-air. It was a swing for a child. It hung over a hollow in the hillside from a high oak branch. I walked up to it and gave it a gentle push.

It was heavy and slow like somebody was sitting on it. I watched it go back and forth, listening to the steady creak of the branch above. I stayed there for a while, pushing it away, and catching it as it fell back, over and over. I gave it a big, solid push before I left and when I glanced back up the hill a few minutes later, it was still swinging. Anyone who stumbled across it from the other direction would wonder where it had got its momentum from when there was nobody around.

I don't know how long I was gone but when I got back there was a car parked outside the cottage. Joe's car? His black coat was on the back seat. Our house keys were in the cup holder. None of this made any sense.

I opened the cottage door and he was standing just inside with Anna. She looked like she'd only just woken up.

He said, 'You're back.' As if it was me who was out of place here, not him. He put his arms around me in a long, firm hug.

Joe was here in Scotland. I hadn't asked him to come. I was sure of it. 'What are you doing here?'

'I came to see you.'

'Why?'

His eyes kept moving away from mine. He had drank too much coffee and not had enough sleep. He looked out of the window, then at me for a second, then over towards Anna who was doing something in the kitchen, her hand on her forehead.

'What are you doing here?' I was so confused. I saw a look pass between him and Anna. 'What's going on?'

Anna said, 'Nothing.' Lying.

'But why are you here? Joe?'

He took a sharp breath in. 'Can you give me a minute, Catherine? I've just done a seven hour drive. I've only had two hours' sleep.'

Anna spoke. 'I asked him to come.' Her voice was gravelly and her face was pale. She said, 'I was worried about you. You're not yourself. You're ill.'

'I'm ill? It's you who looks like you're about to throw up.'

Joe said, 'Mentally ill.'

Oh. Okay. I laughed and they stared at me. Those two words. They sounded so reasonable and that was their power. I said, 'It's funny how you all say exactly the same things.'

'Catherine.' Joe put his arms around me. I stood still until he let go. He said, 'We just want to help you.'

'Help me?' I went to the sink and turned on the kitchen tap. I watched the murky water pooling into the plastic bowl. 'Have you seen this, Joe?'

He didn't answer.

'The water. Have you seen it?'

He started rubbing his face in that anxious way he had. 'We both think you need help. Anna can see it after being with you just a few days.'

I filled a glass and held it up to the light. 'Would you drink that?'

No one answered. Joe took the glass out of my hand and poured the water away then placed the glass carefully on the sideboard and kept his eyes fixed on it. He was doing some kind of controlled breathing exercise and it was filling me with dread.

He said calmly, 'If your husband and your sister are both telling you the same thing, don't you think it might be worth listening to?'

I said, 'Did Anna tell you my daughter hacked my emails, found out where I would be, then came up here to find me?'

He took another deep, slow breath.

'Did she tell you she has a baby who looks exactly like she did when she was a baby? Anna, where's that picture of Fleur?' I spotted the sketchpad under some books. I held up the drawing for Joe to see; Fleur's arms bent at the elbows, her fists by her ears as if she was falling, about to land. I said, 'Anna recognised her as well.'

He shook his head. 'It's not her.'

Such an abrupt dismissal. It infuriated me. 'Where's your room for doubt? Isn't that what you always ask me–'

'Catherine. We've been through this before.' He kept his voice quiet and steady. He would tell me to stop shouting in a minute. 'It's not her. This girl isn't your daughter. Just like Sophie in London wasn't your daughter. You're seeing her everywhere and it's just not her.'

'I'll show you the email.'

'The email from who?'

'From me. To Anna.'

'No, it's irrelevant. I don't want to see it.'

'You're always asking me for evidence. When I give you some, you refuse to look at it.'

Joe closed his eyes for a long moment. 'Your daughter said no, Catherine. You put in the request to contact her, and she said no, she didn't want to meet you.'

Anna interrupted, 'Hang on. *You* contacted *her*? I thought you said *she* found *you*.'

'She did.'

'No she didn't,' Joe snapped. 'You filled in the form to

request contact. The Adoption Register sent you a letter back saying she doesn't want contact with you. I should have kept it. I didn't know you would get this confused. I should never have put the idea in your head.'

'You don't put ideas in my head. As if I'm that easy to influence.'

'I wish you were. Then you might listen to what I'm saying for once.'

It was the start of a familiar complaint. But if I never listened, how did I know exactly what he was going to say next? We'd had this conversation hundreds of times before.

He said, 'Every suggestion I make, you ignore it. You ignore me.'

'I don't ignore you.'

'You do.'

'When?'

He paused. 'Now.'

'I'm looking right at you.'

He closed his eyes again. He didn't want to see me. Then he went outside and got something from the car, I couldn't see what it was. Oh yes, of course. Was this why he'd driven three hundred miles in the middle of the night?

He put the pills the doctor had prescribed on the table in front of me. When I'd googled the brand name, it described them as 'antipsychotics'. I'd thrown them away. Joe had got them out of the bin. He'd been pulling them out in arguments like this ever since.

'What's that?' Anna said.

'It's medication. For Catherine.'

'I'm not ill.'

'*Yes you are.*' His voice cracked in the middle.

'Having a different opinion to you doesn't make me mentally ill.'

211

'It's not your opinions, it's your whole understanding of reality.'

'My daughter is real. She's called Leonie and she works in the café at the beach. She's a real person, walking around, making drinks, looking at me, carrying a baby.' I looked from him to Anna. They were both frozen in place. 'Let's go and see her if you don't believe she's real.'

I waited for a retort from Joe but he didn't have one. I'd shut him down. Then Anna stepped in. Two against one. She said, 'Leonie is obviously real. What Joe means is that the idea she's your daughter, and that Fleur is your granddaughter – that isn't real. It's not a fact, it's just a theory, and, well, *it's wrong.*'

I said, 'If you're both so sure about that, why don't we go and ask her?'

'No.' Joe turned away, his head in his hands like he was trying to hold it in place. It was manipulative, an act. He remembered the pills and tried to hand them to me. He said, 'I need you to take one of these.'

'No.'

'I don't know how else to fix this.'

'Fix me, you mean.'

'I mean us.'

'You mean me.' I went into the bedroom and shut the door.

———

There was a time when I could tell Joe everything. I trusted him not to take what I said and store it away in his head, ready to be presented back to me when he had a point he wanted to make. A point about me, and how I thought, or what I thought.

When your perceptions are constantly being questioned, you make them firmer. And the firmer they are, the less convincing they sound to other people, and even to yourself, if you haven't the awareness and strength of character to resist. I know this. It's how I've been able to survive within it. I've held my position but only by putting up a wall. I know they want to get in my head and start digging around but why would I agree to an intrusion like that? The thing I want most of all is privacy.

I went to the doctors, years ago, to say I thought I was suffering from depression. I wanted something that would fix it with minimum disruption, within a few weeks. He prescribed me a course of antidepressants. They worked and after six months or so, I stopped taking them and I was fine. But then every time I went to a GP, they brought up my medical records and saw my complaints through a filter of 'mental illness'. Every issue I had, they related it back to that one low winter.

I had a spell of migraines; they suggested a mindfulness course. I had an aching in my limbs that lasted for months; they suggested psychotherapy. I said, it's my legs that hurt, not my soul. They tested my blood and found I had a vitamin D deficiency because I hadn't been getting enough sunlight.

It was a problem with the weather, not with me. It was out there, not in here, contrary to what they wanted me to believe.

I prefer to self-diagnose nowadays rather than talk to a GP. It's the privacy issue again. They jab their keyboards while I talk, creating a record to use against me in the future, just like Joe does. It makes me never want to speak again. It's amazing, the power they have to reduce a person and make them doubt themselves. I am careful not to let that happen. It's one reason I write everything down. I've got my own records to refer to while they look through theirs. I could read back through my journal now and it would tell me exactly what happened and what didn't.

There was never a letter from her telling me no. There was a lighter placed casually in the cottage where I slept. There was the way her gaze followed me across the café. There was a child with her eyes and mine.

I tried to contact her, that part is true. And the truth is, I got nothing back. And that is not 'no'. It is a loaded, stony silence. I found out that long before I'd requested contact, she had stipulated that she didn't want any. Because she knew that the best way to hurt someone is to shut them out completely.

It was what she had done last night. It wasn't 'no'; it was her way of controlling the conversation.

She knew that the distance she held between us made us closer. It was why she did it. She kept herself in my thoughts. She made herself present by her absence.

I needed my journal but it was in my bag which was in the other room. I stood in the doorway and neither noticed I was there. Anna was looking out of the window. Joe was studying something on the table, where my bag was. It was the drawing of Fleur.

I said his name. He didn't answer, just kept staring at her face, a question in his eyes. When he looked over at me it was as though he was still struggling to process what he'd seen. I felt the same way the first time I saw her. It was how I knew she was mine.

I said, 'You recognise her.'

He didn't say anything.

I said, 'You can see the resemblance.'

He swallowed. 'No.'

I nearly laughed. I said, 'Joe, I can tell from how you're looking at her.' I smiled. It was so obvious.

'I don't know what you mean.'

But he knew her. I could see it. Why was he pretending otherwise? I didn't understand. I snapped. 'Why can't you just accept that I've found my daughter? Is it because you think I don't deserve her in my life? Do you think I don't deserve a happy ending after what I did?'

Anna said, 'Nobody thinks that.'

'All I want is for everyone to stop judging me.'

'Nobody is judging you,' she said. 'Apart from yourself.'

'Then why won't he admit she's mine?'

Anna said, 'Because she's not yours.'

I said, 'Why are you both pretending not to recognise her?'

'Catherine.' Joe took a deep breath in. 'You're reading into things again. You're seeing something that isn't there.'

They were still playing along with the game. I couldn't believe it. I said, 'You won't make me think I'm crazy. I'm onto you. I know what you're doing.'

Joe said, 'I want you to start taking the medication.'

A blatant distraction. A deft change of subject. 'No.'

'Then we can't keep going with this.'

Anna said, 'I'll get out of your way.'

'Stay,' Joe said quickly.

'You two need to talk on your own.'

'I want you to be part of it,' he said.

'I just don't think I have a role to play in this.' She went towards the bedroom.

He said, 'I need you to look after Catherine.'

'*Look after me?*'

He said, 'She's ill and I can't take care of her anymore.'

'I'm not ill.'

He sat down on the sofa and put his head in his hands. Was he crying? No. He looked across the room at me. 'I don't know how else to say this.' He stopped. He said, 'I want a divorce. I'll stay at my brother's while we sort out what to do with the house.'

'Which brother?'

'Gavin. I can have his spare room until I move back to

London.'

'You're moving back to London?'

'Yes.'

'Well, I'll come too. I don't want to live in Manchester anyway.'

'You can't.'

'Why can't I?'

He spoke quietly. 'Because I'm leaving you. That means you can't come with me.'

My eyes were on his for a moment. I couldn't work out what he meant. Then I looked down and it was as though I couldn't look up again. I couldn't look at his face. Did he say 'divorce'?

He said, 'I thought Anna could move in with you for a while so you're not on your own.'

Anna started talking. 'Joe, just stop a minute. This isn't a solution to anything. I mean, what about relationship counselling?'

'We've been down that road.'

'Catherine's going through a really bad time here. You can't just abandon her.'

'I have to think of my own mental health. I can't deal with this anymore. I don't want to. You're her family. And there's your mum and dad.'

'But you're her husband.'

'She doesn't listen to me. She lives in another world, in her head. I honestly don't think she'll notice that I'm not around.'

I heard Anna say, 'Of course she'll notice.' And I heard Joe say, 'We're out of milk. I'm going to the shop.'

'You've asked for a divorce and now you're restocking the fridge?'

'I can't find my shoes.'

Anna threw them across the room at him. He put them on without speaking and went out into the rain.

12

ANNA

Wednesday. Sunrise 04.29. Sunset 22.21

The cottage had been claustrophobic with just myself and Catherine. With Joe here as well, it was suffocating. It wasn't just the lack of space, it was the atmosphere, which was airless and prickly and impossible to escape. We all stayed in bed longer than normal, probably all wishing the day didn't have to start. Catherine was asleep on the bottom deck when I slid down. In the living room, Joe lay on his back under the blankets on the sofa, his eyes open. It took a moment for them to fall on me.

'Morning.' I don't know why I sounded so cheerful.

'Morning.'

Oh, for an electric kettle. The stove was running low on wood and the rain sounded like pebbles falling on the roof. I put my boots on, pulled on Catherine's waterproof jacket, and went to get more logs. The cloud was low, blocking off the view. Sheep sheltered under the trees by the track. I filled the basket at the woodpile and went back inside. Joe still hadn't moved.

He'd been gone for hours yesterday when he went to 'get milk'. When he finally returned, he said he'd been for a long drive, to clear his head. He didn't mention divorce and neither did Catherine. We spent the evening acting like that word hadn't been said. I made dinner. Catherine and Joe read their books. Then we went to bed. And I started to think that maybe they had that kind of argument all the time, and it was completely normal for one of them to throw ultimatums down like that and stalk out into the rain.

I started filling the furnace with wood. 'Did you sleep okay?'

'Not really. I'm not looking forward to that eight-hour drive.'

I turned. 'Are you going back today?'

'I think so.'

'Oh.' I didn't like the sound of that. I didn't want to be left alone with Catherine and her illness. I watched the flames take hold of the kindling, not saying anything.

'You figured out how everything works, then?' He sat up. He'd slept in his clothes. It was cold at night when the fire died down.

'Catherine did.'

He came to stand next to me at the stove and said quietly, 'This Leonie that she talked about?'

I turned to face the bedroom door, aware Catherine could walk in at any moment. 'She's just a girl who works in the café at the beach. We saw her outside one morning after some stuff had been knocked off the picnic table in the night. It was probably a pine marten but Catherine decided that Leonie did it. All this... it started from there.'

'Leonie came here to the cottage?'

'She was just out for a walk. It was pure coincidence. But Catherine doesn't believe in coincidences. I mean, they're *all* I believe in. There's no secret plot joining everything together. Sometimes things just don't make sense. They end on a question mark in the middle of a sentence. There's no full stop.' I was talking about punctuation because he was a writer and I wanted him to understand what I was trying to say. I was so tired. I sighed. 'Anyway. Leonie isn't anyone. Just some lonely girl with a baby that Catherine's got a weird obsession with.'

Joe sat back down again. His face was the kind of weary that comes from months of worrying, not just one sleepless night on a lumpy sofa. After a while he said, 'If me and Catherine had had a baby, none of this would have happened.'

I wasn't sure what to say. 'You might still have one.'

'No.'

'She's only thirty-eight.'

'Yep.' Like he'd tuned out already.

I sat down next to him, and he snapped back into focus. I said, lower than the sound of the rain, 'Did you mean it when you said you want a divorce?'

He took a deep, defeated-sounding breath. 'I can't see any other way through it.'

'Through what? What's actually wrong with her?'

In a flat, tired voice he told me it was something called 'delusional disorder' and she'd had it 'on and off' for about three years.

I'd never heard of it. He said I should google it. I said how can I when there's no fucking internet, then I apologised because I didn't think he meant to sound dismissive. He was worn out, and I was scared and panicking; the strange way my sister was acting had a name and a list of symptoms. But didn't that also mean it had a cure?

'The medication might help,' he said. 'But she won't take it, and nobody can make her. Unless they section her. And they won't do that. I've tried.' He met my eyes for a moment then looked at the floor.

Sectioned? How bad had things got with her? 'What happened?'

'I went to see her doctor when she got laid off from work. He said she isn't ill enough to be sectioned because she's not a danger to herself or other people.' He sounded almost bored with the subject but I think it was a defence mechanism. 'She's not lost it completely. Which means there isn't much they can do, without her consent.'

'But she's really ill.'

'Not compared to some people. And she can hide it, when she wants to. He said she wouldn't be able to do that if it was really bad.'

'But she's not hiding it.'

'Not from us. We're not her doctor.'

I thought about that. 'She's not stupid, is she?'

He shook his head. 'She doesn't want to get better. Nobody wants their reality pulled out from under them. Imagine what that would be like.'

It would be like realising you'd been living a lie; one you'd told yourself rather than had told to you. You'd feel embarrassed, ashamed. But worse than that, you'd feel like everything around you had fallen away, like there was nothing solid to hold on to, in the outside world, and in your head.

No wonder she didn't want to give up her delusions; she'd made them who she was. If she let them go, she'd lose herself.

Joe said, 'If they sectioned her, they'd put her on a hospital ward with the psychotics and schizophrenics. She'd hate it. And only a doctor could undo it. We couldn't go in and get her if we changed our mind. We might not be able to get her out again.'

I felt sick and frightened and so utterly sad for her. And what could we do? What? Grind up a pill and sprinkle it over her food? Dissolve it in a drink? She thought she was being poisoned, and here I was, thinking of ways to poison her. She thought people were scheming behind her back, and here we were, whispering about locking her away, while she slept in the next room.

He said, 'There'll be times when she seems fine for months. But then it comes back. Or she just stops hiding it from me. It's usually when I've just started believing it might be gone for good.'

'I read her journal. The one you got her at New Year.'

He shook his head. 'I don't want to know what's in there.'

I didn't either but I couldn't unread it now. 'Okay.'

He said, 'I gave it to her as a life planner. I've tried so many ways to get her back on track. Healthy food, exercise, therapy. Moving house.'

'You moved house because of this?'

He nodded. The anxiety radiating from him was catching. 'I thought a change of scene might... jolt her out of it. But she just brought it with her.'

'You can't leave yourself behind. It doesn't matter where you live.'

'No. You must know that with all your travelling.'

'I used to think you could. If you had a completely new start with new people, a new job, a new country. It doesn't work. I guess we'd all be doing it if it did.' I turned to him. 'Did you say she lost her job?'

'Didn't you know that?'

'No. I thought...' I sighed. 'I thought she had a good job.'

'She did until she got ill. They didn't sack her, they "managed her out".' She thought one of the interns, Sophie, was her daughter. And she thought Sophie was orchestrating a plot against her at work, even though she wasn't even there anymore.

'They gave Catherine some time off. Sick leave. As though they cared about her getting better. Everyone thinks charities will be such a nice, caring place to work but they're a business like any other. They wanted her gone so they passed all her responsibilities to other people while she was off. When she came back, she had nothing to do. No projects. No team. They should have just been straight about it all. It made her paranoia worse because, she was right, they were trying to get rid of her behind her back. She quit because she couldn't deal with the stress of it.'

'I didn't know any of this.'

'She hides things.'

I said, 'It sounds like she had a similar thing going on with Sophie as she's got with Leonie.'

He was silent.

I said, 'It's weird that she's doing the same thing again, but with a different person.'

He got up then. 'That's not weird, Anna. It's human nature. Everyone does it.'

Catherine came in, her eyes on us. Had she been listening? She sat at the table and brushed the box of pills to one side as if she was only half-aware of them.

Joe said, 'Did you sleep okay?'

'Yes thanks.'

The kettle started whistling. I made cups of tea for us all and went to get dressed. I couldn't hear what they were saying, if they were saying anything at all. Then I heard the front door open. I looked out. Joe was walking over to his car. He put his bag on the back seat. Then stood there in the mist looking at where the sea would be. He was about to leave.

In the living room, Catherine was still sitting at the table. She was a too-full cup of water that would spill if you tried to pick it up. Except she must have moved at some point because now she had the box of pills in her hands.

I said, 'If you take them, he'll change his mind.' Wasn't that the gist of it? Take the drugs or I'll divorce you. It was cruel but a part of me understood. Imagine the loneliness of being married to someone who didn't share the same reality as you. Whose view of the world was so skewed by all this loss and guilt they were carrying. Of course he wanted to leave. In my experience romantic love was delicate, fragile, never unconditional. It didn't survive long distances and these two were miles apart.

Catherine looked at the box in her hands. 'But I'm not ill.'

'Take one anyway.'

'You want me to take medication for an illness I haven't got?'

I remembered saying to Ade, 'I seriously think I'm going crazy,' after a particularly busy few weeks of partying had left my head frazzled. And he'd said, 'The thing about crazy people is, they don't know they're crazy. If you know, then you're not.'

Catherine didn't know and that was the most disturbing thing about it. Because how can you get yourself better if you don't even realise you're ill?

I said, 'It'll be like taking paracetamol when you've not got a headache. It won't have any effect.'

I had no idea if this was true or not. And, well, it would have an effect, and maybe then she'd start to see that she felt differently, more herself even, afterwards.

She said, 'You take one then, if that's the case.'

I paused. 'All right. I will.' I took the box and unfolded the leaflet inside. The drug had a name full of Z's and X's that made it sound like the last resort, the end of the road. The font looked like a lightning strike. Zap and you're cured. Side effects included sleepiness and restlessness (at the same time?), weight gain, unusual body movements. Like twitching? I stopped there. There was such a thing as too much information.

I poured two glasses of water and put one in front of Catherine. I popped out two tiny white pills. I pushed Catherine's across the table to her.

She ignored it.

I picked up the other pill. Okay. I could do this. It was probably nothing compared to some of the drugs I'd willingly taken in the past. Though they never came with a list of off-putting side effects.

Catherine was watching me. 'Don't, Anna.'

I put it in my mouth. I washed it down with water. 'Done.'

She said, 'It's different for you. Nobody is telling you you're crazy.'

'But if you're totally healthy, it won't make any difference. You could see it as a way of proving you're not ill. You can say, it didn't do anything because there was nothing wrong with me in the first place.'

There were a lot of holes in this argument but I just needed her to take the pill and stop Joe from leaving. *You're here*, he'd said yesterday. But I wasn't, not really. I might want to go somewhere else. I couldn't be relied on to look after her. He'd said I had Mum and Dad to help but they were too old to deal with this kind of thing. We ought to be looking after them, not the other way round. Mum would go to pieces. Dad would deny there was a problem.

I said to Catherine, 'Your marriage will end. Do you really want to turn your life upside down like that?'

'If he loved me, he wouldn't force me to do something I don't want to do. It's blackmail.'

No, if it was just a threat he wouldn't be about to move in with his brother. He wasn't playing games or trying to force her hand. He'd already walked out the door.

I said, 'He's saying this is what he needs to be able to stay.'

'But it would be as if I was saying he's right. He's not right. She is my daughter. It's a fact.'

I didn't have the energy to argue about who Leonie was or wasn't. It wouldn't get through to her so what was the point?

'Look, I've taken one. And it's fine. Not a big deal. Can't you...' I sighed.

She shook her head once, her posture held tight. We sat there not speaking. After a while I got up and went into the bedroom to finish getting dressed. There didn't seem to be much else I could do.

I sat on the top bunk. I could see Joe outside, still standing there in the mist and I didn't know whether it was the side effects of the pill or just the situation but I was feeling kind of sick and anxious. Because realistically, what was I going to do if he got in his car and drove back down to Manchester to leave Catherine for good? How would I get her to a doctor? How would I get her to accept help when she was adamant she didn't need it? And as for moving into her house... it would be worse than living with Mum and Dad. Their brand of insanity; Dad's irrational fear of motorway service stations, Mum's silent wars with the neighbours about wheelie bin retrieval; they were easy to deal with compared to this.

Antipsychotics. Did that mean my sister had psychosis? I didn't even know what that word meant. I knew that nowadays we were all supposed to be okay with mental illness, as though it was no worse than a cold or a bout of hay fever. But I wasn't okay with this. I couldn't accept this strange, awful person my sister had become. She was self-obsessed and cynical and angry, and far too sensitive, and she saw the worst in everyone and every situation. People on social media might be okay with mental illness, but they weren't living with someone who thought the tap water was poisoned. They weren't employing them, or relying on them, or married to them. And talking about it wasn't going to help. Joe said it just made it worse.

The only thing we had was medication. But she wouldn't take it and we couldn't make her. And this was my problem now. And there was no solution to it. And no support because she was ill but not ill enough.

I felt like crying. It wasn't a side effect. I got myself dressed and washed, going in and out of the other room where Catherine was still sitting wordlessly at the table. At first I thought she was staring into space but then I realised it was at the door.

All these years, I'd blithely assumed she was okay. I never went to visit her and Joe in London. I never invited them to visit me in Banff. I had no idea anything was wrong and this thought jagged in my chest. I remembered Catherine saying all those years back that Mum had told me she was pregnant so she'd have someone to talk to about it. I'd failed her then and I'd been failing her ever since, through all these years when this guilt was growing unchecked inside her, twisting and flowering into strange stories about hacked emails and funeral plans.

I was still a child when she got pregnant. It was understandable that I wouldn't know how to handle it. But I was thirty-four now. Why didn't I feel any more capable than back then? And why did I still feel this huge resentment that she was messing up my life as well as her own?

I heard Joe come back inside. I decided to stay in the bedroom and listen but neither spoke. What were they doing? Was Catherine okay? I looked in. Joe was gathering up his phone and keys and cashcard. Catherine was watching him.

She said, 'Joe?' He turned to her. She had a pill in her hand. She put it in her mouth and swallowed it with water. And there was something so defeated in her expression, I almost wished she hadn't done it. She'd given in. She never gave in. Joe watched her with his stupid phone in his hand. For a moment, I hated him.

I said to him, 'So you're staying, then? She took the pill. Like you wanted.'

He hadn't expected it. He frowned. 'Yes.'

Catherine pushed out her chair. 'I'm going to get dressed,' she said quietly. She moved past me into the bedroom and pulled the bedroom door shut, as if to say discussion over, problem solved.

I was itching to get away from them. With all the stress of Joe's arrival, I hadn't had time to think about Callum but it hadn't escaped my notice that he didn't call round yesterday. I remembered our conversation underneath the music at the ceilidh and couldn't decide whether I should be embarrassed or not. 'Whenever you want,' he'd said, as if we had all the time in the world.

The rain had stopped. I set off towards his house. I didn't want to spend the next few months wondering what it would feel like to kiss him and run my hand around his waist. I didn't want to drive myself crazy with desire for someone hundreds of miles away. When I got back, I had to get a job, find a place to live, build my entire life up again. I didn't have time for a long-distance crush on someone who didn't have a phone signal or internet access or even a road to his house. Someone who might as well be living on the moon.

When I reached the woods, I saw him on the path below me, a rucksack across his shoulders. If I hurried, I could catch him, or I could shout. Both options seemed a little keen. He climbed the stile and turned and saw me. He waited for me on the other side of the wall. 'Are you coming to see me?'

Clearly I was and he was happy about it, I could see it in his eyes. I said, 'Just out for a stroll.'

'But you'll be calling in for a cup of tea?'

'I thought I might.'

We walked down through the pasture. The sea glinted in the distance and the smell of ferns rose from the ground.

'Where have you been?' I asked.

'To the centre to check my emails. They've said I can hot-desk. It means I can take some work on, stay up here a wee bit longer.'

'Is that your plan?'

'I reckon. I'm not ready to go back to Glasgow yet. I don't need electricity, clean water, central heating, that kind of thing.'

Oh, it was a relief to be with someone normal. I said, 'I'll think of you when I'm back home, leaning against a radiator.'

'Radiators.' He said it like it was a word from a foreign language. 'I'd forgotten they existed.'

'Electric kettles, electric blankets.'

He laughed. 'Electric blankets? Where do you live, the 1950s?'

'Toasted sandwich makers. The 1980s.'

We'd reached the wooden walkway. He stopped so I could go first. 'I make a mean toasted sandwich in a frying pan. I'll demonstrate when we get in if you want.'

'Anyone who manages to cook anything edible on a Rayburn is a genius.'

Behind me, he said, 'Dad was an expert at it. He taught me. Him lying on the sofa, giving step-by-step instructions. He wanted me to stay here, after.' We climbed up the hill to his house. There were patches of blue in the sky bringing moments of bright sunshine.

'On your own?'

'He said you never know what'll happen.' He held open the front door, looking down at me. 'Or who might get washed up with the tide.'

'Washed up?'

'I meant washed in.'

'Right.'

He led us through to the kitchen. 'Are you hungry?'

'Not really.'

'Do you fancy taking a walk with me?'

The way he was smiling at me... I tried to keep my face expressionless. 'We could do.'

'I'll make us a flask.'

I watched the back of his neck as he made coffee in a jug and poured it into a Thermos. I didn't want to go for a walk. I wanted to run my fingers down the long muscle on his forearm, take his hand, take him to bed. But he turned around with a look of such contented innocence on his face that I couldn't look him in the eye. He put the flask in his rucksack. 'There's a beach you really need to see before you go.'

'And you're telling me about it on my last day? Will I wish I'd been going there all week?'

'You'll wish you'd been going there all your life.'

We followed a faint, overgrown path that led up behind the house. Ferns brushed our legs and there was only space to walk single file. For a moment, I thought of Catherine and Joe and the delicate truce they'd formed before I left. I pushed the thought away, out into the sea, which filled the view to the right of us. Callum stopped to take off his jumper then set off again sure-footed and fast. I imagined lying next to him in bed. The buzz I'd get from using my lips to explore his lips, his chest, his hips. How good it would feel to be turned on next to a beautiful man who was hard and waiting to be touched. Today, it had to be. This afternoon.

The sea was hidden by a hill then back in view. I saw the islands in the distance, Callum's shoulder blades through the thin cotton of his T-shirt. We clambered over a stream at the foot of a waterfall. He stopped suddenly when we rounded a hillside and I almost walked into him. 'There you go,' he said. 'Nice, eh?'

'Oh.' The beach was below us. 'Why have you been keeping this a secret?'

He laughed. It was one of those Scottish beaches that looks like it's in the Caribbean. Surf lapping white sand, shallow water of every shade of green and blue. And empty apart from a few seabirds by the shore.

We reached a shelf of cotton-grass just above the beach. I took off my Converse and walked barefoot onto the sand. Callum sat on the grass, leaning back on his hands, his face in the sun. I felt drawn back to him and drawn to the sea, like a tide on the brink of turning. I paddled in the cold water for a while, poking my toes in the long ribbons of seaweed, sinking them into the soft sand. When I looked back, he was looking at me and from this distance, it was easy to hold his gaze. I walked towards him, he watched me all the while. I sat down next to him, closer than you would sit with a friend. Not touching but almost and he was holding his body very still, his eyes resting on my legs next to his. I didn't speak. He didn't speak. Then there were voices, out on the water. Four kayakers were paddling towards the beach.

He shifted his eyes to look sideways at me. It was very hard not to kiss him. The kayakers were getting out of their canoes, dragging them through the shallows onto the sand. I lay down on my side and turned away from him. I heard him greet the first one. I wasn't sitting up to say hello.

I listened to them spreading out over the beach. They were taking photographs, exploring the rock pools. They were establishing a colony here and they were never going to leave.

He said, 'Usually this place is empty.'

I closed my eyes. I wished the sun would come back.

'I've not been here for a while.' He hesitated. 'I need to

though. I want to make it a happy place again. It just reminds me of my dad.'

I turned over to look at him. 'Did you used to come here together?'

'Every day. But then he went downhill. The nurse said he would. But we weren't expecting it to happen so suddenly. I wasn't, anyway.'

I put my hand on his where it rested on the grass. It softened under my palm. He said, 'One week we were coming to the beach nearly every day. Then the next week it was too hard for him. He didn't have the strength to get up the hill. He used to tell me to come here to stretch my legs, get some fresh air. I'd go and sit in my car instead. I didn't tell him that.'

'Like when I found you the other night.'

'Yeah.' He looked down at me. 'But now I'll have something else to think about when I come to the beach.'

'What?'

He stroked the side of my face and it felt like being warmed by sudden sunshine. The breeze blew my hair over my mouth and he brushed it behind my ear. I loved the attention he was giving me. If I just stayed still and quiet, maybe he wouldn't stop.

He looked towards the shore. 'We're going to get wet.' He nudged me gently on the shoulder when I didn't show any sign of getting up. 'It'll be pissing it down in a minute.'

I sat up reluctantly. Out at sea the sky fuzzed into grey where rain was falling. The kayakers were getting back in their boats and pushing off from the sand.

Callum stood and held his hand out to pull me to my feet. I felt the warmth of it, the mixture of soft and callused skin. The rain started with big heavy drops and quickly became a downpour. By the time we reached his cottage we were soaked through. We hung jackets and jumpers and socks on the drying rack that hung over the stove. My jeans were wet and heavy and my T-shirt was cold across my shoulders where the rain had got through. Callum handed me a towel. I squeezed the ends of my hair in it then handed it back. He said, 'Come here,' and he rubbed it over my head, messing up my hair then smoothing it back into place. I couldn't help moving closer to him. He ran his fingertips from my shoulder, down my back, to my waist.

I said, 'My jeans are soaked.'

He unfastened the button, pulled down the zip. 'And there's no radiator to dry them on.'

My eyes were level with his neck. I lifted my face so he could kiss me and the hunger it created surprised me. It was just his mouth on mine but the desire was intense. He pushed my jeans down to my feet. Jesus, even my underwear was soaked through, and my skin was cold and clammy where the denim had clung to my legs.

He pushed up my T-shirt and I lifted it over my head and it was lucky we were already half undressed when we started this because there were too many clothes to get rid of. He was looking at me with his eyes kind of heavy. He pushed me down onto the sofa and knelt on the floor beside me, kissing my mouth, my collarbone, my shoulders. I felt warm where he was touching me and cold where my skin was still damp. It heated up underneath his hands.

We stayed on that sofa a while. Sex with him was like being somewhere else. Maybe it was an effect of the pill I'd taken but I felt like I was slipping away and he kept tugging me back into myself. It was a weird feeling. I liked it. It slowed everything down, made it harder to come. It prolonged it, which felt fucking amazing. We moved into his bedroom and slept and fucked again and slept. Sometime in the middle of the night, when we were doing neither of those things, just lying in bed talking, he pulled me close to him and stroked my neck.

He said, 'So you're leaving tomorrow?'

Today. 'Oh God.'

I'd become good at saying goodbye to people after so many years of moving around. I knew how it went. The ache in the throat, pushed down with a shove. The last hug before I got on the bus. I could even tell in advance how long I'd be sad for. A day, a week, two weeks. But when I tried to picture saying goodbye to Callum, I couldn't.

'What'll you do when you get home?' he asked.

'I don't know. Get a job in a bar. Look for a house-share. I don't know.' I couldn't even remember what I'd been planning when I'd decided to move back from Canada. I'd wanted roots. Connection. Family. But when Joe had tried to hand me responsibility for looking after my sister, I'd felt this panic, like the locks were sliding shut on all the doors.

I said, 'I thought I was going to have to move in with Catherine this morning. She's got this illness.'

He shifted so he could see my face. 'What's wrong with her?'

I didn't know how to answer. What was the term Joe had used? I said, 'Her husband drove up yesterday and brought these pills for her from the doctor.'

'What kind of pills?'

'Antipsychotics.'

His eyes opened a little wider.

I said, 'I had one this morning, just to persuade her to take one. And she did, thankfully.'

'You've taken an antipsychotic pill?'

'Yeah.'

'I hope you're not going to regret this when you come down.'

'I'm not high. They're sedatives. They're supposed to make you calmer.'

He ran his fingers across my stomach. 'You need a stronger dose.'

'Maybe they're not very powerful? Maybe the doctor thinks she's not that bad?' It was possible, wasn't it? Apart from those bizarre jumps of logic. And the way Joe wasn't shocked and surprised by them but resigned and worn out.

Callum said, 'But what's actually the matter with her?'

I felt the tightness in my chest return. 'I don't know.'

'What does her husband say?'

I wasn't sure I wanted to talk about this. But when I started, I couldn't stop. 'He said she's been like this for a while. And yesterday, he said he was going to divorce her, and that I'd have to look after her from now on because I'm her sister. But then she agreed to take the medication, and he changed his mind, and now he's staying. I'm so relieved.'

'He was going to divorce her?'

'Yes but he's not now.'

He paused. 'It sounds like it's going in that direction, though.'

'No, it's not. He can't walk out on her. She's really confused. She reads into everything that happens in such a sinister way. She doesn't know what's real and what isn't.'

'What would it involve, looking after her?'

'I don't even know.'

His eyes were searching my face. 'Could you talk to someone who knows about this kind of illness? You might feel better if you had more information.'

'But I'm not going to be her carer. I've got my own stuff to deal with.'

'I know a girl whose brother has schizophrenia. I could ask her if you could contact her, if you want.'

'It's not schizophrenia.' My voice wasn't quite steady. 'Joe said it's not as bad as that. She doesn't hallucinate or believe in aliens or mind control or things that don't exist. It's all stuff that could be true, but isn't.'

'Things like Leonie breaking into your cottage?'

'Yeah.'

He was quiet for a moment. 'That scratch on your car.' He paused. 'That was Tom, not Leonie.'

'Tom?' I moved away from him by instinct.

'Yeah.' He waited, watching my expression. 'And the first night, pulling the tablecloth off.'

I sat up. This bed seemed too small all of a sudden. 'You didn't tell me.'

'I wanted to stay out of it.'

Where was this awkwardness coming from?

He said, 'I'm sorry.'

Tom scratched the car. Then he must have been the one banging on the door as well. I said, 'What was he trying to do? He scared the shit out of us.'

'He's an idiot. Daft lad was drunk.'

'But what had we done to him?'

'He thought...' Callum changed tack mid-sentence. 'He didn't know there were two lasses there on their own.'

I watched his face. He wouldn't meet my gaze. The mental acrobatics here were beyond me; two minutes ago I was relaxed and happy, snuggled up to his chest. Now he was, not lying to me exactly, but definitely withholding information.

He said, 'That's why I got him to fix it.'

'Did Leonie know about it?'

'No.' He looked down at the stretch of sheet between us.

'So who did Tom think was at the cottage?'

There was a gap before he answered. 'I don't know.'

Did he think it was Joe's parents? Or his brothers? Or last summer, Joe? He was here a year ago with his youngest brother, Gavin. Catherine had told me they'd wanted some 'quality time' together so they'd spent a week here fishing and hiking. She'd stayed at home, painting the new house and unpacking boxes. It wasn't long after they'd moved up from London.

Callum reached towards me. I shifted to the edge of the bed. I thought of how Leonie had paused when I'd asked her when Fleur was born. And her quick, considering look when she said, February. I counted the months from June in my head.

I looked at Callum. 'What aren't you telling me?'

'Nothing.'

'I don't believe you.'

He said, 'I can't deal with this.'

'Neither can I.'

'This is why I tried not to get involved with you.'

'We're not involved.' I got up. My clothes were still in the kitchen. My jeans and underwear were in a crumpled, wet heap by the stove. They felt cold and tight when I put them on.

Callum came through, half-dressed, his skin radiating heat. 'Don't leave.'

I pulled on my T-shirt and socks, shoved my feet in my Converse.

He said, 'It's five in the morning.'

He'd kept things from me. Huge, important, life-changing things. And he was still doing it now.

I couldn't think about that. He wasn't my main concern. Through the window, the walkway and marsh were coming into focus as the sun climbed above the horizon.

'I need to get back to my sister,' I said.

13

CATHERINE

Thursday. Sunrise 04.29. Sunset 22.21

I dreamt of the red buoy that hung from the oak tree in the woods but when I woke up in my bunk bed I could still hear the branch creaking as it swung back and forth. The sound was distracting to say the least. I couldn't believe I hadn't noticed it before tonight and now that I had, I couldn't unnotice it. Like when you hear a pattern of words in the babbling of a stream and you can't switch them off again. It was especially loud when I closed my eyes. It made it impossible to sleep and according to my phone, it was just before five, so I'd only had two hours. We were leaving today. I had to pack, drive to Inverness, return the hire car, catch a plane. I couldn't do it on no sleep. The only solution was to go out there and make it stop.

Anna wasn't in her bed so I didn't need to worry about waking her. I pulled on some socks and a jumper over my pyjamas. I wouldn't be out long. I just needed to stop the swing from creaking then I could get back in bed and go back to sleep.

But how would I stop it moving? I couldn't control the wind.

I'd need to cut the rope. I pulled out the axe from under the bed. It was sharp enough. I took it through to the living room and looked around for my trainers. Joe was asleep on the sofa. I'd almost forgotten he was here.

He breathed soundlessly, lying on his back, and for a moment I thought about lying down next to him. I could fall asleep beside him. He'd think the pill was working its magic already. He'd think my insomnia had been cured. He says it's a 'symptom' but I've been a light sleeper my entire adult life. Throughout our marriage, and before that when we were living together, and before that when we were living separately but dating. It wasn't a 'symptom' that needed to be fixed or balanced out; it was a part of who I am. For him to see it as an indicator of mental illness was offensive to me.

The things that made me 'me', the things I had always been, he wanted to erase with a sedative. Because that's what the pill was, despite its zappy name. Its ultimate aim was to slow my thoughts and unstick them from each other so that they floated without connecting, unable to join together into a coherent meaning. Joe had said to me once, 'Don't connect the dots.' He was quoting from a recruitment advert for air traffic controllers. I said it was a very tasteless image. He said, 'I'm just asking you to stop jumping to conclusions.'

The pills were meant to stop me from reaching any conclusions whatsoever. Either that or they would smother my thoughts completely, which essentially meant they would smother me. Because you are your thoughts. Take them away and you're nothing, a zombie stumbling around not even realising you're dead.

One pill hadn't done that. Two pills wouldn't. I knew that before I took it; I wouldn't have done so otherwise. It was a strategy to stop his plans in their tracks. This was how I had to operate nowadays because it was how I was operated against. I had two or three weeks before the pills would take their full effect. In the meantime I could look forward to a dramatic increase in appetite and sudden, involuntary body movements, like an addict.

My husband wanted to turn me into a fat, stupid, twitching freakshow. And I had thought he'd loved me as I was. But the main problem with all this was: how would I know when the pills had started working? How would I know where I ended and they began? How did I know that the thoughts I was having now, in this instant, were my own, authentic, genuine thoughts, or chemically-manipulated thoughts caused by the suppression of certain responders in my brain?

It was another reason to keep up with my journal. I know who I am because I've got it written down, and anyone who thinks that is extreme has never been under attack like I am. When people close to you consistently try to break you apart, you do all you can to hold yourself together. I needed to write that down. These were thoughts that needed to be recorded. I found my journal. Joe slept on. Although he could be pretending, like when he'd pretended he didn't see me in Fleur's face.

He sighed on the sofa and turned on his side. The axe was lying on the table next to my journal. I'd put it there but I couldn't remember why. I was going to use it to cut something. I couldn't recall what it was.

Then I heard the branch creak with the weight of the buoy. I remembered why I'd got out of bed: to make it stop.

I hid my journal under the mattress then slipped outside, opening and closing the door softly so Joe wouldn't hear. The morning was grainy and grey like an untuned television. I took the path into the woods. The trees moved in the wind and it sounded like rising applause, then the breeze shifted and it became a hiss. The leaves rippled and quivered like they didn't want me to get a good, clear look.

I followed the path until I glimpsed the ball of red suspended amongst the green. It was moving like someone was on it. Like someone was pushing a child from behind. I edged closer, trying to stay hidden behind the tree trunks. I stopped and listened but I couldn't hear the branch creaking. I stepped out and looked into the hollow where it hung.

There was nobody there. And the swing was still. It didn't make a sound. It was so quiet out here in the woods. I couldn't remember why I was there.

———

I walked back the way I came, aware that whoever was behind this was no doubt watching me with a satisfied smile on their face. Somebody was clearly playing a joke on me and I was annoyed with myself for getting sucked in by it. It was never just a joke though, was it? There was always an objective behind it. I knew that by now. Why had they wanted to draw me away from the cottage and into the woods? To laugh at how easily manipulated I was? To make me doubt my own sanity? Or because there was something happening back there that they didn't want me to see? What were they doing while I was gone? I walked faster, the axe bumped against my legs. I stopped when the cottage came into view.

Leonie's silver car was parked at an odd angle outside.

I crept up to the passenger window. Fleur was strapped into her car seat in the back. Her eyelids lifted as if she was just waking up from a deep sleep. I touched the glass and she turned her head towards me. Her eyes met mine for a moment before they closed again, and her head slumped heavy towards her chest.

Over at the cottage, a curtain moved. I dropped down behind the car. I saw Leonie peer out through the living-room window. And was that Anna behind her?

My daughter, my sister, my husband, all gathered together behind my back. All next of kin, making a plan for what to do about me. Where to put me.

Leonie moved away from the window and the curtain fell back. I watched Fleur sleeping through the glass. She was my blood, my genes. She was a part of me and when she looked at me, it was without judgement. I tried the car door. It opened. I released the straps across her front and felt the warmth of her skin through her sleepsuit as I lifted her out. Her breathing was deep and her head dropped onto my shoulder as I stood up. All her muscles relaxed as she rested on me.

I picked up the axe and followed the path into the woods, walking slowly so as not to disturb her. I made a sling out of my forearm and she fitted into it perfectly, her chest against my chest. I could feel the blood pulsing between us. I felt my ribcage relax along with hers.

We were out of sight now so I sat down on a rock and lay her on my lap, my hand under her head. Her sleepsuit was covered in a pattern of tiny tulips. Flowers for Fleur. Her skin was blushed and dark under her eyes. She had the kind of complexion that would change with her emotions, with her surroundings even, like an octopus that hides itself against the sea-floor.

I remembered looking into the glass cot in the hospital after she'd gone. I was leaving too. I was only waiting for a nurse to sign a form. I remembered the towels she'd been lying on, and the feeling of lightness when she was no longer there. I remembered the wave of relief because it was all over and I could go back to being who I was before. I'd asked myself if I had any sadness or regret and the answer was no.

A leaf floated down from the tree above us. I stroked the smooth skin on the back of her hand. Her fingers curled around mine.

The answer was no but now I thought, if I had held her for longer. Over a few days, or a few weeks. It would have been different and something would have grown between us and I would have been devoted to her entirely. I was sensible; I hadn't allowed that connection to develop. But it was as if the space it would have occupied was already established within me, and without her it was empty, and essentially that has been the problem all along.

She frowned in her sleep then settled again. I sat very still, not wanting her to wake up. I thought of that night when she'd needed to be fed and I couldn't do it, I didn't do it. If she woke now, she would be hungry. What would I do to calm her back into sleep? If she cried, they would hear her and find us, and we'd be separated again.

I must have tensed up; she sensed a change in me and opened her eyes to see what was wrong. She looked at me. She began to whimper. I made a shushing sound and it seemed to still her a little. I remembered Anna telling me something Leonie had said. 'She always sleeps by the sea.'

I carried her down through the woods, avoiding the cottage and the road. I thought the movement might rock her back to sleep but it had the opposite effect. She started to twist in my hands. I whispered it was okay, she was where she was meant to be. She started to cry and by the time we reached the cliff top, it was a wail. She was hungry, she wanted milk. I felt her stomach tense and her shoulders writhe away from my hands.

I would take her to the sea and the sound of waves would send her to sleep. I followed the path down the cliffside to the beach. She was hot and heavy as we wove between the rocks to the shore. I said, 'Here we are, here's the sea.' But it was still and silent like glass all the way to the islands.

I needed something to distract her, a pretty stone or a shell, but all I could see was litter and kelp and the plastic bottle with a warning sign on the label. I crouched down and picked it up and held it against the sky. There was no top on the bottle yet a tide of liquid moved inside; something oily and heavy travelled in a slow-motion wave. I said, look at this. It wasn't what she wanted. All I could hear was her cries which were loud and desperate, as if she was burning up inside. Then someone said my name and I grabbed hold of the axe.

Anna. She was out of breath. She'd been running. She stopped a few metres from me. 'Catherine?'

Fleur gulped between cries. Her shoulders rose and fell.

She said, 'Is she okay?'

'She's hungry.'

'Come on.' She took a step towards me, 'Let's get her back to Leonie.'

I took a step back and nearly slipped on the rocks. 'No.'

For a moment, she couldn't seem to find any words. 'Catherine, she'll call the police. You've taken her baby.'

I said, 'She left her on her own. I'm looking after her.'

'But she's not yours.'

'She is mine. I've not taken her, I've brought her back to where she belongs.'

'But she's not related to you.'

The hair on the back of Fleur's head was wet with sweat. 'Of course she is. We all see it. You see it. Joe sees it.'

Anna took a deep breath like she was struggling to get enough air in her lungs. 'No, that's not what Joe sees.'

I didn't understand. There were people up on the cliff top. I was trapped between them and the sea and I realised, too late, that this was the worst possible place to come to. And that it had

243

been their plan from the start. They'd even warned me: the computer, the ropes, the cages and nets. All ways to pursue and restrain.

I said, 'Who's up there?'

She looked back at the cliff. Someone moved fast down the path. She said, 'It's only Joe, it's okay.'

'What's going to happen?'

'I don't know.'

'Tell me. What's the plan? I need to know.'

She said, 'There isn't a plan.'

Joe had reached the rocks. I held Fleur tighter to me. She was still crying but without the energy she'd had before. Joe slowed to a walk, keeping his eyes fixed on me as if he was approaching an animal he was a little bit afraid of. He looked at me like he didn't know me. He said, 'What have you done?'

Anna spun to face him. 'What have *you* done?'

What *had* he done? There were messages moving between them and I couldn't catch on to what they meant. What was the plan they'd made in the cottage? What was he going to do to me?

I said to Anna, 'Don't let him take my independence away.'

He said, 'I just want my baby.'

I said, 'You mean my baby.'

'No.'

Anna swiftly moved forwards and took the axe from my hand.

Joe said, 'There's something I need to tell you.'

I was trying to think but my thoughts kept slipping out of place.

He said, 'She's mine. Mine and Leonie's.'

Fleur had stopped crying. I looked at her face. Joe's eyes, not my eyes. Leonie had come here for him, not me.

He said, 'I'm sorry.'

'I don't understand.'

Anna took Fleur from me and gave her to Joe. He cradled her in his arms and they stared at each other and there was something between them that wasn't there when she'd looked at me. An acceptance. A recognition. It was so clear and true, I couldn't unsee it, even when I turned and fixed my eyes on the outline of the islands in the distance.

I heard Anna say, 'Leonie's coming down.' I heard Fleur's cries building again, getting rawer and angrier. Joe hushed her with a sound like waves on the shore. Anna took hold of my hand and pulled me away.

AFTER

ANNA

One of the most disturbing things about working in a coffee shop in the town where I grew up was the number of old school friends who came through the doors. I half-recognised them, and they half-recognised me, and sometimes they remembered my name, and occasionally I remembered theirs, and there was always a conversation about what we were up to now, and where we lived, and how such-and-such was, and even though it happened so frequently I had all my answers lined up and ready, it wore me out every time.

I used the word 'temporary' a lot in these catch-ups over the counter. Living with my parents was temporary, this job was temporary, Catherine was home too, but it was temporary. And I wasn't sure whether they envied or pitied me because in contrast, their lives were so permanent and set. They were on their second or third child, I was on my second or third new start. They had buggies, book bags, even *teenagers* in tow; straight-haired girls who delicately spooned the cream off their hot chocolates. Some looked a lot like their mothers did the last time I saw them; it was how I knew who they were after all these years. And when they mentioned other girls we'd known at school, I struggled to work out who they meant because they all had different surnames now.

They had husbands and homes, I had a list of countries I'd lived in. Relationships that weren't worth mentioning. Jobs like this one, just in better places. Capital cities. Beach bars. Skiing resorts. Places where anyone might wander in, and none of them would have been there that night in the park when I was fourteen and so drunk on Diamond White that I threw up on the slide. How did people remember that far back and in that much detail? I'd need hypnosis to recall some of the things they did about our school days.

Today it was one of Catherine's old friends who came in. Rachel. The same willowy figure and chewed fingernails, but now with slightly greying hair and a baby in a carrier on her front. I knew her straight away by her tallness, but it took until she was collecting her drinks for her to place me. She smiled suddenly, shyly, before she sat down with an older lady, probably her mum.

She came over a few minutes later, while her mum fed the baby from a bottle. She said, 'It's Anna, isn't it?'

'Rachel. I thought it was you.'

'You look exactly the same.'

I laughed, incredulous. 'Except without the dungarees and spiral perm.'

'You were always the complete opposite of Catherine. How is she?'

'Fine,' I said. 'We're both staying at our parents for the summer.'

'She's here? I thought she lived in London.' She added, 'I don't know how I knew that.'

'Facebook, probably. She's just home temporarily. I'll pass on your number if you want.'

'Okay. Yeah.'

I handed her a pen and an empty loyalty card. The last time I saw her was in exam season, the spring after Catherine had her baby. All her former friends had been bunched together outside the sports hall, looking pale and serious as they waited to be called in and take their seats. Catherine stood on her own staring straight ahead, a clear plastic bag with her pens inside, her expression unreadable.

Rachel handed me back the card with her number on. She said, 'I've always felt bad about how we–' She paused. 'How we stopped being her friend. We weren't looking down on her but I'm sure she thought we were. We were probably just jealous.'

'Jealous of a teenage pregnancy?'

'We felt like she'd left us behind. It was such a stupid reason to fall out.'

'You were only fifteen.'

'It's so young.' She looked over at her mum who was bouncing the baby up and down, trying to distract it from imminent tears. 'Is there a baby change in here?'

'In the disabled toilets. Congratulations, by the way.'

She looked confused. 'Oh. Thanks. She's my first. And probably my last.' She looked like she was about to say something more but changed her mind. 'Well, nice to see you again.'

I put her number in the back pocket of my jeans. I wasn't sure whether I would pass it on or not.

———

That night when I went upstairs to get changed after work, Catherine was in my bedroom, doing a forearm plank across 'her side' even though she had her own room next door.

She raised her head when I walked in. 'I'll be done in a minute.'

I glanced at the stopwatch counting down on her phone. 'Forty-three seconds.'

Her face was calm but her shoulders trembled with the effort. She managed to say, 'How was work?'

I sat down on the bunk bed. 'I'm pretty sure they'll sack me soon. I'm kind of looking forward to it.' I wanted to get changed. She was in the way of the wardrobe. I said, 'Rachel came in.'

She looked up for a second. 'Rachel?'

'Rachel White. She wants you to call her. I've got her number.'

Her shoulders were shaking. Her eyes were on the floor. Another five seconds counted down. 'I probably won't.'

'I know.' I added, 'She probably doesn't really want you to.'

She laughed then, sort of, and I thought, that's a good sign. A month ago her eyes would have taken on that alert, suspicious look and she'd have demanded to know what was going on. Her phone beeped and she collapsed onto the floor. 'One minute forty-five seconds.'

She'd started a thirty-day plank challenge the week after she came out of hospital. This was day twenty-eight or twenty-nine. She was trying to stop herself putting on weight but it wasn't really working. She said her medication made her constantly hungry. She kept a packet of ginger biscuits by her bed, like when she was pregnant. She left the top button of her trousers undone.

I'd suggested we take up running but she wasn't interested. She said strength training made her feel focused. I thought she was swapping the emotional pain of her divorce for the physical pain of a plank hold. She had a very strong core and a broken heart.

'Are we heading out?' I asked, edging round her to get my jeans and a fresh T-shirt. 'It's sunny.'

'I've not been anywhere today.'

'What have you been doing?'

'Nothing.'

I had a look in her room before we went downstairs. There were files spread across the floor and bed. House deeds, letters from solicitors and surveyors, statements from the bank. I said, 'No wonder you're in my room.'

'Can I sleep in the bottom bunk tonight?'

'Yeah, if you want. Imagine the stress dreams you'd have sleeping amongst all that.'

'It doesn't make me stressed,' she said.

That's because you're sedated, I thought. *The house could be on fire and your expression wouldn't change.* I said, 'Let's go before Mum and Dad get home.'

I couldn't talk her into running but most nights we went out for a walk. We wandered up through the estate to the lane that curved around the edge of the town and onto the moors where the heather was just beginning to flower in the dips and hollows. Soon whole hillsides would be shaded with purple, and dusk would fall earlier and earlier, and then what would we do with our evenings?

Maybe by then we'd have left. It wouldn't be hard for me to find a job and a house-share in Manchester but I wasn't sure about Catherine. I was staying for her sake. I was a buffer between her and my parents, who were still getting to grips with her 'episode', as the nurses on the ward had called it. I needed to figure out a way of being there for her, without losing my own sanity in the process. I thought that once she'd sold her house and had some money, we could both move to the same neighbourhood in the city, be close by without living under the same roof, start to build up our lives again.

She'd gone to the doctor voluntarily when we got her home from Scotland. Sort of voluntarily. She knew she'd crossed a line by taking Fleur, and that she'd been lucky Leonie didn't have a phone signal to call the police when we first found her gone. We used this; this unspoken threat of arrest and imprisonment. I didn't know how else to get her to accept help.

Once she was admitted to hospital, it became clear that the pills she'd been prescribed weren't right for her at all. They stopped her sleeping. Made her hear and see things that weren't there. She was right to refuse them for all that time. In fact, I was starting to think she'd been right about a lot of things, because even in the midst of her delusions, her instincts had been spot-on. She'd seen a threat in Leonie when I'd thought there was none. She'd known something was going on when I'd said it was all in her head. She didn't get the details right but her intuition worked perfectly. It seemed a little one-sided that she'd been labelled as delusional; it didn't take into account all the deception swirling around us at the time.

I wanted to keep everything out in the open now and give her no reason to develop any more suspicions, but the nature of her illness made that hard. It was a sneaky, secretive disease that turned everyone around you sneaky and secretive in response. I often thought of that Nirvana lyric about how being paranoid doesn't mean that they're not after you. But I'd go further than that and say 'It's *because* you're paranoid that they're after you'. The sad thing is, they're only trying to get you to a GP.

I spoke to Joe on the phone, secretly, when Catherine had gone to bed at night. He called every few weeks to ask how she was doing. I never knew what to say. I remembered how he'd used her mental illness to discredit her when she got too close to the truth about him and Leonie. How he'd told her she was reading into things and seeing something that wasn't there. It was useful to have a wife who nobody believed. You could deny everything, even a child, until it turned up on your doorstep.

I didn't ask Joe about Leonie but he seemed to want to explain. He'd slept with her last summer when he was at the cottage with his brother and I guess that was why her lighter was there, amongst all the other junk. Joe and Leonie hadn't stayed in touch. She had a visa to move to Brazil; he never expected to see her again. He certainly never thought she'd be back in Scotland a year later. Likewise, she had no interest in seeing him again, even when she found out she was pregnant. She wanted to raise the child on her own and not involve him at all. But then she had the baby and something changed her mind. She'd gone back to where she'd met him like a migrating bird. It was more of an instinct than a plan. And maybe it was the right one, I don't know.

Joe went quiet after he'd told me all this. 'I barely knew her,' he said eventually. 'I still barely know her.'

I moved the conversation on. I didn't see any point in making him feel bad about what had happened, but I didn't have the energy to make him feel better either. My sister was my priority. Sometimes I ended the call by saying I thought I'd heard her getting out of bed, which was a lie. There was no waking her nowadays until she'd had about twelve hours. She took her medication just before nine and it knocked her out for the whole night and half the morning. She was never awake before I set off for work.

I hadn't expected the changes to be so dramatic. She'd lost her sharpness, her edges, her wiry way of walking. She moved slower, spoke slower, turned her head slower if I asked her a question. There was always a two-second gap before she responded, like she was stoned or on a long-distance call.

She'd swapped one bubble for another. She wasn't living inside her delusions anymore. But she wasn't quite here either.

We walked alongside each other but I still had no real idea where she was.

These moors reminded me of the sea and maybe that's why I kept dreaming about it. I was at the beach watching the water change from grey to petrol blue to turquoise as the clouds moved across the sun. Or I was on the swings in the playground by the pub, flying out towards the waves. I decided it was because I was still in a bunk bed. It wasn't normal to be sleeping that far off the ground as an adult.

And the way we'd left so abruptly. No final look at the view. No goodbyes.

I handed Fleur to Joe, her daddy, and for a moment they just stared at each other, both with these wide, full eyes. Then something seemed to snap in Fleur and she became more and more angry with every second. The noise she was making; it was so loud, it was hard to think of anything other than the fury coming from her little body. Joe held her out in front of him, awkwardly shushing her, and she screamed full-throttle back in his face. An all-out tantrum. A pre-verbal accusation: where the fuck were you?

He looked like he was in shock, though surely, it wasn't that big a surprise. If I'd worked it out, he must have too. But the realness of it. A daughter who you didn't know existed until a few days before.

Catherine was very still, staring out to sea, but I sensed something shifting beneath the surface, as if she was disintegrating from the inside, turning from rock to sand. I took her hand and she looked at me as if she wanted me to tell her what to do. I led her away across the rocks to the path. Leonie was on her way down and I still had the axe. I threw it into the grass out of sight. She didn't need to know about that. I'd felt sick when I saw it in Catherine's hand, Fleur in the other.

We met her on the path halfway down the cliff. She said, 'You took my baby.' I said, 'You fucked her husband.' And Catherine just blinked at her, like she'd just woken up, which in a way, she had. The pull towards Fleur was too strong for Leonie to stop and say anything more.

Back at the cottage I packed for us both; throwing our clothes into bags in whatever order I found them. I wanted to get out of there before Joe and Leonie returned. I thought, drive then fly and land in another country away from all this. It was my default plan.

But Callum. That night, half-night, in his bed. He knew Fleur was Joe's child from the start. And he knew Tom thought it was Joe staying at the cottage when we first arrived. I imagined Tom being drunk and jealous, trying to scare Joe away, thinking he'd come back to Scotland to reconnect with Leonie. Maybe Leonie thought the same when she heard there was someone staying there, and that's why she'd turned up next morning. She was looking for Joe but instead she found Catherine. His wife. And Catherine was showing way too much interest in Fleur, like she thought she had a claim on her. No wonder Leonie was on edge.

And Callum knew all this long before I'd worked it out yet he didn't tell me. Was that why he'd been into me one minute and distant the next? Some sort of internal conflict he was working through? Or was I giving him too much credit, and he'd not really thought about it much at all?

I didn't know. I didn't even know how I felt about it. Everything was about Catherine. There was no space for anyone else.

When I looked back at those weeks when she was in hospital, life had the dislodged, unreal quality of a bad dream.

Her paranoia was intense and far-reaching; it covered me, the doctors, our parents, Joe, the nurses, pretty much everyone she came into contact with. And when she discharged herself a few weeks later, I'd thought she was going to kill herself and it was a fear unlike anything I'd experienced before. I felt it in my chest and in my throat, a sudden, tight panic, out of nowhere, several times a day. I checked her room when I woke up at night. I dreaded a phone call at work. I texted her every lunchtime to make sure she'd not overdosed and died in her sleep.

I knew that the only way out of this nightmare was forwards. We needed to leave Scotland and everything that had happened there behind us, and Callum was included in that.

And, well, I just didn't have the words to talk to him about what was going on. Maybe if we'd been in the same place, the same room, it would have been okay. But not over the phone, on a bad line, or in an email I didn't know how to start.

Besides, I didn't know his number. I looked for him on Facebook but I couldn't find him. And I thought, that's that then. Except for the dreams. Not every night but most.

I turned to Catherine. 'Do you think it looks like the sea up here?'

We were trudging slowly upwards towards the highest point on the moors. They stretched for miles around us; waves of grass and heather, a vast, open space, dried to a tinder by months of sunshine and no rain.

She said, 'A bit.' A few minutes later, she said, 'It's more like a desert than a sea. Or a sea that turned into a desert.'

A desert? Hmm. Flat, empty, unending; the kind of place where you'd slowly die of thirst if you languished there alone for long enough.

I said, 'I'm thinking of sending a letter to the pub for Callum.'

'What's wrong with Facebook?'

'He's not on there.'

'He is.'

I stopped. '*Is he?*'

She got out her phone and I watched as she brought up his profile. In his photograph he was sitting on the bench beneath the whalebone, squinting into the sun.

I said, 'I looked for him for about an hour and couldn't find him.'

She shrugged.

I said, 'Should I send him a friend request?'

'I don't know.'

'I don't want us to be "Facebook friends".'

She nodded and started walking again. I mean, what if he didn't accept? We stopped at our usual spot: a flat rock jutting out over a ridge where we could sit with our legs dangling over the drop, the last of the sun warming our backs. Beneath us was moorland that turned into farmland. Meadows where the grass was still uncut and woodland half-strangled by rhododendrons.

I said, 'I could send him a message without being his friend. But what would I say?'

'Hi.'

I got his profile up on my phone. I typed 'Hi' in the message box. I wasn't going to send it.

Catherine looked at it. 'How are you?'

I put the phone down on the rock. 'It's impossible.'

She picked it up and pressed send. It took me a few seconds to realise what she'd just done. 'Catherine!'

She gave me the phone. 'You'd better add something else.'

'Oh my God. Why did you do that?' And now the signal

had gone. 'It only said hi. It wasn't finished.' I put my head in my hands. 'You absolute nut job.'

I looked at her and away. 'Nut job' wasn't something you should call someone on antipsychotics who thought everyone was in on a plot against her. Who thought there were messages for her in the rubbish washed up by the sea.

But she was gazing at the view, unconcerned. We watched a crow chase a kestrel across the woods below. Used to think. Not anymore.

AFTER

CATHERINE

A kestrel landed on the house with the glass roof. A smudge on a spire. I always meant to bring binoculars so I could see it more clearly but I always forgot.

Down there it was sloping fields and woods but up here it was flat all the way to the horizon. A desert or a sea, Anna said. There was nothing up here. It was why I liked it. It reminded me of my head before I fell asleep at night.

The kestrel had gone. I didn't see where. I squinted at the glass roof. Was it still covered in moss and algae like it had been that night? The stars were blurred by it. The moonlight was tinged green. Our breath clouded the air, it was so cold.

There were no blankets so he covered me in jumpers from his suitcase. His mother had packed them. She'd put a teddy in there too. He blushed when I saw it.

I remember he covered me in his clothes. And I remember he told me his mother worked in a bijouterie. And I asked him what 'bijou' meant and he said, 'You are a bijou,' and smiled but didn't tell me what one was. And I remember his eyes were blue, like my daughter's, though Anna said they may have changed.

Anna wanted us to go home now. 'I don't want to be benighted,' she said.

Benighted. Caught out by the falling night. The house with the glass roof had faded into the trees. If you didn't know it was there, you wouldn't see it at all. I got to my feet. Miles away, in Manchester, sunlight glinted off a tower block. A single, strong bead of light, like somebody was signalling to us with a torch.

Anna saw it too. 'It's like a lighthouse,' she said. 'And all the land between here and there is the sea.'

I followed her down the hill. I'd sent that message when she didn't want me to. I did it without thinking. It didn't matter. But I shouldn't have done it. And now she kept checking her phone every few minutes.

I said, 'Sorry I sent that message.'

'Fuck it. It was a dead end anyway.'

The lights were on in the town. From up here we could see the gap where the chimney used to be. Dad said they'd taken it down piece by piece. He said, your campaign worked in the end. I didn't understand. He said, your posters, your petitions.

I'd drawn posters at school when the air was sour with chemicals. We all had, hadn't we? They'd stopped using the chimney but they'd left it standing there, until last year. And now it was gone and there was nothing to anchor your eyes on. The town looked like a different place.

Anna was asking me a question. 'What do you feel like eating? There's leftovers from last night in the fridge.'

'Toast?'

'Just toast?'

'Or cereal.'

'This is tea not breakfast.'

'I missed breakfast.'

'Lucky you, sleeping the day away.'

'Well, I can't help it.'

'I know.'

'It's like being made of lead.'

'It's worth it to get better though, isn't it?'

I didn't answer. The question didn't make sense.

'You're not going to stop taking them are you?' Anna had stopped. She was looking at me. 'Because they seem to be working. You seem better than you were.'

I said nothing. She sighed. I said, 'In what way?'

'You know what's real and what isn't. With Joe and everything. It's like you accept reality as it is, rather than making it into something else in your head.'

That light was still shining at us from the city. It was a window glinting in the sun.

She said, 'I feel like you're facing up to things a bit more. Like, what you've lost and how you feel about it.'

What I've lost? Did she mean Joe or my daughter? Or both? Both were right. Both hurt. That was why I took the pills. They were called antipsychotics but to me they were painkillers. At first, I'd dreaded them working then I'd counted down the days.

'Please keep getting better, Catherine. Don't stop taking them.'

'I won't.' Not for a while anyway.

We reached our house. She said, 'No car. They must still be at the 'Spoons. It's steak night.'

'Oh yeah.' I'd spoken to Dad earlier. Last week, we'd all gone. You could order your food on your phone but Dad said he didn't agree with it. He went to the counter instead. He'd asked if I was going with them tonight. I must have said no. I was trying to read a letter from the bank at the time. I couldn't focus on two things at once anymore. I could barely focus on one.

In the kitchen, Anna's phone buzzed. 'Message.' She took a breath. 'Callum.' She read it, her bottom lip turned down. 'He's not very happy.'

She stood against the radiator tapping fast on her phone while I put bread in the toaster. She said, 'I can't do this in a DM. I need to talk to him.'

'Ask him for his number.'

'I have.'

I was spreading Marmite on our toast when Mum and Dad came in. They looked at us like they still weren't sure why we were there.

Dad said, 'You'd rather eat toast at home than steak with your mum and dad?'

'Were we invited?' Anna said.

Mum said, 'You don't need an invite to spend time with your parents.'

Another message came through on Anna's phone. She read it then smiled round at us all. 'We'll come next week. It can be family night.'

'Family night?' Mum raised her eyebrows.

Anna shrugged. 'Why not? I just need to make a phone call.'

She went out into the back garden. I watched her through the kitchen window while I washed the dishes. She touched the leaves of the apple tree with one hand, the other held the phone to her ear.

'She looks happy,' Dad said.

'She's in love,' I said.

'Oh.' He squinted out at her. She saw us all watching her and turned her back on us.

Mum put her hand on my shoulder. 'And how are you feeling?'

'Fine.'

She left it there for a moment before she moved away.

My room was a mess. I'd left paperwork all over the floor. I was going to sleep in Anna's room, wasn't I? But she was in there talking and laughing with Callum on the phone.

It was nine o'clock. I cleaned my teeth and washed my face and put on my pyjamas then sat on the edge of my bed, waiting for her to finish her conversation. I liked to go to sleep early nowadays because I missed Joe most when I was tired. I swallowed a pill with water. Soon I wouldn't care that my bed was covered in bank statements and letters. I'd fall asleep amongst it all.

What had Anna asked before? Were the pills worth it? I wasn't sure of the answer. There was the zombie feeling. And the extra stone in weight, increasing every week. And I couldn't think properly so how would I ever get a job again? Anna said I didn't need to worry about all that yet.

She thought they were working. All I knew was that I was starting to see a then and a now. They'd drawn a faint line between the two and I saw it as my job to keep going over it, pressing my pen into the page, making it firmer each time.

All that fear I'd had. It had seeped in and discoloured my entire world. I couldn't see outside that dark, sprawling version of events. But the pills had made that story shrink and the space it left was vast. And what was going to fill it? Disjointed memories of things I'd rather forget? An awareness of an ache I'd managed to ignore until now?

What was the space for? That was what I wanted to know. And was I just supposed to live in it, this sea that became a desert in the time it took from spring to turn to summer?

Anna seemed to think so. She'd said, 'Things don't stay the same, Catherine. It's not how the world works. I'm not saying things always get better but they do always change. So the way you're feeling will change.'

'You're saying I might feel worse?'

She thought for a moment. 'How much worse can things get? It's more likely you'll start to feel better.'

She said just wait and watch, and be aware when something new starts to grow.

Be aware or be alert, I can't remember which one she said.

She was still on the phone. I could sleep in here if I moved this stuff off my pillow. Bills. Bank statements. I put them in the wardrobe. Some of my old things were in there. A-level text books and coursework. I opened a ring binder with a Nuclear Free City sticker on the front.

Inside were revision notes for *Hamlet*. He went crazy but nobody made him take antipsychotics. What kind of play would that have been? Just sleeping and eating and looking at people like you're seeing them through glass.

That was what I'd wanted to find. My snow globes. They were piled together in a cardboard box at the back of the wardrobe. I pulled it out and found the one with the beach and the boat. The one with the Eiffel Tower. The one with the house in the woods with logs stacked by the door. It was the only one with people in it. In front of the house there was a man and a woman standing together. She had a baby in her arms.

I took it back to bed and brought it close to my face and tried to imagine what they might be saying. I held it in my hands. I turned it upside down. I made it snow.

'Are you still awake?' Anna was in the doorway.

I'd been drifting off. I'd forgotten to turn out the light and I still had the snow globe in the palm of my hand. 'Yes.'

'Callum's coming to see me.'

'That's good.'

'Yeah. Just for the day. Next weekend.' She sat on the end of the bed. 'Are you sleeping in here or in my room?'

'In here now.'

'Shall I move this stuff off your bed then?'

'Okay.'

'We'll sort through it all tomorrow. There's a letter you've not even opened here.'

I felt the mattress lift as she stood up. I heard her shuffling about. The tear of paper. I let go of the snow globe and sank down into the covers. I suddenly felt incredibly tired. It hit me like a six-foot wave every night.

'Catherine, don't go to sleep.'

Too late, I thought.

She stood by the side of the bed. 'Catherine. I opened your letter, sorry. It's from a charity that works with people who were adopted.'

I opened my eyes. Anna was staring down at me. She read from the piece of paper in her hand. 'It says, Your daughter has asked us to initiate contact with you, her birth mother. She would like to write to you in person, with the hope of meeting face to face in the future, if you both agree.'

I pulled myself up. A smile spread across her face. She said, 'Read it. It's real.'

THE END

ACKNOWLEDGEMENTS

Thank you to everyone who helped with this book, especially Nicola Mostyn, Maria Roberts, Emma Jane Unsworth, Joanna Swainson, Adele Coulter, Janet Tierney, Alan Thompson, and Marianne Thompson.

A NOTE FROM THE PUBLISHER

Thank you for reading this book. If you enjoyed it please do consider leaving a review on Amazon to help others find it too.

We hate typos. All of our books have been rigorously edited and proofread, but sometimes mistakes do slip through. If you have spotted a typo, please do let us know and we can get it amended within hours.

info@bloodhoundbooks.com

Milton Keynes UK
Ingram Content Group UK Ltd.
UKHW011925150624
444129UK00005B/192

9 781917 214018